EUROPA NIGHTMARE

EUROPA NIGHTMARE

DARK CURTIAN SAGA

WAYNE FAUST & CHARLES EUGENE ANDERSON

MAD COW PRESS
AURORA, COLORADO

EUROPA NIGHTMARE

Copyright 2017 by Wayne Faust and Charles Eugene Anderson

CONTENTS

MAD COW PRESS

Wayne Faust
www.waynefaust.com

Charles Eugene Anderson
www.charleseugeneanderson.com

Charles Eugene Anderson's Mailing List
https://goo.gl/ai9YQj

Valdas Miskinis
Cover art by Valdas Miskinis, miskinis.valdas@gmail.com

DEDICATED TO EDWARD WINSLOW BRYANT JR

A Teacher and Friend to Many

HSWMS SKALBAGGE

Everything went dark on the *SS John W. Campbell Jr.*

Erik Juergenson cursed in two languages. This wasn't the first time the supply ship had lost power. Not even the first time today. He didn't dare take his hands off the controls of his ship, *Skalbagge*. His docking computer would have to recalculate the coordinates if it came back online. He hated to fly blind. Well, only half blind.

Flipping a switch, his smaller craft could go to manual control and he could maneuver out of the path of the much bigger ship. At least he hoped so. Right now it was a monstrous, slate black hulk against a background of glittering stars. They had been only four minutes from docking when the power had blinked out.

Europa Station had called in Juergenson two days ago. The *Campbell* had been racing towards Jupiter, flying erratically one minute and on a perfect trajectory the next. The crew had responded when hailed but their voices had sounded wooden, made no sense. The ship had failed all the normal protocols and procedures on its approach to the planet. As they had gotten close, they didn't correct course. They didn't use Jupiter's gravity to slow their ship down. One hour ago, they pulled away from the planet at an oblique angle. Evidently, that maneuver had used up all their fuel and they were now floating free with no power.

Juergenson let out a deep sigh, and the canned air of the bridge tasted metallic on his tongue. He'd have to perform the docking maneuver all by himself. He needed to get onboard and figure out what in the name of Odin was going on with these people.

He pushed a lever forward. The *Skalbagge* responded as it always did, moving towards the other ship ever so slightly. His ship did what it was told. He'd seen to that every waking hour since he'd left Earth five years ago. The *Skalbagge* was his environment, his safety net, his world. It had grown to seem like a part of his body. Now he pushed a button which would override the *Campbell's* offline docking mechanism. He'd have to eyeball this one and do it the old-fashioned way.

"There we go," he said, staring through the view screen, talking as if to a lover. "Come to me. I want to hold you in my arms."

"Three minutes," said the ship's computer. It had learned to ignore Juergenson's flights of fancy, what he called his 'pillow talk.'

"Inge! Where's your romance?" he said, looking around the bridge as if there were a woman actually standing there. He'd named the voice on the ship's computer Inge after his first girlfriend back in Borås.

"Don't run away from me. I want to feel your touch," he purred.

He pushed the lever another centimeter forward. He had done this dozens of times before. Every ship that approached the Swedish colony was greeted by the *Skalbagge*. The robotic supply ships from Earth didn't need his help. But the Campbell had a crew. It had left Earth six years ago on a journey to the outer colonies at Saturn. Now it was on its way home. Or, at least, it had been trying.

"Two minutes."

Juergenson slowed his ship to match the other. He needed to get just a few meters closer so he could dock. He had time enough to send one more automated message, hoping they would respond. Even with no power, they should still have been able to. Every ship had built in redundancies. But there was still nothing.

"One minute," said Inge's voice.

"Don't be shy, my little Älskare," said Juergenson. "I'll be gentle. I've been waiting two days for you."

"Initiate docking procedures," said Inge. The *Skalbagge* was close enough now. Juergenson made one more, slight change. There was a gentle quake when the two ships finally embraced.

"Ahh, that wasn't so bad, was it, my little Flickvän?"

Juergenson looked at his computer screen. The docking seal was good. In a few minutes, he would be able to go and find out what had happened over there. Everything in his gut told him it was going to be bad. He double checked his space helmet to make sure it was secure and in place. He turned on the light in his faceplate because it would be dark over there.

Amundsen Station on Europa interrupted the quiet. "Juergenson, give us an update please."

He recognized the voice. It was Ljungman. The controller usually made him laugh but now he was strictly business. They were all watching his mission with great interest.

"We have a good seal, and I'm waiting for a pressure match."

"Be safe, my friend," said Ljungman.

Juergenson never had time to reply. His own ship went black. Even the power in his faceplate switched off. He tried to turn it on again but nothing happened. His ship was dark. His spacesuit was dark. He reached for a flashlight but it wouldn't turn on. He hit it but it still didn't work. And there's no dark like the dark of space when you're cooped up inside a ship with no power.

Juergenson was a veteran pilot. He stayed calm. He tried to contact Europa, but his com was dead. He heard a strange pop in his ears. It didn't sound like his ears popping from a change in the pressure of his suit. Then he heard a noise coming from the air lock. A scraping sound. He heard the door to the airlock begin to open. He stared that way as hard as he could, hoping to see something, but it was just too dark. Suddenly, his flashlight switched on. The beam caught the opening door of the air lock. At first, Juergenson was confused by what he saw coming his way. Then he screamed. But that did him no good whatsoever.

Erik Juergenson's days of pillow talk were over.

SENATOR ALAN K SIMPSON

"What's the name of that ship again?"

"It's the *Star Ship John W Campbell Jr*, Sir. It's a long-hauler making the Saturn loop."

Captain Matthew Martin had never heard of the *Campbell* before.

"She's adrift and has no power," said Michaelson. "Sensors aren't reporting any life signs."

Martin had always liked Michaelson. The young crewman was good at his job. And he needed a good crew today. He had known it ever since he got orders from Fleet to intercept the ship. Michaelson had recommended having missiles locked and ready as they approached. That wasn't standard protocol when an Earth vessel approached another Earth vessel. Maybe if the other ship had been from Mars or Luna. But here, near Jupiter, they were too far away from the open rebellion closer to Earth.

"Keep those missiles tucked away in their tubes. Let's not show our teeth just yet. Remember, we're all one big happy family out here," said Captain Martin.

Martin looked over the shoulder of his navigator, Lieutenant Helen Constance, who was monitoring the data on her screen. He knew it was her first time past the asteroid belt. He had been out here many times before but he remembered his first time. She was probably nervous and excited, even though her icy demeanor never showed it.

It was good to be way out here again, away from the politics and chaos closer to Earth. Although the conflict with Mars and Luna was supposed to be over, there was still a lot going on. Earth had subdued the rebellions, allegedly bringing them back into the fold. It had only taken ten months and three dozen ships of Earth's Inner Fleet to get them to settle down. That and sending most of their leaders into exile on mining asteroids out past Saturn. Not a shot had been fired. But Martin knew it was only a matter of time before things flared up again.

Nine souls served on his ship, an ancient frigate named the *Simpson*, after a long dead Senator from Wyoming. Although the *Simpson* was a relic itself. The crew only called it the *Simpson* when they were filling out reports, but onboard, the crew affectionately called their ship the *Homer*, after a character in an even more ancient cartoon show that had been making a comeback lately on SpaceNet.

Even though his ship was a privateer, Martin had secured a Letter of Marque from Earth so they could do what needed to be done out here. It gave him all the leeway he needed to hunt and capture any Martian or Lunar ship that caused him a problem. While Earth kept her fleet close to home in order to protect the planet, ships like his protected their interests further out.

Lt. Constance was second in command. Martin had picked her out of all of the other candidates from her class. She had graduated from the Academy in the class of '74. Earth had just cut back on the Fleet's budget, in spite of the unrest from the inner planets. Martin wondered if there were any senators from Wyoming that had something to do with that. In any event, there were a lot of candidates to choose from for the XO job. The Fleet wasn't hiring, but many Earth privateers like his were. Martin only had to interview a few candidates to know she was the best. And so far, it seemed he had chosen well. She had been the one to lead the boarding party onto a loaded Martian merchantman near Venus a couple months ago while the rebellion was still going on. The captured ship had been turned over to the Earth Fleet Station on Ceres. The auction would take place next year, and there would be millions of credits once the ship was sold, inflating all their bank accounts.

And now they were closing in on another ship, a large, black hulk, floating in space against the stars. Maybe this would be another lucrative salvage job. At least Martin hoped so.

"Bring us alongside. Where did this ship come from again?" asked Martin.

Constance pulled up the *John W. Campbell's* flight plan. "They made the standard run to Saturn with stops at Titan and Rhea. They were heading back to Earth with a stop at Europa. Normal for a long hauler."

"Were they carrying anything unusual?"

"Nothing that's listed. Standard supplies for the colonies."

Martin looked through the view screen at the *Campbell*. "It's a mighty big ship. Looks kind of ominous dead in the water like that." He added, under his breath, "Sometimes Captains don't list everything in their cargo holds."

"Can we take her for our own?" asked Constance. "I mean, Sir, they're adrift. There's no power over there and no communication."

"We might be able to make a salvage claim. But that's a grim thing you're asking. Either they're all dead over there or they had to abandon ship. I'm thinking the worst because none of the hatches for the escape pods are open."

"I've checked...pods are all still aboard," said Constance, looking at her scans.

"Are you up for another boarding?" asked Martin.

"Sure," answered Constance, not showing a hint of hesitation.

"I'm sure you'll want to use the same five crewmen as last time."

"Sure," she said again. "You pick good people. People like me."

Martin glanced over. She wasn't smiling but merely checking her scans one more time. He liked that Constance was so sure of herself. But he was old enough to know that her confidence might get her into trouble. "There could be a ship full of dead bodies over there. Do you think you can handle that?"

"Yes. And I think my boarding party could handle it as well."

"Okay. We're getting ready to dock so we'll both know pretty soon."

Michaelson continued to pilot the ship closer to *Campbell*. When all of the displays were lined up on his screen, he said, "Ready to dock, Sir. Would you like me to complete the mooring?"

Martin said, "Proceed..."

The words had just come out of his mouth when Michaelson cut him off. 'Sir! Their power just came on. My sensors show their primary reactor coming online as well!"

"What? How can that be?"

"I'm showing the same thing," said Constance. "Also, their engines are starting to engage."

"Back us off. Now," said Martin to Michaelson. "Someone must be alive over there after all. How could they get their engines started that fast?"

Neither Michaelson nor Constance gave him an answer. It wasn't possible, was it? Whatever had happened, it was dangerous. Very dangerous. If the other ship fired up engines while they were only meters away...

Martin looked through the viewport and then down at his own sensors. "Reverse full! Get us out of here as quick as you can! Her reactor is heating up much too fast. It looks like she's getting ready to blow!"

Michaelson did as he was told and the *Simpson* began to back away quickly. The *Campbell* shrank in the *Simpson's* view screen. But not fast enough. Martin knew that if the other ship exploded at this distance it would destroy his ship as well. "Give me everything you've got," he said.

"Yes, Sir," said Michaelson. "We're already at one hundred twenty percent...one hundred twenty-five...one hundred thirty..."

The *Simpson* was an ancient ship and Martin knew it couldn't take much more. He had a choice between the devil in front or the devil inside.

"How much longer before she explodes?" asked Martin.

She looked at her readings. "Thirty seconds."

"Distance?" asked Martin.

Michaelson said, "One hundred kilometers."

Were they still too close? How had all of this happened? Martin wasn't the kind of Captain who took chances with the lives of his crew.

The *Campbell* was now just a speck on the view screen.

"One and fifty kilometers."

"Ten seconds. Nine. Eight..."

Martin said, "More speed!"

"Five, four, three, two...one..."

The explosion filled the view screen and the bridge was bathed in piercing light. Martin raised his hands to his eyes to shield them. Or maybe it was to protect him from the explosion. The *Simpson* shook as if tossed across a dance floor by a bad partner. Loose objects flew around the bridge. Martin could smell hot electronics. He thought that at any moment the hull would breach, leading to annihilation for them all. But the hull didn't breach. Within a few moments, the *Simpson* stopped shaking and objects clattered to the deck. Everyone took deep breaths, and there were nervous giggles of relief all across the bridge.

The old battlewagon had held together. They had gotten far enough away from the *Campbell* and they were all still alive.

"Status?" asked Martin.

Constance scanned the data filling her monitor. "Our paint is burnt, but we're unharmed. No systems damaged."

"Nice job," said Martin to the crew. The smell of sweat hung heavy in the air.

"Slow to a dead stop," said Martin.

Martin scratched his unruly, red beard. What had happened? *Campbell* had shown no life signs and no power when they approached. Somehow the crew had fired up the reactor. Cold-started the engines. And destroyed their ship within minutes of being dead in the water. Martin didn't know what to think. Nothing made sense. "Where was the last contact made with the *Campbell*?"

"Europa, the Swedish tending station there. Two weeks ago..."

Constance paused mid-sentence and her mouth dropped open.

"What?" asked Martin.

"Sir put the view screen on full magnification," she said.

"Why?" asked Martin.

"I think you should see this, Sir."

Martin punched some buttons on his console and gaped. There on the view screen, floating in space like a smooth asteroid, seemingly intact, was the *Campbell*.

"That's impossible," muttered the captain. Because it was.

3

BRAHE STATION

"Holy cow, why are they all so damned big on Ganymede?" muttered Oscar Gunn as he prepared to step into the ring. This wasn't his first fight, not by a long shot. Hopefully, it wouldn't be his last fight either. His opponent for this one was huge. Hell, everyone on this moon was big, even the women, the kids, and the dogs. Weight class? No such thing on Ganymede. Why couldn't he fight jockeys, midgets...sorry, little people, or maybe even ballerinas? Oscar always knew he could knock out a ballerina. But such is life as a bare-knuckle fighter. Ballerinas, little people, or jockeys didn't climb into the ring on Brahe Station.

Oscar was surprised there was even a fight ring at all. A true one with three ropes and a flexible canvas floor for good footing. It even had the right dimensions: six meters per side. On most stations, they used chalk to mark out the ring on cafeteria floors. Here on Brahe Station, they had a real gymnasium with bleachers, spectators, and a referee. The large inhabitants of Ganymede put a lot of effort into staging fights. They liked to watch combatants batter each other for their entertainment.

Brahe Station was neat and orderly as far as space stations go, giving the impression of being a safe harbor. But Oscar knew that wasn't the case. Not at all. The nickname for the station was "The Hall of Nine Hostages" and it was the seat of the O'Neil clan. The O'Neils loved mining aluminum, fighting, and taking hostages. Oscar wasn't from a rich family, nor did he have an immediate family at all, so he hoped they wouldn't take him hostage after this fight. Why would they? The O'Neils would have to wait a long time before anyone in the solar system gave them a lunar dollar for Oscar Gunn.

Oscar held onto the rope and looked across the ring beyond his opponent. One of the O'Neil's endless line of hostages was sitting ringside. He had been pointed out to Oscar earlier in the day, a member of a wealthy asteroid-mining family. While there's a certain distinction to being taken hostage by the O'Neils, Oscar didn't envy him one bit.

He leaned his head back and whispered over the crowd to Sean O'Neil, the promoter. He was also a big man but he'd begun to shrink with age. For some reason, people aged faster on low gravity moons. Oscar thought it should be the other way around but then again, he didn't know much about physics. As an eighth grade dropout on Earth, he had learned everything he needed on the streets and in the ring. "What's my take on this fight again?" he asked.

"Twenty-five percent of the house," said Sean O'Neil. "Like we agreed to over the SpaceNet. It's the standard here."

"We agreed on forty," said Oscar. He was lying of course. But the fight promoter was lying too. There was no actual standard, and they hadn't talked about the percentage. It was what you could actually get. On his first fight back on Earth, the promoter in Winnipeg had only given him fifteen percent. He had simply accepted that one, assuming that everyone was just as honest as he was. But when the promoter handed him a pitiful hundred-dollar lunar note, he vowed to always be careful to settle the percentage before the fight started. And the best time was right before he stepped into the ring because there would be no time for the promoter to think about it. Usually, he ran a one-man operation, acting as fighter, promoter, manager and cutman. But on Ganymede, you had to go through the O'Neils. So you had to play hardball.

"Twenty-five percent?" said Oscar, twisting his mouth into a frown. "That's ridiculous. I'm outa here." He picked up his fight bag and made motions like he was going to walk away. That would have been a disaster for the O'Neils. Not that Oscar would really do that, of course. He'd never get off Ganymede alive if he walked away. But negotiations were like a poker game and you had to be willing to bluff.

"I guess maybe it was thirty percent," said O'Neil quickly. He had the look of all the O'Neils, with shifty, rat-like eyes.

"Thirty percent to fight against a monster fighter like that?" sputtered Oscar. He pointed across the ring at his waiting opponent. "You gotta be kidding me. Do I look like I ever lived on the belt?"

O'Neil paused and looked Oscar up and down. "You're solid, I'll give you that. But I'm not sure you'll give my cousins their money's worth tonight. I tell you what. I might be willing to go forty percent but only if you let my boy knock you out. What do ya think?"

Oscar knew what that meant. 'Knockout' meant he'd end up close to dead. Or maybe even dead. If he let that hulking guy connect with even one punch it might be the last punch he ever took.

"I don't take dives," said Oscar. He glanced to the bleachers and saw most of the O'Neil clan. They were tapping their feet impatiently. He had the advantage right now. But he couldn't overplay his hand. He simply waited the promoter out.

"God above all of us," said Sean O'Neil in disgust. "I should take some of this mutton under my shirt and fight you myself. Forty percent! Ya jus' wanna fuckin' spit on me, don't ya?"

Oscar knew when to shut up. The negotiations were working, although he knew the promoter could have dozens of O'Neil thugs here in seconds to take care of him. And before long he'd be pushed through an airlock. But then again, if that happened the fight would have to be called off. So once again, he said nothing.

"You're a greedy bastard, aren't ya?" asked O'Neil. But his voice carried with it a small bit of respect.

Oscar almost smiled at that. What was that old saying, something about how it takes a bastard to know a bastard? He decided it was time to finally say something.

"I'll give you a good show."

O'Neil shook his head and grimaced. "Not the show they really want. What they really want is to see my cousin rip your head off of your shoulders. Is that what you'll give them?"

"How 'bout I catch the morning shuttle and move on?" said Oscar, stepping back from the ring.

"How 'bout we take you hostage?" countered Sean O'Neil. "If you don't bring in any money, we'll make you a slave for our house. It's always nice to have a slave to clean the toilets."

Oscar cursed under his breath. O'Neil had been getting ready to cave.

All through the gymnasium, rowdy voices were getting rowdier. The impatience of the crowd was the only card he held right now. He had been risking a lot to play hardball with the O'Neils. They might have had pretensions of being a fine house, but when it came down to it, they would always be a pack of thugs under the pressurized dome.

The crowd continued to get louder. Catcalls began pouring out from the top bleachers. O'Neil looked around, taking in the whole scene. Finally, he turned back to Oscar and ran a hand through his thinning gray hair. "Okay," he sighed. "We're all here for a little bit a fun tonight.

I'm not trying to be the bad guy. We like to be friendly to one another on Brahe."

Oscar swallowed hard and waited.

"Thirty-five percent. That's the best I can do. You gotta leave me a little meat on the mutton."

Oscar knew when to grab onto a lifeline. "Okay," he said, trying to sound reluctant, even though he knew he had won. "Thirty-five it is. But you'll have to throw in a corner man. I'm on my own."

The promoter nodded his head. He looked over into the crowd and whistled. A teenage O'Neil came out of the crowd and ran over to the two men. Oscar didn't like the look of the kid. He had the same rat eyes as all of the O'Neils, but he also looked eager to please. Oscar knew he could never trust him. He was an O'Neil after all, but he only needed to trust him for as long as it took to finish this fight.

"He'll do," muttered Oscar.

The promoter shook Oscar's hand and smiled with relief. He went over to join his clan in the bleachers. Would he still be smiling when the fight was over? Definitely not.

Oscar handed the boy his bag. "Don't let this out of your sight. Keep it right next to you at all times. Got it?"

The teenager nodded and smiled. He was definitely a smiler. A real people pleaser. Or maybe he was just an idiot and that's why the promoter had picked him for the job.

Oscar gave him a stern look. "You're in over your head. If you knew what was going to happen tonight, you wouldn't be here. You'd be far away."

The boy continued to smile. "I've seen plenty of fights and plenty of fighters. What makes you so special?"

"You've never seen me fight. I'm going to give them something that no one on Ganymede will ever forget."

The smile left the boy's face and Oscar chuckled to himself. He had gotten the boy's attention with that one. Maybe he wasn't such an idiot after all...

4

EUROPA STATION

Aaron Ljungman was normally a very calm person, at least outwardly. Like most Swedes, he kept his emotions beneath the surface. But right now those emotions were percolating way down deep in his gut and threatening to erupt like an Icelandic volcano. Erik Juergenson was his best friend way out here on Europa. In fact, the two of them had been boyhood friends in Borås, following the same path through school and graduating from the same class in the Swedish Space Academy. All Swedes had to stick together in space. They were a small minority compared to the Americans, Russians, Japanese, and Chinese. But Erik was more than just a countryman. And now he had gone missing.

Nobody got along with each other particularly well out here. There were too many conflicting interests and too many national characteristics that clashed with each other. So it was up to the Swedes on Europa to play their historical role as diplomats. Back on Earth, Sweden had managed to stay out of all the big wars, ever since they sat out World War One and World War Two. Okay, they took sides in the early Colonization Wars on the Moon but that was ancient history by now. Since then, they had gone back to being the kind of people who could see both sides of every argument. And they were able to make a lot of money while doing it. The Americans hated the Russians. The Russians hated the Japanese. And everybody hated the inscrutable Chinese. But nobody hated the even-tempered Swedes. So they were rarely in danger. Until now.

"Replay that video again," muttered Ljungman.

"Here you go," said Broberg, and she pushed a few buttons. Both she and Ljungman stared at the screen, Broberg tapping her foot and Ljungman gritting his teeth. They both knew what was coming.

On the video, *Skalbagge* slowly approached the hulking *John W. Campbell Jr* like a beetle approaching an elephant. It was almost as if Erik had known something was wrong and seemed reluctant to get too close. That was unusual for Erik. He was usually fearless when docking. But not this time.

And that's when the lights on the *Campbell* blinked out. Not an earth-shaking development, for that had happened several times since the *Campbell* had contacted Europa Station. But this was right before docking. The com was still open and Ljungman could hear Erik utter curses in both Swedish and English. Normally he would have chuckled at that. But he knew what was going to happen next.

The *Skalbagge* continued to approach and it was clear that Erik had switched over to manual docking. Again, not that unusual. He was good at doing this and had done it a hundred times before.

"Ahh, that wasn't so bad, was it?" said Erik's voice on the video as the two ships docked. Watching, Erik felt a rush of affection for his friend who always talked to ships like girlfriends he was making love to. It was his 'pillow talk.'

On the video, Ljungman heard his own voice say, "Be safe, my friend."

And that's when everything went skit.

"Oh, Helvete! I've just lost power," said Erik's voice, not too loud but with an edge. He was an experienced pilot but he'd probably never lost power immediately after docking. It would be really dark in his cabin, with his ship butted up against the massive *Campbell*, blocking any ambient light through his view screen.

Broberg and Ljungman could barely see the two ships clinging to each other against the black background of space.

"Aaron, can you hear me?" asked Erik.

"Yes, yes, I can hear you," came Ljungman's voice in reply. Erik couldn't hear him. No matter how many times Ljungman replied, there was no response from *Skalbagge*. But the com was still open and Broberg and Ljungman could hear every sound from the cabin. There were small clicking sounds as Erik tried his flashlight, his faceplate light, and several buttons on his console. Then it was quiet for a few moments, with just the sound of Erik breathing. Between engine noise, crew noise, and radios, a ship's bridge is normally a noisy place. But there were no crew members on this ship. It was especially creepy to hear only Erik's breathing, in and out, in and out, faster and faster as he became more alarmed.

Then they could hear another sound. Something was scraping against metal. The metal of the airlock? And then there was a pop like a pressurized can of tennis balls exploding. And then something else.

Ljungman felt sweat trickle down the back of his neck as he listened to this sound. It was almost like...well...like slithering.

And that's when Erik screamed. The sound made Ljungman and Broberg nearly jump out of their seats, even though they had heard it before. It wasn't a soft scream. Not even close. It made the speakers distort. And then it cut off.

All of that would have been bad enough. But what happened next on the view screen was simply mind-boggling. It could have been a trick of the light. It could have. But Ljungman didn't think so.

For a brief moment, the lights of the *Campbell* switched on. They could clearly see the *Skalbagge* silhouetted against it like a small, black bug. And then the *Skalbagge* began to shake. Over the com, they could hear things rattling around on the bridge, as though the ship was in the midst of a meteor shower. Then the *Campbell* began to phase in and out as if there was something wrong with the video. A rift opened all around the *Campbell*'s docking bay, a blacker than black opening larger than a small spaceship, larger than the *Skalbagge*. And then, suddenly, the *Skalbagge* was gone and the lights of the *Campbell* blinked out.

"Slow motion again, please," said Ljungman, his voice low and insistent. He had watched this many times already but he was drawn to it like a train wreck. A train wreck involving his best friend. His buddy. His *kompis*.

In slow motion, it wasn't hard to see what the whole incident looked like, as hard as that was to believe. First, the *Skalbagge* began to vibrate. Then it began to shake like a wet dog. And then a rift appeared in the *Campbell*, looking exactly like a...well...like a mouth. The mouth opened wider and sucked in the *Skalbagge*. Or, rather, it swallowed the *Skalbagge* whole. The mouth closed and Erik's ship was gone, leaving just the floating, dark hulk of the *Campbell* in its wake, hanging in space again with no power, no movement, nothing.

"Odin only knows what happened to my friend," muttered Ljungman.

"Do you think he can still be alive?" asked Broberg.

"There's only one way to find out."

"You're not going out there, are you? Think about what almost happened to that American ship. When it got close, the *Campbell* fired up its reactor and blew itself up. The American ship barely got away."

Ljungman ran his hand through his curly, blond hair. "But it didn't blow itself up. It certainly looked like it did but it's still hanging up there, undamaged."

"Well, something happened. Our sensors showed a huge explosion, as if the reactor had really exploded. Maybe if the American ship hadn't gotten far enough away it would have been pulverized."

"Maybe." Ljungman stared down at the floor.

Broberg reached over and turned Ljungman's face towards her own. "You can't go out there. Space Fleet will never give you permission."

Ljungman sighed. "I don't plan to ask Space Fleet."

"But you'll be drummed out and sent home. That is if you even survive."

"Well, I'm going out there anyhow. They just finished repairs on *Trollslända*. I'll just have to get a crew together. A lot of people on Europa owe me favors."

Broberg gasped. The Swedes were the diplomats of space. They didn't get involved in conflicts except as peacemakers. They were not well represented in Earth Fleet. But they did have a few warships, just in case.

Warships like *Trollslända*.

5

SENATOR ALAN K SIMPSON

Data is data, but sometimes it lies. Martin looked at the vid screen and cursed. If the *Campbell* had really exploded, it would be nothing but space dust now. They had all watched it explode. All their sensors had recorded the core meltdown. The *Simpson* even had burn marks. But improbably, no impossibly, the Campbell was still there on the vid screen. All their sensors verified that fact as well. And now the Campbell was moving again, ponderously heading away from Jupiter towards the inner planets, with Captain Martin ordering his ship to pursue.

Eyeballs also lie. After everything that had just happened, Captain Martin's eyeballs were very tired. He needed to get away from the bridge to study the data someplace quieter. He sent all the sensor data to his laptop. Satisfied he had collected everything he needed, he headed towards his quarters. On the way there he stopped at the mess for a cup of coffee and something to eat.

The *Simpson* was lucky to have a real cook. In fact, they had an excellent cook. The crew of the *Simpson*, including Captain Martin, blamed their extra weight on the Chef. "So, what's on the menu today, Jelly Roll?" asked the captain as he walked into the mess.

Jelly Roll answered by holding out the captain's personal, steaming coffee mug.

"You got radar-mods implanted in your skull or something?" asked the captain. "How did you know I was coming down here just now?"

Jelly Roll winked. "It's my job."

The mug was from the Class of '59.

"Sometimes it's really creepy when you do stuff like that," said Martin. But that didn't stop him from grabbing the mug with his free hand and taking a sip. Jelly Roll always kept the coffee fresh, and Martin couldn't remember a time when there had been old coffee in the urn.

"It's a small ship, Skipper," said Jelly Roll. "I know everyone's footsteps, and how they sound against the metal of the deck plating. Your steps are easy to make out because you drag your right heel a little bit. I'm sure that's the first place you wear out your boot."

Martin looked down and lifted up his right foot. "Huh. You're right. Okay, Sherlock. Maybe you should be the captain of this boat. Or at least head of security if we had one."

Jelly Roll gave a hearty, rolling laugh, true to his nickname. Everything about the cook was too big for the ship, even his laugh. "This mess is command enough for me, Skipper. Every morning I work as if there's a storm brewing and every night after supper I relax as if we're sailing for the Southern Cross."

The Captain took a step towards the coffee urn intending to get cream and sugar, but after his first sip, he realized that Jelly Roll had foreseen that as well. He decided against going back to his cabin to look at the data, but instead grabbed a table in the corner of the mess. There weren't many places on the *Homer* where a crewman could get away, but Jelly Roll made sure anyone walking into his mess felt as if it was their own.

"Skipper, I gotta get ready for supper mess tonight. Forgive me being rude, but I need to check on the roast."

"Roast? Fancy for a Wednesday night don't you think?"

"No, not too fancy if you're getting us another prize."

"Don't celebrate too early. She's one of ours. We probably aren't taking her."

A look of disappointment crossed the chow boss' pudgy face before dissolving into his usual smile. "Then we'll celebrate the upcoming rescue of our Earth comrades from their misfortune." His round eyes blinked a couple of times. "I have baby potatoes and carrots to go along with the roast. And nice homemade gravy too."

"What if our 'Earth Comrades' on that ship are all dead?" asked Martin.

Without missing a beat, the chow boss said, "The crew of the *Homer* will still be hungry. They'll appreciate Old Jelly Roll taking good care of them in their hour of sadness."

The captain chuckled. "Like usual, you have all the bases covered. Are you sure you wouldn't rather be Captain?"

Jelly Roll laughed one more time and headed for the kitchen. As the cook opened the door, the delightful aroma of the roast wafted out. Martin's mouth watered. But he decided against having a snack. He wanted to be hungry when it was time to eat that roast.

He took his coffee and settled into a comfortable chair. He set his laptop on a small table and began to review the data from all the ship's sensors and cameras. There was a critical point when all of the *Homer's* sensors showed the same thing. The *Campbell* should've exploded. But it hadn't.

He went back to the beginning. The sensors showed the engines attempting a dangerous cold start, the core heating up and finally reaching critical mass leading to the explosion that should have pulverized the ship. There was simply no doubt in what the sensors showed.

The cameras showed the same thing. But then he decided to try something on a hunch. He put the time signature up for both the sensor readings and the camera feeds side by side on his screen, superimposed over the images. He ran the sequence. There was a discrepancy. It was very small but it shouldn't have been there in the first place. The sensors showed the exact moment of the explosion .33 seconds before the cameras. Of course, there is always going to be a delay in how long it takes light to travel to the camera. At the last moment, the *Simpson* was not far from the *Campbell*. Only about two hundred kilometers away. The light from the explosion should have arrived at the cameras within a millionth of a second. Even if it hadn't, the sensors and cameras should've been synched. There should be no gap at all. So what accounted for that .33 second gap? False information? But why would anyone want to do that? The obvious answer was to scare them away. And that part had worked. The *Simpson* had backed away as fast as it could go, almost blowing up its own engines in the process. But if there hadn't been an explosion, how did the burn marks on the outside of the ship get there? It was still a quandary, but Martin thought he might be getting closer to figuring it out.

"How does our mystery ship look now, Skipper?" asked Jelly Roll.

Martin had been so engrossed in what he was doing that he hadn't noticed Jelly Roll sit down beside him. The Chef held a plate of fresh baked chocolate chip cookies. The captain grabbed one from the plate and popped it into his mouth. "Just one," he mumbled through a mouthful of cookie. "I don't want to spoil my dinner when we eat that delicious roast. So when did you have time to bake these?"

"It's all in the planning. I have another batch baking right now. I'll take them out of the oven in a few minutes."

Jelly Roll reached across the small table and turned Martin's laptop so he could see the screen. "Mind if I check out the sensor data?"

Martin chuckled. "You make dinner for the crew, you bake cookies, and now you want to analyze our sensor data. Is there anything you can't do?"

Jelly Roll didn't look up from the screen. He stared at it for another minute. "Why did you put the timeline from the camera feed and the sensors side by side?"

"I was just curious."

Jelly Roll nodded. "And they don't match up, do they?"

"No." The man was amazing.

"So," asked Jelly Roll, "any idea what's going on over there?"

"I wish."

The cook turned the laptop away and looked off into the distance for a moment. Then he turned back to Martin. "Well, it's clear to me that you have a cake problem."

Martin had just finished eating his chocolate chip cookie and paused before taking a sip of his coffee. "A cake problem? What's that?"

"You should spend more time in here with me. You'd learn how to conquer the whole solar system. I've only got another minute so I'll make this quick. A cake problem is...no matter how many cakes I've baked in my life, I still need to stick in a toothpick to make sure they're cooked all the way through before I take them out of the oven. Even after all these years, I still have to do that every time. If I don't, the sponge will usually be either undercooked or overcooked. If it's undercooked, the sponge will collapse in the middle. If it's overcooked, the sides will get too brown and it'll be too dry when it's ready to serve. The trick is to pull it out exactly when it's done. Not too soon and not too late. That's the secret of a good cake. And you can't do it without checking it with a toothpick."

Martin scratched his head. "That's very interesting, Jelly Roll. But what can that possibly have to do with the mystery ship?"

"It's a cake, Skipper. You need to take a toothpick and stick it in its middle to see what's really going on."

"Huh," muttered the captain. "Good analogy."

The captain mused on that for a few more moments. Then he said, "I think I might have the right toothpick."

Martin reached over to a nearby com-box and called the bridge. "Lt. Constance, I need you to start gathering your boarding crew. We're going back in to dock with the *Campbell*. I want to know what's going on inside that ship."

The speaker crackled before Constance's voice answered. "But Captain, we got close once already and it almost blew us up."

"But it didn't. I'm still working it out, but that ship didn't explode. That's obvious because it's still out there. Somehow...somebody did something to our sensors and cameras so we just thought it exploded. Some sort of defense mechanism on that ship, although not one I've ever heard of. But I think we can modify our sensors to protect against false readings. I'll explain more in a bit. Out."

Martin turned off the com-box and smiled at his cook. "A cake problem, huh?"

"That's one sharp toothpick you're going to stick in that cake, Skipper."

"The sharpest," said Martin, reaching for another cookie.

6

BRAHE STATION

Fighting is a simple sport. All it takes is a few meters of floor and two people willing to punch and kick each other into oblivion. Weight class? That was a luxury left behind on Earth. Back home in South Carolina, Oscar Gunn would be a Cruiserweight at ninety-five kilos, but this was Ganymede. Here, he was just over fifty kilos. There were gravity plates under the floor, sure. But they weren't set to 1G. Nope, it was something less. Of course it was. Less gravity would make Big O'Neil look better. He could jump higher, launch his kicks from further away, and make more of a show for his clan tonight.

The bell clanged to start the first round.

Oscar took a small step forward. He knew he had to keep his feet firmly planted on the canvas floor if he wanted to land any decent punches. From the opposite corner, Big O'Neil stepped forward as well, but then immediately jumped a meter into the air in a spinning hook kick. Oscar grunted. What a showoff. There was no way he could connect with a kick like that from across the ring. He was obviously just playing to the crowd and it worked. They all cheered, whistled, and stamped their collective feet.

He was not intimidated. At least not yet. He moved towards the center of the ring. He needed to find out just what the big man really had.

Big O'Neil executed another spin kick.

Oscar had been expecting this and slid back, but the low gravity fooled him. At the last second, he had to put up a hand to protect his face. Big O'Neil's foot glanced off his chin. When the big man landed back on his feet, Oscar used a bolo punch to hit him in the gut. He heard a whoosh of air escape from the big man's lips. He felt a momentary rush a pleasure from landing the blow, but there was no time to savor it. Quicker than Oscar would have expected, Big O'Neil fired back with an odd punch of his own, a one-hand back fist that caught Oscar just below his left eye. He felt something trickle down his cheek.

A cut. Blood already. It was below the eye so he could still see. Lucky.

Big O'Neil smiled like a wolf getting ready to devour his kill. He came in hard and fast, using all his punches, wanting to end the fight. He kept his feet grounded and began pummeling Oscar, hitting like a maniac.

Punch, block, punch.

Oscar fended off each blow, both to his face and midsection. The big man wouldn't beat him this way. Even though Oscar was big, he was smaller and quicker than this monster of a man. Oscar waited for an opening. When one came he lashed out with an overhand punch, illegal on Earth. But this was Ganymede. He connected and hit the big man in the right eye.

Now there was more blood, but this time, it was from O'Neil.

The big man shook his head. His left eye widened while his right eye began to swell. His mouth hung open. He wasn't used to getting hit by a smaller opponent. But then his lips compressed into a snarl. The man was getting pissed. Oscar felt a rush of elation. It's never a good idea to let your emotions take hold of you in a fight. Oscar thought he could take advantage of the big man losing his head. But he had underestimated.

Before Oscar knew what hit him, Big O'Neil executed a nearly perfect Jujitsu move. Oscar was thrown down onto the mat with the big man's tree trunk legs wrapped around him. Soon he was being crushed between the man's legs and smothered with body blows. It had all happened so quickly that Oscar felt disoriented, as if this was all a dream. The rank odor of the big man was nauseating. He felt the man's sweat pouring down onto his own skin as he got pummeled. He knew he wouldn't last long under these conditions.

Oscar glanced beneath Big O'Neil's armpit towards his own corner. His bag was still there covered by his robe, still next to the teenager. In the midst of his difficult situation, that made him feel better.

The body blows continued to rain down on Oscar. Although he was able to fend most of them off with his arms, some were connecting with his midsection, his legs, his head. It was time to do something, anything.

Oscar was just able to force his elbows under Big O'Neil's thighs. Then he grunted and lifted the big man's hips into the air. Thank God for low gravity. He grunted again and was able to throw Big O'Neil off.

He bounced to his feet, finally able to breathe fresh air again, or what passed for fresh air on Ganymede. Big O'Neil got to his feet just as the bell clanged.

The first round was over.

Oscar stepped towards his corner. It was time to do what he had come here for in the first place. The O'Neils not only enjoyed fights, but they enjoyed booze and drugs. Oscar knew that half the clan would already be too wasted to interfere.

The O'Neils made high quality fuel and mined high quality aluminum. But they also made their living taking hostages, the richer the better. They traveled the solar system looking for human prizes to bring home to Ganymede. Most of the richest families had no problem paying huge ransoms to get their loved ones back. For the most part, the O'Neils treated their hostages kindly. Among the uber-rich, it was a badge of honor to have been held hostage by the O'Neils.

Nonetheless, not every family was willing to pay. Either they stood on principal, or they were not as well off as they let the rest of the solar system think they were. When that was the case, they hired someone like Oscar Gunn to bring their loved-ones home at a much discounted price. Some people called Oscar a 'Special Negotiator.' Everyone else called him 'The Surgeon,' because he didn't mind slicing through a problem to make it right.

And that's why he was here on Ganymede.

Oscar reached his corner. It would have been much easier if the O'Neils had brought his hostage to the fight tonight. But they hadn't.

The rat-faced O'Neil boy stood up from the trainer's chair and grabbed Oscar's elbow, trying to get him to sit down so he could help him with the cut under his eye. Maybe the kid was a virtuous lad after all, unlike the rest of his clan, but Oscar waved him away.

He climbed through the ropes and out of the ring. His bag was still waiting under his robe where he had left it. The teenager had been too wrapped up in the fight to get curious and check it out. Good.

Oscar grabbed his robe and put it on. The spectators sitting closest began to grumble. "What's he doing?" muttered someone. The bell clanged again to announce the second round.

He didn't head back towards the ring but tied his robe around his waist.

Sean O'Neil was in his face in a few moments. "Where do you think you're going?" he shouted over the now-escalating din from the spectators. "Get back in there and fight or you'll give up your money and I'll kick your ass myself!"

Oscar didn't reply. He simply reached down and unzipped his bag.

"Are you deaf? " shouted Sean O'Neil. "You promised us a good show. Now get back out there and give us one!"

Oscar pulled a gun out of the bag. He pressed its barrel against Sean O'Neil's forehead. "This is a pistol," he said tersely. "A Saeilo K25. Made with care on Mars. It's loaded." He cocked the trigger with a click that was audible even over the chaos in the room.

O'Neil's eyes opened wide. "How did you get that in here?" he said in a tortured voice. He held his head still. Sean O'Neil was afraid.

"It's made of Bryantonium," said Oscar. "Maybe you've heard of that. They mine it on Janus. It's stronger than tungsten. And impossible to detect. Now let's go. Just you and me."

Sean O'Neil found his voice again. "I'm not the only O'Neil here. There's a whole clan looking at us right now. And you're just one man with a pistol. How far do you think you'll get?"

He bent down and reached into the bag with his free hand. He pulled out a bomb. It wasn't just any bomb. It was a Scott-Key Mark 7, used mainly by miners on the asteroid belt. Very small and very powerful. He held it up so Sean O'Neil could see it.

"This is a bomb. It's made out of Bryantonium too."

O'Neil pursed his lips. "Oh."

Oscar pressed his face closer to the other man's face. "I have a client on Mars. You're holding his daughter hostage. I'm here to take her back."

"A girl? Which one. We're holding three. May the crows curse you."

"Molly Mackintosh. Take me to her." Oscar motioned for Sean to turn around and pointed the gun at the back of his head, holding the bomb high with his other hand so the entire O'Neil clan could see. It grew quiet as everyone in the gym realized what was happening. The two of them began walking away from the ring.

"You would want Molly Mackintosh," muttered Sean O'Neil over his shoulder. "She's our most valuable hostage. We were hoping to get a pretty penny for her. Maybe we can make some kind of a deal. But, you should know she's not worth the trouble. She's a bad one. We should have put her out the airlock months ago, even if she's a pretty lass to look upon."

"Move," said Oscar through clenched teeth.

In a few moments, they were out into a dark, smelly hallway as all hell broke loose behind them in the gym.

7

EUROPA STATION

Aaron Ljungman hunched over his Krater beer and gazed out through the huge picture window of Pappalardo's Bar, which overlooked the sprawling complex of buildings at the edge of the Tyre impact crater – the massive drills at the center of The Bull's Eye, the Hydroponics Quadrant, the star-shaped Hammarskjöld Residential Building, the Ikea Terminal Complex, and on and on, all sitting on top of 20 kilometers of ice. With its underground ocean containing three times as much water as Earth and its endless supply of geothermal heat, Europa was the jewel of the Jupiter system. All the colonies on the other moons relied on Europa's riches to survive. Any craft from out beyond Saturn had to refuel and resupply here. Europa was like an ancient crossroads city on Earth, where travelers all had to stop on their way to someplace else. And Sweden had cannily developed Europa for their own.

As a Swede, Ljungman was proud of all that, of the riches and influence his native country had achieved here. They had done it by keeping a low profile, by getting along with anyone and everyone, by making themselves useful. They were classic politicians. But, like every native Swede, his genetic makeup still contained the DNA of a Viking warrior. And a Viking warrior needed a ship...

Aaron took another gulp of beer and chuckled. He supposed that was a ridiculous analogy. After all, the Vikings were more than a thousand years into the past. Look how far the human race had progressed since then. Wasn't he sitting here in a bar 390 million miles from Earth? But some things were eternal, like loyalty to your best friend. And Erik

Juergenson was his best friend. It wasn't like Aaron could just walk out into space and rescue him from whatever was inside that black spaceship.

That's why he had called on a VIP to meet him here tonight at Pappalardo's. And also, on three other cohorts to meet him at midnight inside the Terminal Complex. *Trollslända* normally fielded a crew of ten. But Aaron was a former pilot and he knew the ins and outs of Swedish spaceships better than most. He could get by with a three-man crew. He needed help with sensors, engineering, and life support. He would pilot the ship, manage the weapons, and navigate.

He had worked in Central Communications for the past two years, monitoring every ship that came and went. He knew just about everybody who had anything to do with the Company. Many people who fled Earth to work far out in the solar system were not necessarily people of the highest moral character. Aaron knew who had been skimming off the top from the Company books. He knew who had been sleeping with somebody else's wife or husband. He knew who was involved in the black market. The people he had contacted this afternoon owed him their very freedom. Aaron's silence had been keeping them out of asteroid prison.

"*Hej*," said Alrik Nyland.

Aaron hadn't noticed the other man come into the bar. He flinched and stood up. The two men shook hands amiably and sat back down. Aaron motioned for a waitress and ordered them four shots of Aquavit. He would need all the help he could get tonight.

"What can I do for you?" asked Nyland. He was the man who oversaw all the comings and goings of spaceships on Europa. It was a lofty position and he made a lot of money. But in the past few years, he had sent home more than twice as much as he had made. Aaron had stumbled upon his financial records during an end of the year audit. Since he and Nyland were drinking buddies, he had tweaked the records so no one else would find out. But he had made sure to let Nyland know that he knew. Yes, they were drinking buddies but information was valuable on a small moon like Europa.

"I need to ask you a favor," said Aaron, his voice calm, as if he were going to ask Nyland to watch his cat while he took a trip to Ganymede. But Nyland wasn't fooled. His face went as pale as the ice beneath the building they were sitting in.

"What kind of favor?"

Just then the waitress showed up with their shots. Aaron set two shots in front of Nyland and two in front of himself and waved the waitress away. He raised one shot. "*Skol*."

"*Skol*," echoed Nyland in the ancient, time-honored way. They both drank. And then they drank the second round. The Aquavit at Pappalardo's was some of the strongest in the solar system and they each struggled not to cough.

Aaron cleared his throat. He leaned forward and spoke softly. "This is going to sound crazy. But I need a spaceship. And I need it by second midnight tonight."

Nyland's eyes got as big as potato dumplings. Then he leaned forward and whispered, "A spaceship? What, like a runabout or something? Are you a smuggler?"

Aaron shook his head. "No. I'm an honest fellow. Unlike some people around here."

This time Nyland's face flushed as red as the spot on Jupiter, which was hanging in the sky outside the big picture window. "Are you threatening to..."

"Forget that," interrupted Aaron, putting his hand on Nyland's arm. "I wasn't talking about you. Not really. I just mean that we're friends, right? And friends help each other out. And they keep each other's secrets."

Nyland looked sick to his stomach. It probably wasn't from the Aquavit.

"I need a ship tonight," whispered Aaron through clenched teeth. "A certain one. They just put it in the hangar this morning after two months of repairs."

Nyland looked confused as he struggled to understand. Then his mouth dropped open. "You're not thinking about..."

Aaron nodded his head and stared directly into Nyland's blue eyes. "We're friends. We do each other favors. And I need this."

"You want *Trollslända*," the other man muttered, seemingly to himself. "You want the *jävla Trollslända*."

"I'll bring it back," said Aaron. "I promise."

8

SENATOR ALAN K SIMPSON

"Make no mistake, I want you in and out of that ship as soon as possible," said Captain Martin to Lieutenant Constance, who was standing near the airlock with her boarding party. "We just need to know the situation over there. Are they alive or are they dead? If they're alive, who's in control? Were they hijacked? There are just too many unknowns here. But the main thing is, I don't want any of you getting hurt. Understood? None of you gets hurt. If you have to, get the hell out of there at the first sign of danger. We have plenty of juice over here if we need to blast the *Campbell* to kingdom come and this time for real. I'll do it if I have to. I don't like to be fooled."

After his conversation with Jelly Roll, Martin had scrolled through his ship's computer code for hours, especially the code that was responsible for the ship's sensors and camera feed to the view screen. He knew his ship's computer code better than anyone, but still, he'd overlooked the anomaly the first twenty-five times that he scrolled by. Someone had made a very subtle change, just two lines of code buried deep.

His ship had been hacked. Presumably, someone on the *Campbell* had made that change. That had never been done to a ship captained by Matthew Martin before and it really pissed him off. It was as bad as if someone had snuck a camera inside his pants.

The tiny bit of code they had inserted had allowed the hacker to project a false image onto *Homer*'s view screen, so it would show the *Campbell* exploding. It even projected false images of burn marks on the outside of *Homer*'s hull. But none of those images accounted for the turbulence that almost shook the *Homer* apart after the 'explosion.' After many more unsuccessful attempts, Martin found two more lines of hacked code in the feed to the stabilizers. That would certainly account for the turbulence that had tossed objects around the bridge and made them all think the explosion was real.

It had been a well-orchestrated ruse by someone who really knew what they were doing. But to what purpose? After the ruse was over and the hacked code had done its work, they could see the *Campbell* still intact on the view screen, floating in space. Did the hacker think that the *Homer* would just run away and keep on running? Did they think that the *Homer* would tear itself apart trying to back away in the first place? It almost had. Well, whatever its intent, the scheme had failed and Martin had removed those lines of code. And now, pissed off as he was, Martin would never leave this sector without finding out who was on that ship. And this time, the view screen and sensors wouldn't be fooled by a few lines of damned code, because he had removed the offending ones and had done a search for any other lines of code like them. What the view screen and sensors showed now was what was really out there.

He gazed at the boarding party. As always, they looked formidable. Leopold Jagr and Abdul Haleem Karam stood behind Constance lugging AK-5s, their proven weapons of choice. The Bofors automatic rifles had been effective during the last boarding. They had scared the crew of the Martian ship so badly that no shots had to be fired, which was a side benefit of such fearsome-looking weapons. Behind the two was the other female of the group, Silence Bohannon. She was a large woman who carried a SAAB CBJ-MS. The small submachine gun held rounds with a tungsten core that could penetrate most body armors. The weapon seemed slight in her big hands. Standing by the airlock, Constance carried the smallest weapon, her Saeilo K25 sidearm. Unlike the other three, her weapon was still in its holster.

Constance was calm and focused as usual and focused her entire attention on her boarding party. "We're here for a recon only. Captain's orders. We don't want a shooting gallery over there."

Abdul double checked his rifle. "If they start something, we'll give them a hundred dicks right back. We'll put it up their asses if we need to. It's been awhile since I've had a chance to use this weapon. I have a feeling today might be the day."

The rest of the team laughed but Constance held up her hand. "Recon and rescue. That's all. Is that clear?"

Disappointed, the others nodded.

Martin knew this was a good team. While the three crew members

Constance had picked might be crude, they would still follow her orders. Martin reached for the com-box to talk to the bridge. "What's the distance to the *Campbell*?"

Michaelson answered in his flat, matter-of-fact voice. "Two hundred and fifty kilometers, Sir. Do you still want us to dock?"

"Yes, start the approach. I'll be there in a minute. Out."

He thought of giving Lieutenant Constance and her team a pep talk, but he didn't want to break up their routine, so he turned towards the bridge. Behind him, he heard Lieutenant Constance say, "Five minutes. We're going by the book. The way we practiced. I don't want any screw-ups over there. Is that understood?"

Martin smiled. Constance had been a great hire for the ship. But now he needed to get back to the bridge. He passed the crew quarters and mess. The aroma made him want to go inside, but food would have to wait. Hopefully, this would all be over in an hour or so and he could see what Jelly Roll was cooking up...

An explosion rocked the ship. Martin fell to the deck. He struggled to get back up as the ship reeled like a sailboat in heavy seas. The lights went off for a brief second before coming back on. Had someone hacked into the ship's computer again? That seemed doubtful because this time the entire ship was shaking. Alarms sounded, calling everyone to battle stations. He knew he had made a mistake in coming down to see Constance off. He should have been on the bridge. Neither he nor his executive officer was there. Only Michaelson. He started running.

There was another explosion. The ship rocked and bucked like a bronco. This time, the lights went out for five seconds before the backup generator kicked in again. He kept his feet, reeling like a drunk. He could see the bridge up ahead and could smell burning electrical components. Acrid smoke swirled through the air. The *Campbell* must have fired on his ship. But what kinds of weapons did it have? It was supposed to be a common freighter.

The loudspeaker sounded. "Captain to the bridge! Captain to the bridge!" Michaelson's usually even voice was filled with panic.

Martin charged through the doorway. "Report, Mr. Michaelson. What the hell is going on?"

"They hit us with their Gaston lasers. But they've been altered or something. They fried most of the electronics to our lasers with their first shot."

"Isn't our hull plating polarized?"

"Of course, Sir. And the polarization is still operational. But somehow they fried our lasers. I haven't seen that kind of firepower since the war with the inner planets. One more shot and they're going to split us in two!"

"Shall I ready our missiles?" asked Crewman Oceanus Clements. He had taken Lieutenant Constance's station. Martin rarely had the same duty rotations as the younger man, so he didn't know him well. He knew he should be annoyed with him for speaking out of turn.

"Negative. We're too close...we'll blow each other out of space."
Martin found his captain's chair. He liked to know all the facts before making a decision. Looking at his monitor, he was overwhelmed by all the information that flooded his computer screen. He knew he had to make a decision from his gut. And he had to make it fast. "Get us closer. I want us so close that their forward battery can't shoot at us. I want us to kiss them if we can. We still have engines, don't we?"

"I think so, Skipper," said Michaelson.

Michaelson punched a few commands to take the *Homer* off autopilot. He grasped the yolk in his sweaty hands. "It's not responding, Sir. It feels like something else is controlling the ship. And the *Campbell* is maneuvering closer. It's almost like they're attempting to dock with us."

Martin gritted his teeth. From the way the other ship was moving, he knew that was exactly what was they were doing.

A female voice sounded through the com. It was Lieutenant Constance. "Sir, do you need me to return to the bridge?"

"No, stay where you are. It looks like they're going to try and board us. I want you to give them a nice welcome. Do not let them onto our ship."

"Aye, aye, Sir," answered Constance.

"The hunters have become the hunted," muttered Michaelson, still gripping the useless yolk.

By now the blackness of the *Campbell* filled *Homer*'s view screen. Something shimmered in the blackness as if some hull lights were blinking on. But they weren't solid lights. They shimmered and seemed to phase in and out in a circular pattern. No, that wasn't right. It was more like an oval that grew wider by the second, resembling a huge mouth. There seemed to be something inside that mouth, menacing and sharp. It looked like shiny, metallic teeth.

The mouth opened wider and made ready to swallow Captain Martin's ship.

9

BRAHE STATION

With each step, Oscar thought he might have to shoot someone. He was surprised when he didn't. None of the O'Neils followed him out of the gymnasium. The corridors to Brahe Station were silent. That made Oscar nervous. His own hostage, Sean O'Neil, hadn't said a word. That was practically a miracle for the fight promoter, so it made Oscar even more nervous. He had let Sean lead the way and he knew he was being led into a trap. When and where would that trap spring? That was up to the O'Neils. How he was going to avoid it was up to Oscar.

He had a gun, a bomb, and a prisoner. The O'Neils would take those things into account.

Finally, Sean O'Neil said something. "I know what you're planning. We're not going to let you walk out of here alive."

"We'll see."

Sean laughed. "It would have been much easier for you to take the fight money. It's still not too late to do that. I'll make sure my family lets you live."

Oscar liked it better when Sean wasn't talking, but he didn't think he could shut him up again if he tried. He was that kind of man. Maybe he would have to kill him to get him to be quiet. One of the hazards of the job was listening to ugly and venomous toads like Sean O'Neil.

They came to an intersection of two corridors. One headed towards a section of living quarters. The other headed towards the shuttle bays. Sean O'Neil stopped. It must be here that something was supposed to happen. But nothing did. Sean looked left and right and pursed his lips.

If this was where the ambush was planned, someone hadn't gotten the message.

Oscar pressed his pistol to the back of Sean's head again. "Let's go. Take me to Molly."

Sean hesitated. Evidently, he didn't have a Plan B.

Oscar clenched his teeth. "I said, let's go. Or I'll have to fire this pistol. I think I can find Molly on my own from here."

"Okay, okay," muttered Sean. "I just needed a little rest."

"Yeah, right."

They continued down the corridor towards the living quarters, which is where Oscar knew Molly would be. His sources had even told him which door. With a big clan like the O'Neils, there was always a way to find things out. They walked in silence again. Oscar wondered how long it would last this time. Not long.

"You shouldn't interfere with my family's business," said Sean.

"Not everyone likes your family's business," answered Oscar. "And that's why they hire someone like me."

"You aren't nothing but a three-inch fool if you think we're going to let you walk out of here."

"Yes, you said that before. And I'm still alive. Stop here."

They had arrived in front of a blue door. Oscar had been silently counting as they walked along and he was pretty sure this was the one.

Sean pulled up. "Why here?" He was trying to act nonchalant but he wasn't that good of an actor. Oscar felt a rush of elation. He just might be able to pull this off.

Before Oscar could do anything else, the door opened. A big cloud of gas wafted into the hallway along the floor. A big man with a gun staggered out. Instead of pointing the gun at Oscar, he dropped his weapon and fell to the floor, choking. Another figure came out in a cloud of yellowish gas. As she burst through, Oscar saw that it was a small woman wearing a gas mask. The mask was made out of a clear, two-liter soda bottle with rags stuffed at the bottom. It was a real homemade job, but it seemed to be protecting her from the fumes, which were now wafting up to towards Oscar's nose. He smelled chlorine and began to cough.

The young woman grabbed Oscar by the hand and pulled him away from the door. Through tearing eyes, he saw that she had curly, red hair. It was Molly Mackintosh. He let go of Sean O'Neil and allowed the woman to pull him away.

Behind them, Sean sputtered and coughed, sounding like his lungs were going to come out of his throat. He managed to wheeze, "What the fuck's going on here? What the fuck did you do?"

They left him standing in front of the blue door, bent over with his hands on his knees. They ran back to the junction of the two corridors. Molly ripped off her gas mask and let go of Oscar's hand. "Give me your bomb," she said.

Oscar didn't argue. This seemed like the perfect time to keep his mouth shut. He handed her the small bomb.

"Let's go," said Molly, as she took off running towards the shuttle bays. "I need to find the power relay for this corridor. You're going to fly me out of here, right?"

"How did you know I was coming?" asked Oscar, struggling to keep up with her.

"That's why my father hired you, didn't he? To rescue me? What a waste of money. I thought I was doing a pretty good job of rescuing myself until you showed up. But since you're here, I might as well take advantage."

As they jogged along the corridor, Oscar asked, "What was that gas? How did you do that?"

"Easy. Can you believe they left me access to cleaning supplies? Vinegar and bleach. It made enough chlorine gas to kill most of my guards. But the last one made it out into the hall. He'll live. Maybe." Molly stopped in front of some panels marked with the universal symbol for electricity. She opened one up. There was enough space inside to hold the small bomb. She set the timer and closed the panel. "Even if they find this, they won't be able to turn it off in time. But they're probably not smart enough to find it in the first place. Let's go. Here they come."

Behind them down the long corridor, three more O'Neils rounded the corner.

"You're going to blow up this whole section?" asked Oscar as they ran.

"That's the idea. Most of the O'Neils are too stoned and drunk in the gymnasium. Those that aren't will be too busy trying to save their station to bother with a missing shuttle. You were planning to steal a shuttle, right?"

"Of course. But I wasn't planning to kill anybody."

They pulled up in front of the shuttle hangers. Molly looked at him as if he was a small child. "The man doth protests, too much, methinks. Now come on. They're right behind..."

The corridor exploded behind them. Molly flung open the shuttle bay doors and pointed. "Let's take this one."

Oscar followed her into the shuttle bay, head spinning. Molly pushed a button and the doors hissed shut behind them. Alarms were going off all over the station. He was usually the one doing the rescuing but instead, he was trailing this red-haired, crazy woman, doing whatever she said. But there was nothing else to do. Her plan seemed to be better than his. The explosion had probably blown a gaping hole in the station and the air would be gone soon.

They climbed into the shuttle. Oscar tried to sit in the pilot's chair but Molly elbowed him out of the way. "I've got this," she said.

Of course, she did.

Oscar took the co-pilot's chair and watched as Molly went through the launch procedures like an experienced pilot. She switched on the ignition. The shuttle groaned, sounding like a bear waking up from hibernation. But the engine didn't fire. She tried it again. This time the groaning was a little louder. But then it died out. That wasn't unusual for some of these old shuttles. They got a lot of use. You had to nurse them along. But Molly's face was turning as bright red as her hair, and her mouth set into a thin line. At that moment, she looked like she could have been five years old.

"Come on, you son of a bitch!" she yelled. Then she began pounding on the control panel.

"Give it a chance!" pleaded Oscar. "Hitting it's not going to do any good. Let me try."

But Molly kept right on pounding.

Oscar sighed. Yes, Molly was a good looking lass, just as Sean O'Neil said. But mainly, she was turning out to be the most difficult hostage he had ever rescued. And sooner or later, she was gonna get them both killed.

10

EUROPA STATION

Aaron Ljungman checked his watch. 19:40. Twenty minutes to midnight. Things would happen fast now if they were going to happen at all. He had to rely on three other people, which put things way out of his comfort zone. He had always been something of a loner and only let a few people get close. Erik Juergenson was one of those people and that had taken a lifetime of friendship to develop. Jenny Broberg was a friend, ever since they had begun working together. Actually, she was more than a friend. Most people needed someone to warm their bed way out here, but those kinds of relationships didn't last long on Europa. Tours of duty tended to be short. And Broberg's personality was much different than his. She was way too sensible to get involved in something like this. But he could count on her to keep her mouth shut.

He took a deep breath and headed down the long hallway to the Terminal Complex. Like all the connecting walkways on Europa, it felt claustrophobic, and the air was dense and close. Below his feet, he felt the rumbling from the massive drills that burrowed beneath the Bull's Eye, close to this part of the Station. The drills ran twenty hours a day, six hundred twenty-four weeks a year. Long ago on Earth, drills like that would have been used to dredge up fossil fuels, but here they drilled for water, always water. Among the outer planets and moons, it was the most valuable commodity there was.

Aaron reached the entrance. Above the door and just below a large, blue and yellow Swedish flag was the word Avslutande. Below that, like everywhere else in the solar system, was the English translation,

"Terminal." In English, that word could also mean the end of life. As in death. He hoped that wasn't an omen. What he was about to do could well be the last thing he ever did.

He opened the door to the Terminal. He had been on Europa for over four years but the view in front of him still took his breath away. The plastisteel ceiling was much higher here than on any other building on Europa. It was quite an achievement for Swedish engineering to design such a large space, and then to constantly manufacture enough air to fill it. The Terminal Station was a dome over a half mile in diameter, with the main walkway down the center, and pathways branching off in all directions. Each walkway led to a series of individual hangars of various sizes, stacked on top of one another, with plastisteel elevators going up to each level. All the hangars had an airlock from the inside, and a clear plastisteel door to the outside, so spaceships could come and go. It looked like the largest Lego set in the universe, with all the Legos made out of clear plastic, and spaceships tucked neatly into hangars like flies in amber. Above all was the blackness of space with a rich tapestry of stars, and Jupiter hanging on the horizon like a giant rubber ball.

But there was no time to stand and admire the view. It was now ten minutes to midnight. He would have to hurry. Trying not to draw too much attention to himself, he speed-walked the way he did so often in the Exercise Quadrant. He threw his head back and whistled *Uti vår hage,* an ancient Swedish folk tune. There wasn't a lot of activity at this time of the night. He hoped that anyone inside one of the hundreds of hangars would think he was just out for an evening constitutional. He mentally counted the walkways on his left. Seven, eight, nine...

He turned. His destination was *Sektion* 11, *Nivå* 4. His birthday was 11/ 4. Maybe that was a good omen. He could only hope.

Alrik Nyland was waiting for him by the elevator, looking like he was about to be sick to his stomach. He glanced down at his watch. "You're right on time," he said, his voice cracking.

Aaron chuckled. It was nice to know there was someone even more nervous than he was.

The two of them boarded the clear, plastisteel elevator and Aaron pushed the button for the fourth level. They began to move upward. Aaron glanced around as they went higher, the amazing view becoming more breathtaking by the minute.

"You don't want to do this," said Nyland. "You've got a good career going here. Why would you throw it all away on some crazy scheme?"

"Some things are more important than careers."

"But..."

"Just do your job and shut up," said Aaron.

The elevator doors opened. They headed down the corridor and pulled up in front of Hangar 49. There were four people waiting there. Three of them he expected, one he did not.

"Jenny? What are you doing here?" he sputtered.

"I can't let you do this all by yourself. Your weapons skills leave something to be desired. You'll shoot off your own stabilizers if I don't come along."

Aaron started to object but there was no time. The other three were shuffling their feet, looking like they wanted to be anywhere but here. He had blackmailed them all, just like he had blackmailed Nyland. It would be nice to at least have Broberg along because she had come of her own volition.

"Let us in," he said to Nyland. They had to get off Europa and out to the black ship before anyone knew they were gone.

"Are you sure..." Nyland started to say.

"Do it!" declared Aaron through clenched teeth.

Nyland shook his head, muttering something incomprehensible. He entered his password on the airlock console. The doors hissed open.

"What time does Borstel come in to replace you?" asked Aaron.

"Five in the first A.M."

Aaron glanced at his watch. They had a little less than five hours. He hoped that would be enough. "And no one else will be in the Command Center?"

"Not now. No other ships are due until morning."

"Okay, thanks." Aaron tried to shake Nyland's hand but he pulled it away.

The airlock door began to close. Aaron, Broberg and the other three stepped into the hangar as the door hissed shut behind them. Just before it sealed, he heard Nyland say, "Good luck. You're going to need it."

Aaron turned around and gazed at the ship in front of them.

Trollslända.

The name meant 'Dragonfly.' It was an apt name, for that's what it looked like. As far as Aaron Ljungman was concerned, it was the most beautiful ship in the fleet. Sleek and agile, it had lustrous wings projecting from the top of the hull, making it equally at home in space or on a planet with an atmosphere. Its weapons were tucked away beneath its wings, unobtrusive but deadly. In that respect, it was more like a wasp than a dragonfly, a wasp that could sting over and over again. And Aaron might have to use its sting to blow the black ship into space dust. But not until he had rescued his friend.

"Time to go," he said.

They all grabbed space suits from off the wall. When they had them on, they walked up the metal steps into the ship. Nyland had done his job, getting everything ready for launch. The steps retracted behind them and Aaron made his way to the captain's chair. Feeling a rush of exhilaration, he performed his pre-launch routine. It had been quite a while since he had piloted a ship. Only once had it been a warship, and that was during the Colonization Wars. How many years ago now? Too many to think about.

He radioed Command Center. Nyland answered immediately. "Go ahead, *Trollslända*."

"Ready to launch," said Aaron.

"Affirmative."

The outside hangar door opened with an explosive hiss as the air escaped. Aaron looked through his view screen and saw the icy surface of Europa bright and clear in the lights of the dome, the view not refracted from plastisteel like usual.

"Ready to launch," said Broberg from the navigator's chair.

"Take us out," said Aaron.

Within minutes, *Trollslända* was gliding gracefully into space, heading for the black ship.

11

SENATOR ALAN K SIMPSON

A few centimeters can mean the difference between life and death in space. Inside the *Senator Alan K. Simpson*, Captain Martin knew his crew could live. Outside his ship, they would die, and only the thin skin of his ship protected them.

The two ships were touching. For some unknown reason, the eerie mouth that had opened up on the hull of the *Campbell* had phased out suddenly, and now Martin heard a metallic sound as the two ships scraped against each other. When he was a boy he had run his fingernails against an old-fashioned chalkboard. He remembered the sound sending shivers up his spine. This time was no different. The same sound, and the same shivers, still went up his backbone.

Whoever was piloting the *Campbell* didn't have the skills to dock the two ships. "How's our hull holding up?" asked Martin.

"Okay so far," said Michaelson. "But if they don't get a docking lock pretty soon, we could rupture. Either way, I don't think there's a flake of paint left on that part of our hull."

Martin heard the concern in Michaelson's voice. The man was a professional and he was doing the best job he could under the circumstances. It was hard to know what to wish for. If the *Campbell* completed the docking procedure, *Homer's* hull would be fine but who or what would board them? While the two ships were scraping together there was a very real danger of a hull breach. Martin wanted to curse but the others were relying on him, taking their mood from his reactions. He had to remain calm and professional. At times like this, he fell back on his training. When stressed, he made himself do a mental checklist. The first duty of a captain was the condition of his ship.

The power to their primary systems had been taken out, which was why they were at the *Campbell*'s mercy. They still had backup power to their environmental systems and lights. As long as they had that they could survive. Without that, they would only have at most a day's worth of oxygen. Then they would have to abandon the *Homer*, but as long his ship was still intact and they still had air, Martin wouldn't order his crew into the lifeboats. But he still needed to get that main power back online.

He used his combox to call engineering. The ship's only engineer, Silas Onion, worked the frigate's power plant. Martin knew the old engineer must be throwing a fit down there. It was a good thing he was by himself. "Chief, how's it going? How long until you can restore power?"

It took a moment for his chief to answer. An alarm bell was clanging steadily in the background.

"I don't know how long, Skipper," answered Onion, sounding frazzled. "The inductor has been through an all-night tea-bagging bender. Luckily, I have a spare. If I could get one of you sodding shit shark erection herders down here to help me out, I might be able to get things going again before hell freezes over."

"On my way down, Chief. Give me a few minutes."

"Skipper, meaning no disrespect, you might need to stay on the bridge. You can send one of your other sphincter minges to me. All I need is an extra pair of hands. I'll get the inductor replaced, but it's big and awkward."

"I can send you Jelly Roll," said Martin. The chef was the only crew member free at the moment.

"That ginger breaded hole fondler has huge sausages for fingers. He'll never be able to get his hands where I need them."

"Then you'll have to make do with me. I'll be there in a minute."
Martin shut off the combox. Even in space, some things were done the old fashioned way. The *Homer's* engines just required a little extra elbow grease and a big hammer to make them behave.

He didn't want to leave the bridge. But he wasn't doing much at the moment and he could help in engineering. Like it or not, Chief Onion would have to put up with him. Michaelson could handle the bridge, whatever there was to handle without main power. The *Homer's* engines were the priority now. He stood up from his captain's chair.

Just then the *Campbell* bumped his ship again like a shark feeling out its prey, and Martin struggled to keep his balance. The ship's hull screamed like a banshee. The *Campbell* was toying with them and Martin didn't like it one bit.

Michaelson's voice was shrill. "Sir! The *Campbell* is backing off!"

"Now why would they be doing that?"

"Ten meters. Fifteen. Twenty."

The *Campbell* was giving them a little bit of breathing room. As it retreated further, they should've been able to see Jupiter. Or at least some stars. But out past the *Campbell*, the view screen was black.

"What the...?" muttered the captain. "Mr. Michaelson, where are we?"

Michaelson didn't answer. He scanned his sensors. Then he scanned them again. Finally, he shook his head. "We don't seem to be anywhere, Sir. I can't pick up any beacons and I can't find any fixed locations. There's nothing out there for our navigation sensors to grab onto. The only other fixed point I can find is the *Campbell*. And she's now fifty meters away. Maybe she's done bumping into us."

That didn't make any sense to Martin. Space is big. It's endless. But there are always points in the solar system to fix sensors onto. There should be something out there. Jupiter? Jupiter's moons? Mars? Earth? The Sun?"

Michaelson looked into his captain's eyes. "We seem to be nowhere, Skipper. I know space is mostly empty but this is something else. Wherever we are...it's just us and the *Campbell*. And it must have been the *Campbell* that took us there."

Martin flopped back down into his chair and cursed under his breath. He gazed at the mysterious ship on the view screen. "What have you done to us? And what kind of ship are you? I've never..."

Michaelson interrupted. "They're coming at us again. They've lit up their engines. This time they're going to hit us hard."

The captain gasped at the view screen. The black ship really did remind him of a shark, one that was done feeling out its prey and was now coming in for the kill. He grabbed the arms of his chair and braced for impact.

12

BRAHE STATION

The plan had been simple. Rescue the girl. Steal a shuttle. It should have been foolproof. Oscar Gunn had found that simple plans always work the best. He had done it this way a half dozen times. But this time it wasn't going to be simple at all. The problem wasn't his plan or the O'Neils. It was Molly Mackintosh. Sure, he had had to fight Big O'Neil in the ring, at least for one round. He could have died or had his brains scrambled. He had had to take Sean O'Neil hostage so he could rescue the girl. Sean O'Neil had warned him that Molly was more trouble than she was worth. And he had been right. Already she had killed three O'Neils and destroyed a whole section of Brahe Station with Oscar's own bomb.

There had been too many mistakes. The O'Neils were not known for forgiveness. As soon as they saved their station, they would come looking for him. They would seek their revenge. It didn't matter how far he traveled away from this moon, he would have to look over his shoulder for the rest of his life, however short his life turned out to be. That's what happened when you let an amateur interfere with your carefully laid plans. He should have knocked Molly out, dragged her down the hallway, and then found an available shuttle to steal. If he had done it that way, the O'Neils might forgive and forget. After all, they would have only lost a single hostage and a shuttle, instead of three of their clan and a whole section of Brahe Station. But it had all happened too fast. When Molly came bursting through that door with chlorine gas trailing behind her, he had gotten disoriented.

To make things worse, he was now trapped inside a nonworking shuttle with the girl. Oscar was sure the shuttle would have started up fine before she began banging on the control panel after only one misfire. But she had insisted on doing it her way. Now, nothing she tried would work. Finally, frustrated and swearing up a blue streak, she produced a screwdriver and started dismantling things.

"I think I can jimmy this switch under here and get these damn engines to fire. But first, I need to see what's going on," she said, her bright red hair spilling down across her eyes as she ducked her head beneath the console.

"Why don't we just get another shuttle?" pleaded Oscar, looking back towards the airlock. "This bay is full of them."

Molly wasn't listening. Evidently, she was that kind of person. The kind who always had to be right. She kept taking out screws from underneath the forward control panel. Oscar knew if given enough time, the girl might take apart the whole shuttle.

Oscar could pull out his pistol and shoot her. No one would blame him for that. The O'Neils would find her dead body. Maybe then they would leave him alone. Sure, there wouldn't be any money from her family, but getting the O'Neils off his back might be worth it.

Oscar wondered what was happening in the hallway leading to the shuttle bay. The longer it took them to leave Ganymede, the more danger they were in. It wouldn't be long before the O'Neils burst through the door. And then they'd both be dead.

A chime went off in the shuttle.

"What is that?" asked Molly, looking up from the partly dismantled control panel.

"I don't know," said Oscar. The sound had been almost like the chime from his front door on Earth. He aimed his pistol at the entrance portal. "I think someone wants in."

"So open up," said Molly, sounding more annoyed than anything else.

Oscar moved towards the door. It seemed too early for the entire O'Neil clan to have made it past the explosion site. So who could be out there? He hit the button. The door hissed open as Oscar increased the pressure on his trigger finger. But instead of an entire mob of O'Neils, there was only one O'Neil standing there. It was the teenager that had helped Oscar during the fight.

The rat faced youth held Oscar's fight bag in his left hand. He smirked. "I think you left this back in the gym." He held up a plastic card with his other hand. "You may be a good fighter and a wise guy, but you aren't going anywhere without this."

The boy looked past Oscar and saw what Molly was doing. He ran over and knelt down beside her. "Stop that!" he shouted. "Are you crazy?"

Molly pulled away and gaped at him.

"Thank the saints I'm here!" said the boy. He dropped Oscar's bag and ran his hand through the dismantled pieces of control panel that Molly had scattered on the deck. "You're lucky I got here before you did something truly stupid. You need walls to keep in the air. You need a roof to keep out solar radiation. And you need a coded pass card to work an O'Neil shuttle. Let me get it started for you, you idiots."

The boy settled into the Captain's chair as if he were born there.

"You aren't going with us," said Oscar.

The teen smiled, this time looking like a cat instead of a rat. "Yes, I am. All O'Neil shuttles have been modified, as Molly just found out on her own. We can't have hostages escaping this way. Bad for business and bad for my family. Now, why don't you close the door so we can get going?"

Oscar took a step towards the boy, pointing his pistol. "I'll take that pass card now and you can head back out into the hallway. We'll be on our way and nobody else gets hurt."

"Do you think that's the only modification we make to our shuttles? Even if you get it started, you're going to need me to fly it. Only an O'Neil knows how to fly an O'Neil shuttle, smart guy."

Molly got to her feet and nodded. "The boy is right. I can't make heads or tails out of any of this."

Oscar didn't know if he believed either one of them. But what choice did he have?

The teen inserted the card into the proper place on the control panel. Oscar held his breath, wondering if Molly had messed up whatever made the engines start. But they fired on the first try.

"We're ready to rock n roll," said the teenage O'Neil. "If I were you, I would strap myself in because this bird wants to fly. And it's got some kick. Oh. And I'll ask you again. Do you think you could close the door?"

Oscar did as he was told and then strapped himself into a third chair, while Molly took the co-pilot's seat. He wondered exactly when he had lost control of this mission. He had become simply a spectator to a smart-ass teenager and a red-haired psycho girl from hell. Why was the teenage O'Neil helping them?

He felt the shuttle rumble to life as the boy goosed the throttle. The craft leapt forward like a springing leopard and Oscar felt himself thrust back in his seat. The shuttle truly did have some kick, and it would get them far from Ganymede before long. His gym bag flew up to the ceiling, along with all the control panel pieces that Molly had dismantled, and for a moment it was like a small meteor storm swirling around them. But then they were weightless, and everything settled into a lazy drift. Oscar reached out and brought his gym back into his lap. Through all this confusion, he had forgotten he was still wearing his fight robe. As soon they were well away from Ganymede, he would change back into traveling clothes.

He was glad the kid had brought his gym bag along. With luck, he hadn't discovered the remaining surprises hidden inside.

13

HSWMS TROLLSLÄNDA

God, it was good to be at the helm of a spaceship again, especially a warship. Aaron Ljungman liked his job on Europa, but it was basically an office job. Oh sure, it was exciting to help ships from all across the solar system come and go. Maybe it was like working at a world class resort back on Earth. But nothing could compare with the feeling of having a spaceship under your control, especially a graceful, elegant, man-of-war like *Trollslända*.

When they had first glided into space an hour ago, Jenny Broberg had settled into the seat in front of Weapons Control. Heidi Herko was down in engineering. Peg Rasmussen manned Sensors. And Mats Renberg was monitoring life support. It had been audacious for Aaron to take *Trollslända* into space with just himself and a four person crew. The ship called for a crew of ten. But, like every other ship of the fleet, regulations called for duplication in case anyone died or became incapacitated. And Aaron didn't plan on having anyone die. If all went well, they'd be back in the hangar on Europa by early morning when the shift changed at Command Center.

Aaron had been dreaming about the Vikings lately. Maybe it was from a book he had been reading, or one of the Viking history shows on SpaceNet. Either way, he'd started to sense his ancestors poking their way into his consciousness from over a thousand years ago, as crazy as that sounded. But this wouldn't be a Viking raid where they would pillage and loot and attack with overwhelming force. He planned for a stealth operation, a get-in-and-get-out mission. He needed to somehow find his way on board the black ship and rescue his friend Erik Juergenson, getting him out of there before whoever was on that ship knew what had happened. But if he had to fight his way in, he was prepared to do that like a Viking. Especially after what Broberg had just shown him.

"So the rumors were true," she said when inspecting the weapons console after they had gotten into space.

"What?" he asked.

"Those were more than simple repairs and maintenance they were doing the past couple months."

It's hard to keep secrets in any military or diplomatic organization. Swedish Space Fleet was no exception. For years there had been rumors that Swedish engineers had come up with a brand new weapon, one that would make Gaston Lasers and Phillips' Missiles look like pea shooters. There was supposed harmony among the various factions and nationalities that made up Earth fleet. But there was always competition. And when any one faction had a monopoly on something valuable, like the Swedes had on Europa, someone was always casting a jealous eye. And you had to be ready to protect your interests.

"What do you see?" asked Aaron.

Broberg pointed to a symbol on the weapons console. "I've been on a lot of Swedish warships and I've never seen that before."

Aaron walked over and glanced down. There was a large button tucked away beneath all the usual controls for weapons and shields. A strange symbol, looking like a Greek letter, was stenciled in green on the face of it.

"What do you think it is?" he asked.

"It must be the new weapons system. I don't know how it could be anything else."

The butterflies which had been flying around in Aaron Llungman's stomach for the past few hours began to do gymnastics. It was scary enough stealing a warship in the middle of the night. But it was absolutely terrifying to know that they had access to a new, secret weapon. What did it do? How powerful was it? "Well, let's hope we won't need anything like that," he muttered.

"I agree with you there," answered Broberg. "Maybe it's not a new weapon at all. Maybe it's a self-destruct module or something. I know I'm not going to push it."

But it was time to focus on the task at hand. They had closed to within a hundred kilometers of the *John W. Campbell Jr.* It was hanging motionless in *Trollslända*'s view screen like a black monolith, silhouetted against the star-studded shroud of space behind it. Ljungman swallowed hard as he stared at it. How was he going to get in there undetected? He had watched the slow motion video of the *Campbell* swallowing his friend's ship, the *Skalbagge*, like a shark swallowing a minnow.

"Hang in there, Erik, my friend. We're coming for you," he whispered.

He punched a few buttons on the glittering, modern console. "I'm cutting all power," he said, both to the three on his bridge and by radio to engineering. "We're going to glide in from here. Odin knows what kind of sensors they have over there. I'm hoping we can catch them napping. Ms. Broberg, be ready to fire up weapons at a moment's notice."

"Yes, *Kapten*."

The ship's engines went silent. The lights on the bridge dimmed to emergency power levels, leaving the multicolored lights on various consoles as the brightest in the room. On the view screen, the *Campbell* grew larger.

"Easy, big fellow," muttered Ljungman. "We're just a clump of space dust. Nothing to worry about here."

"Fifty kilometers," said Broberg. "Forty."

Ljungman stared at the dark bow of the *Campbell*. Nothing seemed to be happening over there...

Suddenly all the lights on *Trollslända*'s bridge switched on full. Ljungman looked up and blinked. "Who did that?" he asked in a voice that sounded too loud in his own head.

No one answered.

"Broberg, did you turn the power back on?"

"No, Sir!"

He called down to engineering. "Herko, what's going on?"

"I don't know, Sir," came a voice over the com in a lilting Laplander accent. "I yust been monitoring the engines and suddenly everything came on by itself."

Ljungman looked down. His console was lit up like a Yule tree. "Who's doing this?" he asked in exasperation.

They were accelerating, the engines whining in a higher and higher pitch. They headed straight for the *Campbell* like a bullet fired from a gun.

"Brace for impact!" shouted Broberg.

At the last second, *Trollslända* veered to starboard, missing the black ship by what seemed like inches. *Trollslända* continued to accelerate on the other side before rotating one hundred and eighty degrees and racing back the way they had come. Again the black ship loomed large in the view screen as they watched helplessly, with Ljungman frantically pushing buttons on his console to no effect. Again they narrowly missed the *Campbell* as they raced by. Then they turned around once more. It was like being on an out-of-control roller coaster. But this roller coaster had no track and there was no guarantee they wouldn't smash into the larger ship.

As they raced towards the *Campbell* for the third time, *Trollslända's* engines suddenly wound down and went into reverse, stopping them. They hung motionless in space with the *Campbell* a hundred kilometers away, as if someone had pushed a reset button on this whole scene.

"What in Helvete is going on?" sputtered Ljungman in exasperation.

"Our main power is still on," said Broberg, her voice cracking.

Ljungman heard a humming sound from above his head. Even though this was his first time on *Trollslända*, he recognized the familiar sound of torpedo bays opening. On this particular warship, sharp, prickly points would be thrusting out from beneath its dragonfly wings, betraying the real nature of the beautiful craft.

"Broberg! Did you just start our weapons firing sequence?" he shouted.

"I'm not doing a thing!" she answered, both hands held up in the air.

There was a sharp, explosive sound as a space torpedo launched from *Trollslända*. On the view screen, they saw a bright, pinpoint of light head towards the *Campbell* like a firefly. It hit the black ship on its port side and there was a brilliant, yellow flash. The *Campbell* remained dark, with no apparent debris or damage that they could see.

Then *Trollslända's* Gaston lasers began firing, one after another, with Broberg still gaping helplessly at her console. "I swear I'm not doing this!" she sputtered.

On the view screen, the lasers sped towards the *Campbell* in long, red lines. When they hit they black ship, they left momentary, deep black breaches in the hull, which immediately closed up again as if they were flesh wounds touched with läkning cream.

"Kap...Aaron, you need to see this!" shouted Broberg.

He got up from his chair and stumbled over to Broberg. She pointed down below the weapons console. The light with the mysterious, green symbol had begun to blink on and off.

"Whatever this new thing is, I think it's getting ready to fire," said Broberg.

Blink...

Blink...

"Can you do something to stop it?" asked Ljungman.

"I wish," answered Broberg, hands flying over the keyboard. "Nothing's responding."

A strange, high-pitched wail erupted from the console itself. The eerie, green light began to blink faster.

Blink, blink blink...

Broberg threw her hands in the air. Ljungman braced for whatever was going to happen. Was this a self-destruct sequence? Were they all about to die?

The button settled into a solid, green glow. A deep, moaning throb came from beneath their feet, like a bear waking from hibernation. They heard a sound like an ocean wave crashing against a rock. On the view screen, a giant globe of greenish light burst from *Trollslända*, heading towards the *Campbell* like a butterfly net. It enveloped the black ship, and veins of pulsing green swirled around the outside. Beneath it, the black ship began to shudder. Holes appeared in its hull and bits of debris filtered into space, as if the strange, green net was crushing the massive ship. Whatever this new weapon was, it was about to destroy the black ship, killing Erik Juergenson along with it.

"No!" shouted Ljungman.

But then the green swirling stopped. The bits of debris that had filtered into space were sucked back in through the hull breaches. The holes closed again, the way they had after the laser bursts. And suddenly the green light was gone.

Trollslända nudged forward and began to creep towards the *Campbell*. "Jenny, have our engines fired up again?" asked Ljungman.

"No. The *Campbell* seems to be pulling us in. And something is opening up in their hull."

Ljungman gasped. That same, ominous mouth they had seen in the video was forming on the hull of the *Campbell*. Though they were barely moving, it was already growing larger.

There was only one thing left for him to do. "I'm going down to the cutter," he said.

"What?" asked Broberg.

"I'm not going to let that monstrosity swallow *Trollslända*. I'll get there first. One way or another, I'm getting inside that ship and I'm going to stop this. If I fail, do everyting you can to break free."

14

SENATOR ALAN K SIMPSON

Captain Martin feared for his crew. He had taken every precaution, and yet he couldn't prevent what had happened. His ship was in danger. They were lost. His ship's computers couldn't figure out where they were. The nav-computer had nothing to lock onto because wherever the Campbell had brought them was a void.

There was nothing out there, no place for them to go. If they couldn't find their way out of here, wherever 'here' was, they would die. They would eventually lose the power from their engines. The *Homer's* environmental systems would shut down. Without that recycled air, they would die from carbon dioxide poisoning. But they had a lot of time before that happened. Without any solar input, the environmentals would still have power for more than a year. So that was the least of the worries on his mental checklist.

The next thing to worry about was food. They had enough for six months. With rationing, maybe eight or nine months. The same for water. They could stretch it out also, but eventually, they would consume more than their ship could recycle.

Captain Martin sat at his station on the bridge and gazed at the *Campbell*, hanging there in the black void, lights twinkling on and off like stars. Minutes ago it had been racing towards them on a collision course, a devouring course. Everyone on the *Homer* had been cringing, bracing for impact. But then it just pulled up short, as if it had hit a wall. Now it was just hanging there again. It was maddening. Nothing to do with this mysterious, black ship made any sense, not how it had behaved, and not where it had taken them. It had done everything it wanted to do to his warship. It had shut down his weapons. It had kept his crew from boarding them. It had even pushed them out of the solar system to this place. It was playing with them like a cat plays with a mouse.

Back on Earth, when Martin was a boy, he had spent a summer on his aunt's farm in Florida. There were cats that never came inside. His aunt called them her 'feral creatures.' Martin wanted to catch one but they never let him get close.

"They just want to be left right alone," his aunt had told him. "Some animals should never be touched."

Martin hadn't listened. He chased them all over the farm. Once, he trapped one in the corner of the barn. It was a gray and white cat with only one eye. It hissed at him as he crept closer. As he stared at its empty eye socket, he wondered what had happened. Had it gotten into a fight with another cat? In any event, it seemed to see him just fine with its remaining eye. It hissed again as he continued to close the distance between them. He held out his hand and made soft, soothing noises. He wanted the cat to know it was all right. He had been lonely all summer and needed a friend. But the closer he got, the more the cat protested. It even showed him his claws...

Lt. Constance broke his reverie. "Maybe I could manually launch a missile. If I pull one back out of the number one tube, I could reprogram the launcher and the guidance system. What do you think?"

Martin didn't answer. He was still thinking about that one-eyed cat. There was a dead mouse splayed out in the dirt in front of it. Of course, there was. Barn cats loved to catch mice. He had watched them do it from up in the hayloft. The cats would hit them on the head to stun them. Then when a mouse started to come back to its senses, the cat would hit it on the head again. The same thing would happen over and over. In the end, the cat would become bored with the game and kill the mouse...

"Sir?" asked Constance. "Did you hear what I said? About launching the missile?"

Martin remembered sunlight pouring through one of the many holes in the barn. Why hadn't the cat run away through one of those holes? Something was keeping it pinned where it was. In a moment, he found out what.

An alligator blasted through the old boards of the barn with a crash. Martin fell backward in surprise, his mouth open. He hit the floor and felt bits of hay in his fingers as he scooted away from the reptile. The gator was lightning fast. Before he could blink, it had grasped the shrieking cat in its jaws, swinging its head back and forth. Within a few seconds, the cat was gone.

The cat had known that there was a monster lurking outside the barn. That's why it hadn't run away through the holes in the boards. But the monster had come for it anyhow. And now that monster stared at Martin with unblinking, prehistoric eyes that knew nothing but killing. But it didn't come for him. It must have been satiated because it simply turned around and crawled back outside through the hole it had created.

The bridge of the *Homer* was quiet. Martin looked over at Constance. "Did you have alligators where you're from? On Earth, I mean?"

"Alligators? What are you talking about?"

"Did you?"

Constance looked confused. "I'm from Alaska. No alligators. Why?"

"Well, we had them in Florida. They sometimes came around my aunt's farm. Big ones."

Martin felt a rush of blood to his head. A plan was taking shape in his brain. "I'm tired of being the mouse," he said as he pointed to the view screen. "I'm sick of that cat hitting us on the head. We've forgotten something. Out here in space, we're not a mouse. We're not even a cat. We're a big ol' Florida gator. And that cat out there has been treating us like we're a mouse. "

"I don't understand," said Constance.

"You will," said Martin. He stood up and went to a spot behind her. He allowed a smile to crease the corners of his mouth. "Now. What were you just saying about manually overriding those missiles?"

15

SHUTTLE

Usually, space travel was boring. It took weeks to get anywhere. Sure, there was SpaceNet, but after a while, that got boring also. Oscar had always thought he should write about some of his many adventures but he'd never gotten around to doing that.

Oscar didn't know if his current adventure would warrant an episode of some show on SpaceNet, but it certainly had been interesting. There were still a lot of questions in his mind that needed to be answered. How had Molly known ahead of time that he had come to rescue her? Why had she been so brutal to the O'Neils, killing three of them when she didn't have to? Why had the teenage O'Neil come along to actually help them escape? And why was the boy running away from his family?

Clearly, there was a larger plan in place. What was that plan? What was really going on here? As Oscar sat in the shuttle, speeding away from Ganymede, he started to get angry. When Oscar Gunn got mad, he wanted to hurt somebody. He wished he was someplace where he could make that happen. But he was cooped up in a small shuttle with a teenager, who happened to be the only one who could fly the thing, and a crazy, red-haired woman. He would rather have been back in the ring with the Big O'Neil.

He had already cleaned himself up and changed back into his traveling clothes, even before the artificial gravity had switched on. Now he reached into his gym bag and got out his pistol. He checked to make sure there was ammo in the clip. Feeling clean, Oscar hoped he wouldn't have to use it. He needed to calm himself down. He knew he hadn't been

56

thinking straight; the feeling of being out of control had fed his anger and now he needed to calm himself down. He took a deep breath and put his pistol back in the bag. He didn't even know the young O'Neil's first name. Shooting the kid was the last thing he needed to do. Besides, who would fly the shuttle?

Oscar walked up to the front of the craft, where Molly and the young O'Neil were laughing at something together. When they looked up and saw Oscar, their laughter died and smiles froze on their lips.

"What's your name?" said Oscar to the kid.

"O'Neil," said the kid with a smirk. "Like all the rest of my family. Didn't you notice that we all have the same name?"

"Not everyone," said Oscar, his anger returning. "I think your name is Smartass." He grabbed the boy by his collar and lifted him up out of the pilot's seat. The boy's legs started to kick wildly, but the fighter didn't care. Unlike Big O'Neil, this wimpy kid was not nearly strong enough to wiggle out of his grasp.

"I'm an O'Neil!" shouted the kid. "I swear to the Mother Virgin. I'm an O'Neil all the way to my bones!"

Oscar pulled the boy's face close to his own until he was just inches away. "O'Neils are loyal. They're famous for that loyalty, especially on Brahe Station. The only outsiders allowed in are hostages and an occasional fighter like me. Their motto might as well be 'Blood is thicker than water.' So I'm thinking something is wrong here. Because you're definitely not loyal."

The kid paused. Oscar could smell garlic on his breath. "It's not what you think. I am an O'Neil. Tormod O'Neil. But I'm not like the others."

"I'm going to break you in half if you don't start making sense," said Oscar, clasping his left hand around the boy's throat. Tormod didn't weigh much. Oscar knew he could hold him in the air all day if he needed to in the shuttle's lower gravity settings.

"He's right," said Molly. Oscar had been wondering when she was going to speak. She hadn't exactly been the shy, retiring type so far. "Tormod is different than the other O'Neils. He was the only one I could trust on Brahe station. That's why he helped us escape."

Oscar tightened his grip. The boy began to wheeze, struggling to take a breath. "I've been played for a fool by the two of you," said Oscar. "It's beginning to look like this whole thing was just a setup."

Oscar squeezed harder. He knew it would be ridiculously easy to break the kid's neck and his anger had turned into a red cloud behind his eyes.

"You don't understand!" screamed Molly. "Let go of him and I'll tell you whatever you need to know!"

The boy's face had turned purple. Oscar relaxed his grip slightly and the boy gasped and coughed until red flowed back into his cheeks. Oscar looked inquiringly at Molly. "This better be good," he said.

"I knew I could trust him because he's my brother."

Oscar let go of the boy and the kid fell to the floor in a heap. This was her brother? Oscar hadn't been expecting that one. He didn't know if he believed Molly or not, but she had certainly gotten his attention. The wheels turned in his brain. If this was true, then maybe her father, no, their father, would pay him to double his fee for getting them home...

Molly rushed to the boy's side and knelt down. Tormod was still coughing and gasping. "It's gonna be okay," she said, actually sounding like a big sister.

"But you're not an O'Neil," said Oscar to Molly. "Your last name is Mackintosh."

Molly looked up at him. "This is one big family fight you walked into the middle of. I'm half O'Neil on my mother's side. My father is a Mackintosh. The two families go way back, to olden times on Earth, centuries before either clan ever dreamed of venturing into space. My mother left Brahe Station years ago after she married my father. After she died, my father went back to Brahe to take another bride. His new bride had other ideas, and she wouldn't leave her family, so my father eventually left her. But not before they had Tormod. He's my half-brother. And that's why he's helping me. Because he favors the Mackintosh side."

Molly's face had turned as red as her brother's. She was clearly angry at Oscar for almost strangling her brother. She might have been angry at herself for letting her brother get hurt in the first place.

Oscar decided she was telling the truth. Which meant that he had been played for a fool by Molly's father. "Why me? he asked. "Why did your father want me to be involved in this little escapade? And if you're all family, why were you a hostage in the first place?"

"My father has been on the outs with the O'Neils for a long time, so they grabbed me, partly to get money and partly to get back at him. He wanted to make sure we really did get away so he hired you. But you showed up sooner than we thought."

Tormod raised himself up and coughed once more. The kid was going to be okay. Molly pressed her hand to his back and helped him to his feet.

Oscar was still struggling to digest all of this information. "I still don't get it. Your father would know about Tormod. He would know that the two of you could have escaped without my help."

"Freeing me isn't the only reason you're here. We need you for something else."

"What?" sputtered Oscar.

"There is a ship out near Europa. It has a valuable cargo. A very valuable cargo. A cargo that nobody has seen in the solar system before. My father trusts me. He trusts Tormod. And for some reason, he trusts you, if only because you can make way more money doing this than you'd ever make rescuing hostages. We're heading out to intercept that ship."

"What ship?" asked Oscar.

Molly gave Oscar a cold look and said, "*Campbell*. Have you heard of it?"

16

CUTTER

There is an unwritten maritime law that says a captain should always be the last to leave his vessel, or, if necessary, to go down with the ship. Every captain in history knew this. Which is why Aaron Ljungman was in agony. He had just left his own ship, *Trollslända*, aboard the small cutter, which was mostly used for quick landings on planets that didn't have docking facilities for larger spaceships. The cutter could also be used as a lifeboat in the event of a catastrophe, but that wasn't the case here. At least not yet. *Trollslända* was still intact, hanging in space like a paralyzed dragonfly, being pulled ever so slowly towards the *John W. Campbell Jr.* Whatever was on that black ship was controlling *Trollslända* like a puppet. It had fired the Swedish warship's new secret weapon, along with its Gaston lasers and torpedoes, like a child playing with a new toy to find out what it can do.

The black ship had left Aaron with only one option. He had launched the cutter in the hope that the *Campbell* wouldn't detect such a small craft. And now he was getting ready to pilot it right into that ugly, gaping mouth. Once inside, he might be able to find whoever was controlling things in there. And then? Well, he didn't know what he would do then. But anything was better than twiddling his thumbs on *Trollslända* while it met whatever fate the *Campbell* had in mind.

So far his plan had worked. In the few minutes it took him to traverse the hundreds of kilometers of space between them, nothing unusual had happened. The cutter's controls were working smoothly and it was still responding like a finely-tuned rover heading across the ice plains of Europa.

Aaron swallowed hard. He was now within a kilometer of the black ship. Through the plastisteel bubble in front of him, he could see that ghastly, black mouth gaping, the edges phasing in and out like an electrical storm. It looked big enough to swallow *Trollslända* whole, so the cutter would be like a flea in comparison. The inside of the mouth was like the black of deepest space, only instead of stars, Aaron saw a spattering of glowing green specks. They reminded him of the phosphorescence he had seen while scuba diving at night in Aruba during his university days.

Aaron pulled back on the throttle and the cutter slowed. What could those green specks be? They were the exact same color as the light from *Trollslända's* secret weapon. Was the black ship somehow digesting the matter from that weapon? Any spaceship that could do that was a terrifying monster indeed. And Aaron was getting ready to sneak right into its belly.

"Oh, *Helvete*," he said aloud, repeating one of his friend Erik Juergenson's favorite words,"there's no time like the present."

He goosed the throttle and the cutter responded, leaping into the open mouth like a puppy into water.

And then suddenly the cutter was gone, along with Aaron's spacesuit and helmet. He found himself standing at the edge of a peaceful pond. A dusting of new snow coated the ground. There was a clump of evergreen bushes to his right. The air tasted fresh and crisp. It was the first non-manufactured air he had breathed since...

Earth.

Not just Earth. A special place on Earth. He gazed across the reflecting waters of the pond and saw a cluster of quaint buildings in the tidy, timeless, Swedish style. One building had a steeple that thrust up into a clear, blue, early winter sky. There were trees here. It had been forever since he'd seen trees growing outside of a dome. Birds chirped from their branches. The whole scene felt achingly familiar.

A steel bridge crossed the pond in the distance, leading to a snowy path. He knew that path. It would take him right into the center of Old Town. Old Town Borås.

It was the town he and Erik had grown up in, just the way it had looked on the early November day they had left together to attend the Swedish Space Academy.

Aaron scratched his head as a breeze ruffled his blonde hair. What was going on? A second ago he had been aboard a spaceship, and now...

Tears came to his eyes. It had been so long since he had been on Earth. Since he had been home. Without being aware he was doing it, he started walking towards the steel bridge. Then he broke into a run. Maybe his family was there waiting for him, just past that steeple where the launch pad was.

"No!" shouted a voice. Aaron stopped in his tracks. His friend Erik stood on the bridge, now just fifty yards ahead. The sound of Erik's voice continued to echo, the way it would in the fjords. "No...no...no......."

But the tone of the echo wasn't what you'd hear on Earth. It was more like an echo in a large gymnasium on Ganymede. Or maybe in the empty storage bay of a space freighter.

"It's not real," said Erik.

His voice was weak and strained. His face was as white as the snow that covered the railing of the bridge. He began to sway as if he were about to pass out. "Don't give in," he said. "Don't believe it. You have to fight them."

Behind Erik, the town of Borås flickered like a video projected onto a sheet in a windstorm. The bridge Erik stood on blinked out, becoming instead a steel support beam, stretching horizontally both directions into darkness. The entire, pastoral scene was gone. Aaron looked down and saw that, instead of a snowy path, he was standing on the metal deck of a space freighter. It was massive, with dark, cavernous passages leading off into all directions. The fresh, crisp air had morphed into the familiar smell of canned oxygen. There were no more birds singing in trees, but instead, a consistent, low humming noise. The smells of the Swedish countryside had given way to the familiar spaceship odors of metal and grease. But beneath that smell was something else. Something clinging. Something foul.

"Stay away!" shouted Erik, just as something knocked him off the support beam and down to the deck below. He picked himself up and waved his arms. "Don't come close!"

Aaron saw something crawl up Erik's leg. It was hard to see exactly what from this distance, but it looked like a slithering, black snake. Its movements weren't smooth like a reptile's, though, but jerky and mechanical as it climbed higher, wrapping around Erik's torso. A triangular head arose, rearing back and swaying in front of Erik's face, seeming to hypnotize him. There was a crackle in the air like an electrical short and thin tendrils shot out from the rearing head. They wrapped themselves around Erik's neck. Then they covered his face like vines, slithering into his mouth and up his nose.

As Aaron watched in horror, Erik coughed and gagged. But before his voice disappeared altogether, he managed to force out one last garbled word.

"Run!"

Erik fell over with his legs kicking as the creature dragged him away. His legs were still kicking as he disappeared off to the right, into the dark labyrinth of the ship.

Aaron's knees began to tremble and he nearly collapsed to the deck in shock. What was that thing? He knew that if he was going to save his friend, he'd have to go after it, but that was the last thing in the universe he wanted to do right now.

His eyes saw movement along the floor, coming from the spot where Erik had just been. Another dark, triangular head was rising from the metal deck, swaying like a seaweed pod on the floor of the ocean. Then it began to slither his way.

17

SENATOR ALAN K SIMPSON

Two things a captain never says in front of his crew: "I wish I had never made that decision," and, "I don't know."

Captain Martin had learned a long time ago to keep his mouth shut when things were going bad. But he certainly wished he hadn't made the decision to approach the black ship in the first place. And there were an awful lot of things he just didn't know right now. He rubbed his temples and wished he could go to his quarters and get some sleep. But there was no one else on the bridge to take his place. And, right or wrong, it had to be him who made whatever decisions still needed to be made.

Lt. Constance was down in the forward missile bay, modifying the Phillips' Missiles for a manual launch. This simply had to succeed, because if it didn't, Martin couldn't think of any other options. If the modifications worked, the mysterious black ship would either be destroyed or disabled and that would be a huge relief. But even that wouldn't solve their other, even bigger problem. Where was this place? Despite having some of the best navigation computers on any ship in the solar system, they still didn't know what part of space the *Campbell* had pushed them into. Would a scientist even call this 'space?' Yes, space was a vacuum, but it still contained planets, stars, meteors, space dust, and much more. Wherever they were now contained none of those things. It was just the *Campbell* and the *Homer* hanging in the blackness, arrayed against each other like model spaceships hanging from a ceiling in some Earth kid's bedroom. And if his navigation systems couldn't discern where they were, how was he supposed to figure out how to get them back to Europa? Or anyplace else for that matter? Martin had taken every course on astronavigation at the Academy in Annapolis and he had never heard of anything like this.

Martin's head down for a moment. He jerked awake and slapped himself. How long would it take Lt. Constance to make those modifications? She had thought it might take an hour, but an hour had already passed. She might have gotten the job done quicker if Martin had allowed his foul-mouthed, chief engineer to help. But Silas Onion had his hands full trying to restore main power. That still had to be the priority. Martin had even sent Michaelson, his third in command, to help the chief in the engine room. That had left Martin on the bridge by himself. It had already been a long day and the lack of anything to do was making it nearly impossible to stay awake.

It was ironic that the captain was the only one on the ship without anything to do. If only Constance was here. He enjoyed his conversations with her. She reminded him of himself when he was fresh out of the Academy. She had been the best candidate in her graduating class and Martin had gobbled her up before anyone else could. After a few tours aboard the *Homer*, she would return to Earth with plenty of experience as a deep space officer. She would have her choice of duties, her pick of stations and vessels. If Martin decided to retire, she might even be able to take his job aboard the *Homer*.

He also liked talking with Michaelson. The man was originally from New Mexico. Every time he returned to Earth, he picked a new spot on the planet to hike. The last time they had gone home, Michaelson had started on the west coast of Peru and hiked over the Andes, making his way down the other side and traversing the Amazon jungle. He was already planning his next trip when they returned to Earth. He wanted to do the entire 2000 miles of the Appalachian Trail. Martin couldn't imagine doing that, but he admired the younger man's sense of adventure.

Martin should call for Jelly Roll to bring him some coffee. But the cook was in his own cabin, trying to get a few hours sleep before waking up to prepare tomorrow's meals.

Martin hated falling asleep lately because of the dreams. The only benefit of their encounter with the *Campbell* was that he hadn't slept, which had kept the dreams at bay. One dream in particular terrified him. He never wanted to have that dream again. But the thought of sleep right now seemed almost irresistible. Maybe if he just put his head down on his console and closed his eyes for a moment...

He is on the bridge of the *Homer.* It's the third watch. He is alone. The bridge of a spaceship can be a spooky place when you're by yourself. So quiet, but yet full of sounds. Creakings and rustlings. of engines. Soft beeping of sensors. He feels the hair on the back of his neck stand on end. His heart beats faster. And then it appears. Again. A disembodied hand floats in the air in front of his face. It comes closer. A grimy, blackened, hooked finger points at him and Martin can't look away. It moves closer. Closer. The finger is aiming for his left eye. Oh no, not again. Always his left eye. He needs to wake up before it touches his eye.

But he doesn't wake up. Not this time. He wants to turn away. He wants to get out of his chair. He wants to run from the bridge. But he can't move. All he can do is stare at that crooked finger, growing larger now in front of his left eye. It is only centimeters away.

"Close your eye! Don't let it touch you!" His mind screams. But his eyelid won't close. It's as if it is being held open by toothpicks. The fingernail in front of his eye looks sharp as a knife. He has seen all of this before, but never this close. He can see something on top of the nail. A single drop of blood, getting ready to roll off and fall to the deck. The nail is eight centimeters away now. "Look away!" But he can't.

Six centimeters.

"Please! Blink, for God's sake!" All he can do is watch.

Five centimeters.

There's someone else here. Martin can sense them but he can't look away from the finger. There's another drop of blood on the foul nail. Now two more.

Three centimeters.

"Wake up!" his mind screams. "You always wake up by now!" But not this time. This time, the claw of the nail moves in.

Two centimeters.

It doesn't pierce his eye. Yet. It wants to do something else first.

Martin knows what the nail wants to do. It wants to scrape the cornea off his pupil.

One centimeter.

Martin knows his cornea will be slowly ripped away, to join the drops of blood on the crooked nail.

Still unable to blink, unable to turn his head, he remembers that someone else is in the room. He manages to shout. "Help me! Wake me up!"

Somewhere, a cup crashes to the deck and breaks. The finger suddenly pulls away. Martin still can't blink. The floating hand slips away smooth as silk and disappears through a hatch above his bridge.

"Captain!" A beefy hand shook Martin's shoulder. He whirled around to see Jelly Roll peering down at him in alarm. The cook looked different as if Martin had one eye closed. Then he realized he could blink his eyes again. The dream was blessedly over. He breathed a sigh of relief.

"Captain, what's going on? Were you screaming?" asked Jelly Roll.

"I fell asleep. It must have been a nightmare. I'm sorry." Martin shook his head. What had touched him? Was he still dreaming? "I'm sorry," he muttered. " I didn't mean to fall asleep on duty. It's just that there was no one here."

"Captain, you're bleeding. Your eye. Oh my God! What happened? I'll get the first-aid kit. Wait here!" The kit was only a few meters away, but it took the large man an eternity to find it. "Captain...Sir. Don't move. Please sit down."

Martin needed to leave the bridge. He needed to find his way back to his quarters to lie down. He stood up and took a few shaky, uneven steps. Some sort of fluid was leaking down the left side of his face. He looked down. There was something on the deck.

It was an eye.

His eye.

18

SHUTTLE

There wasn't much for Oscar to do aboard the stolen shuttle. Molly and Tormod were managing to pilot it towards the *John W Campbell Jr*, wherever that was. He suspected that it was somewhere in orbit around Europa. Every time he tried to help, one or both of them would bark at him, so he simply shrugged and mumbled, "Suit yourselves." Then he went back to reclining on one of the cots and surfing SpaceNet for any information he could find out about the mystery ship. But he didn't find much, just that it was a simple but massive freighter that had headed to the outer colonies near Saturn a few years back. He wondered what they were bringing back that was important enough to get him involved in this crazy scheme.

After the first day, their scans showed no one chasing them. The few shuttles that had halfheartedly tried to pursue had turned back to Ganymede. After the excessive damage Molly had caused, there would be chaos for quite a while. But eventually the O'Neils would come looking for them, there was no doubt about that. Oscar wanted to be as far away as he could when that happened. They would come after him with more than just a shuttle. The O'Neils had access to a lot of spaceships, including full-on warships.

Oscar's original plan had been a simple one. He would just rescue Molly and fly away. No one was supposed to die. No one was supposed to destroy a major section of Brahe Station. But that's not how it had worked out. Who would have thought that Molly would take over her own rescue? Who would have thought she would detonate his bomb, and recruit one of the O'Neils, her supposed 'half-brother,' to help her escape? Oscar still didn't know if he believed her. But the headstrong woman was now in charge of their journey. She wanted little to do with Oscar now that they had escaped from Ganymede. According to Molly, Oscar had been brought along as extra muscle by the insistence of her father. At first, Oscar had found her to be pretty. But she didn't look so good now and he didn't like her one bit. He thought of killing her and the boy. It wouldn't take too much effort to do that and take over the shuttle. He was a fighter after all. But if he did that, he would lose all the money her father would pay him for getting her safely back to Earth.

When Oscar was a teenager in Mitchellville, South Carolina, his grandfather and he were fishing on the open ocean when they were caught by a storm. Waves washing over the tiny boat's sides tried to capsize them. Oscar found his life jacket, put it on, and found another one for his grandfather. The ocean was angry and he was terrified, but when he came forward with the extra life jacket, his grandfather began to sing an old hymn. At the same time, the old man turned their boat towards the open sea instead of home.

'We're going the wrong way, Sir!' shouted Oscar over the boat's engine and the howling storm.

The old man motioned for Oscar to take over steering the boat so he could put on his life jacket. Oscar grabbed the wheel with both hands, clutching it as tightly as he could, afraid that any second it would fly from his hands.

"Sir, shouldn't we turn around?" shouted Oscar.

His grandfather continued to gaze out to sea, balancing like an old fisherman in the rocking boat. He stopped singing and shouted over his shoulder. "Do you know the story of Mitchellville? Do you know where your people came from?"

By now, seawater was lapping around Oscar's feet. Ocean spray was whipping into his face like needles, and he was having a hard time keeping his eyes open. This didn't seem to be a good time for his grandfather to start telling one of his stories.

"It was back in the Civil War," continued his grandfather. "It was chaos. All the slaves had left their masters. They didn't know where to go. But they never lost their faith. They knew that God had finally set them free. The swamps hid them from the overseers but even the swamp couldn't stop the news from spreading. Soon other freed slaves joined them in Mitchellville and the town thrived, becoming a safe harbor for all the slaves from nearby coastal plantations."

Oscar peered into the distance. "I can see something ahead! Is that St. Helena Island? Is that where we're heading?"

His grandfather waved his hand. He never liked to be interrupted when he was telling a story.

"When the Union soldiers arrived, they must have been pretty surprised to find a whole town of self-emancipated men and women. My great-great-great-great-great grandfather was the mayor. He told the Union general to thank President Lincoln for their freedom, but that they'd already claimed it the year before. He said that no one blamed the soldiers for taking so long to get the news down to Mitchellville. Everyone knew that President Lincoln was tall and that his big feet made him a slow walker. Besides, he had never been a runaway slave, so he had never had to move very fast. So we decided not to wait."

There was a pause, and the storm began to abate just a little. "There's a small inlet ahead," said Oscar. "Should I take us in there?"

His grandfather smiled. "A safe harbor from the storm. Sounds like a good place to wait this one out. You're a good boy, and brave. Once we get in there, you can call your father. You know how he worries."

'Yes, Sir. Mother says he's a professional worrier. One of the most talented worriers she's ever seen."

His grandfather laughed. Then he started to sing again in a booming baritone:

> *"Through many dangers, toils, and snares*
> *"We have already come*
> *"'Twas grace that brought us safe thus far*
> *"And grace will lead us home."*

Back on the space shuttle, Oscar smiled at the memory, silently mouthing the words of that ancient song as they traversed the blackness of space. Space was far bigger and broader than any ocean on Earth. But there had been storms just the same. He would patiently wait out Tropical Storm Molly. While he waited, he would continue his search on SpaceNet for any information on the *Campbell*. There hadn't been much so far, but the information you could find on SpaceNet was practically unlimited. He would dig deeper. His fingers danced on his computer pad. He began to sing out loud this time instead of just moving his lips. If Molly and Tormod thought he was crazy, so what? His grandfather would be proud.

> *"When we've been there ten thousand years*

"Bright shining as the sun..."

19

SS JOHN W CAMPBELL JR

Aaron Ljungman felt panic spread through his veins like a creeping poison. His mind was a jumble, threatening to shut down beneath a black curtain. Something was inside his head, prodding, seeking. What was going on? Where was he really? Moments ago he had been aboard the small cutter, launched from the Swedish warship *Trollslända*. Then he had seemingly been transported home to Earth, to Borås. For one short minute, he had been overjoyed at seeing his hometown after so many years on Europa. And then his old friend Erik had appeared, telling him to stay away. The whole scene had then flickered out just as Erik had been swallowed up by that...thing. Was Erik dead? Somehow Aaron didn't think so. If the creature had wanted to kill him, it would have. Instead, it had launched tendrils up into Erik's nose and ears like vines, whisking him away into the dark depths of the ship. But not before he had a chance to warn Aaron. "It's not real," he had said. Of course, it wasn't. There wasn't a power in the universe that could immediately transport them back to Borås like that...

"Oh yes, little BarnBarn, there is."

The voice was speaking English with a Scandinavian lilt, soft and soothing, not in his ears but inside his head. It was the voice of his grandmother, the one who had inspired him to go into space in the first place, telling him stories about her own life as an astronaut in the early days. As a boy, Aaron's favorite place in the world had been sitting on his grandmother's knee.

Aaron glanced down. Along the corrugated, metallic deck of the freighter, the swaying, triangular head was creeping closer. It was exactly like the one that had carried Erik away. Aaron tried not to look at it because whenever he did, he remembered Erik's voice. "Run!" that voice had said. And whenever Erik's voice reverberated in his mind, his grandmother's voice grew softer. In the duel between the two voices, Aaron clearly wanted his grandmother to win, for he longed to hear that voice again. It was the only soothing thing in this terrifying place.

"Don't believe it!" Erik's voice was louder still.

"Don't you want to go home?" said his grandmother, but her voice was fading fast. "I'm waiting here for you. Come to Mormor and..." But her voice faded to nothing before she was able to finish. Those last few words, 'Come to Mormor and...' had no longer sounded like his grandmother but were said in a primitive, mechanical voice, like you would hear from an early prototype of synthesized speech.

"You have to fight them," said Erik's voice, the only voice left now, not mechanical. It sounded like Erik was really speaking to him. "Now you need to run."

The creature along the deck was now only thirty meters away. He twitched in revulsion as he remembered tendrils from a thing just like that thrusting themselves into Erik's mouth and nose. He shook off the stupor and confusion that had engulfed him. He turned and took off running as fast as he could, his bare feet pounding.

He didn't know where he was going. He simply wanted to get away from that crawling monster. He no longer thought about *Trollslända*, or even Erik, although his friend's voice was still inside his head, urging him to run, run, run. He continued for several minutes, crossing an open area large enough to hold an entire warship.

He came to a junction. Pausing for a moment, he looked back in fear, breathing heavily, expecting to see that swaying head nipping at his heels. But there was nothing there. In front of him, pitch black corridors branched off in seven or eight directions. The light here was dim as if this area was being lit by emergency power, but each corridor was dark, looking like yawning, underground caves. Should he venture into one? If so, how would he see anything at all? And what was he looking for if he could see? He had snuck aboard this ship with the intention of finding whoever was controlling it and getting them to release *Trollslända* from its clutches. And to rescue Erik. But how was he supposed to do that?

A light flickered from far down the second corridor on his left. He heard soft footsteps approaching. Someone was coming his way. Or some...thing.

His body tensed. The footsteps didn't sound like one of those creatures. But every fiber of his body told him to run away. If he went back the way he had come, it would take him towards the creature. If he went down one of the other corridors, he would be running blind...

Erik's voice sounded inside his head. "Wait."

He had grown to trust that voice. He waited. Peering into the distance, he saw the flickering light resolve into a small, clear, flashlight beam. There was a silhouetted shape behind the beam. It looked human.

"Shhhh," said a voice.

A woman stepped forward. She was very tall, slim, and dark, dressed in the Kelly green fatigues of Bertholf Mining. Aaron had seen a lot of that outfit over the years as miners returned from the outer colonies with Bryantonium. But this woman's fatigues were torn and blood-stained, and she smelled like she hadn't washed in a very long time. Aaron inadvertently flinched.

"I know, I know," she mumbled in an accent that could have been South African. She talked fast and her hurried words ran together. "I stink. My anties feel like biltong." She he ran her hands across her chest and made a sour face.

"Huh?" asked Aaron.

"Never mind. Just have to put up wid it, Ja, Nee? I'm the only one dey didn' catch. Was with my bru havin' a jol when dey started actin' up. He went to see. Never come back. So I hid. Been wanderin' ever since. Ain't enough of 'em to see the whole ship. Their technology is amazing. But dey don' know everything. So you an' me, we gotta snotklap 'em. Before dey figure out more. Two mo' better den one, Ja?"

"Huh?" muttered Aaron again.

But she had already begun heading back the way she came. She stopped and motioned with her flashlight. "You comin'?"

Aaron shrugged. There was nothing left for him to do but follow her bobbing light down the pitch black corridor.

20

SENATOR ALAN K SIMPSON

Jelly Roll knew everything eventually filtered down onto the deck plating of the Homer. His biggest enemy was dirt and he battled it every morning and every night before he went to sleep. He made sure his kitchen was the cleanest part of the ship. He refused to let dirt migrate from other areas, to creep into his galley. Along with dirt, he battled coffee grounds, bread crumbs, salt, sugar, and whatever else managed to drift to the deck in the ship's artificial gravity. It never took him long to clean his kitchen. The trick was to stay one step ahead of the dirt, to attack it aggressively. He would have rather been in his kitchen right now, disinfecting it, making its fixtures shine like new, but instead, he was on the bridge with cleaning supplies in hand.

Blood was always the most difficult thing to clean up. Jelly Roll gaped down at the aftermath of Martin's terrible 'accident.' All that blood would surely creep into every crack and crevice. And as disturbed as he was about Captain Martin's injuries, he had to admit that the mess they had made disturbed him more.

As soon as the cook had stumbled upon the Captain, disoriented and missing an eye, he had called for help. Michaelson and Constance were the first to arrive. The three of them had taken Martin to sickbay and put him into the AutoMed capsule. A red medical diagnostic blanket covered him as the top shell hissed down to entomb him completely. The AutoMed would repair as much damage as possible. It wouldn't let the Captain out until his wounds had been stabilized. Martin had already been inside there for the last half hour. If his injuries were severe enough, the AutoMed might keep him in there for as long as two or three days. Well, at least he was alive, and the machine would take care of him.

Because there had been nothing else for him to do, Jelly Roll had decided to clean up the blood on the bridge. He had gone back to his kitchen to get the supplies he needed, his mop, paper towels, and anything else he thought he might need. But he hadn't started cleaning yet. As he stood there looking at the blood on the deck, he knew something wasn't right.

From the way the Captain had been acting when they all converged on the bridge, Michaelson and Constance had assumed that Martin had finally cracked under the pressure of what had been going on for the past few days. They'd all seen similar things happen on various missions into deep space. It might have been a stereotype but it was often true – the loneliness and longing eventually got to everyone, especially someone who was in charge of a lot of other lives. It was no different than on long sea voyages of discovery in Earth's past. Crews had mutinied on many occasions when a captain had begun to lose his mind. Oh sure, Captain Martin had never shown signs of anything like that. But that was probably because he was so good at outwardly appearing calm. So finally, he had lost control while alone on the bridge in the middle of a dark night. He had smashed parts of the bridge and injured himself in various places, even clawing out his own eye while still sitting in his chair. It was ghastly but what could you do? He had been nearly incoherent when they had all gotten there. The AutoMed would keep him safe from himself until they could get him to a psychologist on Europa. If they ever managed to break free from the dark ship, that is. Now that task would fall to Lt. Constance, the second in command.

But Jelly Roll had worked out something the others hadn't. During his free time, he liked to read crime novels involving the police, mostly classic novels set on Earth. There was always a crime scene in stories like that, with mountains of evidence in minute details. The authors were often ex-cops or forensic specialists. You could learn a lot from those books. From reading more than one, Jelly Roll had learned that the diameter of a blood drop could tell you what height it fell from. A drop of blood that fell from four feet above the deck was twice as big as one falling from two feet. The further the blood fell, the larger the drop. Most of Captain Martin's blood had fallen from roughly the height of his chair. But not all of it. There were larger drops on the bridge's deck plating. They had come from high above the captain's chair. Clearly someone, or maybe something, had attacked the Captain from above. It might even have plucked out his eye and then tried to carry it away through a hole in the overhead, dripping blood from way up there before dropping the eye when Jelly Roll intruded at the last minute.

"I think he's going to be alright," said Lt. Constance, standing to Jelly Roll's right. "Michaelson is going to stay with him for now. Hopefully, the doctors on Ceres can re-grow him a new eye." A tear rolled down her cheek. "I don't know why the Captain would do something like this. He seemed okay when I last saw him. Yeah, he was worried about the *Campbell*, but I never thought he would harm himself."

"He didn't," said Jelly Roll. "Meaning no disrespect, but look at the blood drops. Something reached in and took out his eye. It came from up above. There are smaller drops close to his chair but they get bigger as they go further away. And look up. There's blood on the overhead. The Captain couldn't have gotten it way up there."

Constance craned her neck. "Huh. I see what you mean. But there shouldn't be anything up there. That hatch has never been opened since I've been aboard. I don't even think the chief has been up there in years. The ship's sensors would have shown any life form large enough to take out somebody's eye. That's one of the reasons we have onboard sensors in the first place, to guard against picking up a nasty pest along with cargo."

"I don't know what it is, but the Captain didn't do that to himself. Something else did."

Constance continued gazing at the overhead. "I'm pretty sure it's just a crawl space up there, maybe some wires and pipes, stuff like that."

"Is there anything above that?" asked Jelly Roll.

"Just the hull." Constance ran her hand through her hair. "I suppose we'll need to go up there. With everything that has been happening with the black ship, maybe they got something aboard that our sensors can't detect."

"We?" exclaimed Jelly Roll. "Not me. I'm just the cook. I'll stay here and clean up. There are far braver people than me aboard this ship. What about those commandos of yours? I'll leave the heroics to you and your people."

"Okay. But maybe you should come with me while I gather them up. If there is something up there, it might come back while you're here alone."

Jelly Roll brandished his mop. "I'll be safe with this. Everyone knows not to mess with old Jelly Roll when he has a mop in his hand."

Constance chuckled and said, "Holler if you see anything."

She walked away, leaving Jelly Roll to begin cleaning up the blood. As he did so, he occasionally glanced at the overhead, ready to bolt at the first sign of trouble.

21

SHUTTLE

What day was it? Oscar had lost track. That was easy to do in space, of course, without the rising and setting of the sun, but all spaceships set their computers to run on Greenwich Mean Time, with twenty-four hour days, seven-day weeks, and twelve month years, just like on Earth. That seemed to work best for the natural rhythms of human bodies and it made the most sense for ships' logs, trade manifests, and legal proceedings. But Oscar hadn't been able to settle into any kind of rhythm aboard the stolen shuttle from Ganymede because he had completely lost himself on SpaceNet.

The deeper Oscar searched on his tablet, the less he found out about the ship they were heading towards. Oh sure, he had found the usual facts that were available for all spaceships. The *John W Campbell Jr.* was a Libertarian Class Freighter. Like the rest of its class, it had been built for the invasion of Mars. That made it an old ship by today's standards, but like all the rest from that era, it had found new life out past the Asteroid Belt. It had been constructed in orbit above Luna by the New Philadelphia Starship Corporation. After the war, it had settled into mundane freighter duties, or at least as mundane as space travel could be. At first, it ran cargo between Earth and Mars. After the shipping lanes opened to Jupiter, it sailed between Mars and Jupiter. It hadn't returned to Earth orbit in over twenty-five years, living nearly all of its life in deep space. None of that was unusual. What was unusual was the fact that after the shipping lanes opened between Jupiter and Saturn ten years ago, the *Campbell* completely disappeared from SpaceNet after just one voyage. Specifically, the ship had vanished from history after it had been sold. And who had bought it? That seemed to be a well-guarded secret. Records had been deleted. False data trails had obviously been set up by somebody. More than once, trying to follow the *Campbell's* trail had given Oscar a migraine. But one name kept coming up, even if it was buried deep in piles of statistics, the Salome Corporation.

Oscar slid sideways out of his bunk and plopped his bare feet onto the shuttle's deck plating. He had only gotten out of his bunk a few times in the past couple of days. The fighter wanted to stay as far away from his traveling companions as possible. They seemed to sense his mood and kept their distance from him as well. He wondered what Molly and Tormod talked about during these long miles in deep space. He would have liked to know more about their plans since he was obviously stuck in the middle of whatever they were going to do. He was still mad at Molly and her father for getting him involved in the first place. This isn't what he had signed up for when he had agreed to rescue the business tycoon's daughter.

He found a clean pair of white socks in his black duffel bag and put them on. He gathered up his boots from under the bunk, leaned over, put them on, and laced them up. After he tied the last knot, he stomped his right foot on the deck plate. It made a loud noise that he was pretty sure Molly and Tormod could hear, but, apparently, neither of them took any notice and the normal hum of deep space travel didn't change in the least. Even though the shuttle was small, it was like he and the other two had carved out completely separate worlds.

Oscar stood tall and stretched. He thought about what he had uncovered concerning the Salome Corporation. It had been mentioned in conjunction with something called Project Lapetus. Lapetus was an ancient Greek word meaning 'The Piercer,' as best as he could tell. There was only one article on SpaceNet about Project Lapetus, and that had been from ten years ago. It referred to a revolutionary proton-fusion drive, supposedly being developed by the Salome Corporation. There was a quote from the CEO of Salome that this could usher in a brand new era of space travel, allowing ships to voyage outside the solar system without having to take lifetimes to do it. This wasn't unusual of course. Over the decades there had been all kinds of rumored breakthroughs in propulsion, but none of them had panned out. Oscar had only found that one mention of Project Lapetus in all his research. After that, there was nothing at all. But he did find another mention of The Salome Corporation. Two years after the mention of Project Lapetus, the CEO of Salome had been fired. Surprisingly, the man's name hadn't been deleted.

Duncan Mackintosh. Molly's father.

"Look who's prepared to join us amongst the living?" smirked Molly as Oscar made his way from the back of the shuttle to the bridge. "I'm glad you're here. We're only a day away from the *Campbell* and I need to tell you what we'll do when we get there."

As usual, Tormod was sitting at Molly's side on the bridge. Whenever he had seen the two of them during this voyage, they were always side by side. Tormod reminded Oscar of the moon he came from, Ganymede, circling Molly as if she was Jupiter.

"I don't expect any trouble docking," continued Molly. "I'll board first to check things out. Then I'll send for you and Tormod. That's why my Dad wanted you along so you could..."

Oscar had advanced on her while she was talking. Now he was so close that she stopped mid-sentence. He could feel the heat from her skin and he hoped she could feel his breath as he leaned down and brought his face close to hers. He didn't speak but simply glared at her.

"What's wrong?" asked Molly, trying to look stern. She probably wanted to start yelling at him like normal. That was what she was used to from her life of privilege and wealth. But Oscar had caught her off guard. He could have reached out and broken her in two if he wanted. He still hadn't made up his mind if he was going to kill her and Tormod because Oscar Gunn was a man who liked to keep his options open.

"I'm glad we're almost there," he said, his eyes locked onto hers. "This hasn't exactly been a pleasure cruise for me. So now you're going to tell me everything you know. About that ship."

Molly looked away. Her face flushed, becoming nearly as red as her hair, camouflaging her freckles. "I'm not sure I know what you mean," she muttered.

To Molly's left, Oscar saw Tormod reach his hand beneath the control panel.

Oscar recited a line from an old movie. "Whatever you reaching for better be a sandwich because you're going to have to eat it."

Tormod pulled his hand away like he had just touched a spent fuel rod.

Molly held up her arms. "Okay, okay. Calm down. Maybe you deserve to have more information. The *Campbell* is a very important ship. Very important. You have no idea where it's been. I'm not sure anyone knows, except for the people that are on it. There's something on board that could make history." She sat back and took a deep breath. "So there. That's all you need to know. I'm not afraid of you."

Oscar clenched his fists. He had the advantage on both of them because they were sitting down and he was standing up, looming over them like a fighter in the ring.

Molly glanced at Tormod and spoke through the side of her mouth. "Don't worry. He won't do anything to us."

She was trying to sound tough but her voice cracked as she said this. Oscar knew he had her rattled. All across the solar system, he had run across plenty of hard cases and she wasn't one of them. Not really. Sure, she was a psycho, but she wasn't all that tough. And, like a fighter in the ring, he knew when it was time to press his advantage.

"Let's talk about Project Lapetus, shall we?" said Oscar. "And the Salome Corporation. That was your father's company, wasn't it? I need to hear more about that. I'm not going anywhere near that ship unless you tell me what we're going there for."

Molly swallowed hard. This time, instead of blushing, all the color drained out of her face and Oscar thought he could have used her freckles to play 'Connect the Dots.'

"How do you know about Lapetus?" asked Molly. "Nobody knows about that."

"Start talking," said Oscar.

And so she did.

22

SENATOR ALAN K SIMPSON

Lt. Constance looked at Jelly Roll and sighed.

"You look ten years older," he said, "but you're still just a kid."

"Thanks a lot," she muttered. She wasn't sure which statement bothered her most, the part about looking older or the part about still being just a kid. Ever since the beginning of this mission, she had attempted to prove herself mature enough to handle her job. But, like most people, she didn't like the idea of looking older either. Well, she'd have a chance to prove herself now. She was going to have to be a badass. It seemed like ages ago when she had been a member of the boarding party that had made ready to dock with the *Campbell* and charge on board with guns blazing. But they had never gotten the chance. The black ship had made other plans, and now here she was with the same boarding party, assembled on the bridge of the *Homer*, preparing to climb up through a hatch and blast the hell out of whatever had plucked out the captain's eye.

Jelly Roll handed her each piece of body armor in turn. The others already had theirs on but she had been too busy checking on Captain Martin in the AutoMed and seeing to the ship's vitals to get ready. Not to mention trying to modify those Phillip's Missiles for manual operation so they could blast the damned black ship to kingdom come. She had been a long way from getting that done when she was interrupted by the call from the bridge about the captain being attacked. She supposed that it was the price of leadership to have to switch directions at a moment's notice. And with the captain in sickbay, she was in charge now.

The boarding party stood around impatiently as she donned her Kevlar vest. They hefted their automatic weapons and grunted. All this firepower seemed huge in the confined space of the bridge. She had directed them to load only standard rounds so none of their shots could pierce *Homer's* Bryantonium hull. That only made sense, since they would be right up against that hull. She certainly didn't need a breech to suck them all out into space. But she only hoped that standard rounds would be enough against whatever they found up there.

It would be a tight squeeze. Four of them in armor would be crammed into the space above the bridge console, along with various wires and pipes and probably enough collected dust to choke a moose. But that couldn't be helped. Somehow, something had gotten aboard ship and attacked the captain from up there. Presumably, it was still there unless it had migrated to someplace else on the ship. And that was something she didn't even want to think about.

As she put on one of her elbow pads she asked Jelly Roll, "How's the captain doing?"

"The AutoMed still has him in her embrace."

Constance smiled and said, "Her? So you think of the AutoMed as a woman?"

"I sure hope so. I've got nothing against a man giving another man a hug, but I don't like the idea of a guy poking around my body like that. Besides, there are lots of ways to tell she's a female. Look at her stance. The way she looks at you from the corner of her eye when you first walk into sickbay. Oh yeah, the AutoMed's definitely a woman. But not a sexy one. More like my mom back in Indiana. You want a mom to take care of you when you're sick. Not only because she'll make you better but you'll feel all warm and fuzzy while she's doing it. I'm surprised AutoMed doesn't bring you milk and cookies."

The boarding party laughed. Constance chuckled as well as she put on her other elbow pad. "I never thought about it like that. I've always thought of her as a machine."

"Hah!" said Jelly Roll. "You just called her a 'her!' Don't deny it! The rest of you heard it too, didn't you?"

The team members all nodded and laughed again.

Constance was glad for a little levity at a time like this. Leave it to Jelly Roll to lighten things up for all of them. She donned her helmet. "Is there any machine you think is male?"

Jelly Roll nodded. "That's easy. My pasta maker. It has to be a guy. Always needs to get the last word. However much dough I put in, all of it ends up coming out of his mouth. We all know guys like that, don't we?"

Constance examined her sidearm, put it back in its holster, and double-checked the rest of her team. When she was satisfied that all was ready, she nodded at Jelly Roll. "That's it, then. Thanks for the help."

Jelly Roll ran a chubby hand over the back of his neck. He puffed some air out between his lips. "I'm just glad I'm not going up there. Well...come back safe. All of you. I'll make you the very best spaghetti dinner tonight."

"I thought you didn't like your pasta maker," said Constance.

"Oh, he's not as smart as the AutoMed, that's for sure. But I'd still rather hang out with him than her. I haven't been inside an AutoMed for twenty years. I haven't visited my mother in twenty years, either. And I've been healthy as a horse all that time, so why change now?"

There were more chuckles all around but clearly, it was time to go. Constance clumsily reached towards Jelly Roll and pulled him close. It's not easy to hug someone while you're dressed in full battle armor, especially if the person you're hugging is as large as Jelly Roll, but Lt. Constance found a way. It was a long moment before she let go. Then she crept up the waiting ladder and turned the circular wheel which would open the hatch.

23

SENATOR ALAN K SIMPSON

Lt. Constance glanced around in the tight space and coughed. Dust motes swirled in the harsh glare of flashlights and the softer light from the open hatch below. Sweat trickled down her armpits. It was hot up here, and their body heat was making it worse. There was more room here than she had imagined, and the Bryantonium outer hull was high enough above their heads so they could stand. The iron deck below their feet was a good thing. When she was a kid, she and a friend had climbed up into the attic of her house. Walking across a couple of beams, she had accidentally stepped between the joists and fallen through the ceiling to the floor below. At least that wouldn't happen here.

She put her hands on her hips. There didn't seem to be anything up here.

They had run gloved hands over all the filthy wires and pipes. They'd crawled along the deck with their lights, trying to find out where something could have come in. They'd scanned every inch of the ship's outer hull above their heads. They'd checked every crevice and corner. There was nothing here. Maybe whatever it was had migrated to another part of the ship and they'd have to do a lot more crawling around…

Leopold Jagr screamed. Constance whirled and pointed her flashlight to the far corner where he was standing. The other two members of the party did the same. Jagr tried to scream again but his voice cut off. Something was wrapping itself around his neck, something with tentacles. A triangular-shaped head hovered in front of his adam's apple like a broach. Tentacles crept up his chin, heading for his nose and ears.

"Shoot it!" shouted Silence Bohannon.

"No!" hollered Constance. "You'll hit Jagr!"

The other member of the party, Abdul Hakeem Karam, dropped his gun and grabbed the triangular-shaped head with both hands and pulled. The thing made a screeching sound and the tentacles withdrew quickly from around Jagr's neck. They whipped into Karam's face and he let go of the head and frantically waved his hands, trying to keep the tentacles at bay. Constance ran towards them, waving her flashlight in one hand and grabbing her sidearm with the other. In the flickering light, she could see the creature's entire length. It was at least fifteen or twenty feet long, with tentacles slithering up and down its body like caressing hands.

The creature pulled away from Karam and raced up the far wall of the compartment. The bottom half of its body disappeared through the outer hull as if there was a hole in the Bryantonium. The front half, including the triangular-shaped head, was still in the room with them. Its body snapped down like a whip and struck Jagr on the back. Constance heard the sickening sound of ribs and spinal cord snapping and Jagr went limp as a rag doll. Tentacles wrapped around his waist and smashed him down against the deck plating with a loud thump, like a dog playing with a shake toy, over and over and over. Constance looked on in horror. She could see that Jagr was still alive but his arms and legs were useless. He looked at her with pleading eyes. But what could she do? She couldn't shoot the creature because she would surely hit Jagr.

After getting smashed against the deck two more times, Jagr's eyes closed and it was clear that he was dead. The tentacles unwound and Jagr's body dropped down like a spent bullet. The creature's triangular-shaped head reared up and waved back and forth like a seaweed pod. It had yellow eyes that twinkled like fireflies back on Earth.

Silence Bohannon fired. The shot missed the waving head and hit part of the creature's slithering body. Black blood splashed the wall. Bohannon fired again and then Karam was firing as well. They were frantic and panicky in such close quarters and a lot of their shots went wide. It was hard to see because everyone except Constance had dropped their flashlights, and in the chaos, the lights were spinning around like strobes. Some shots hit Jagr's body with soft thuds that sounded like pebbles hitting a rotten pumpkin. But many of the shots hit the creature and black blood began to flow onto the metal deck like dark, oily sludge.

The creature shrieked and pulled its entire body up through the overhead hull with an audible pop. And just like that, it was gone.

Bohannon and Karam fired a few shots after it, but none of the standard rounds pierced the Bryantonium hull.

"Cease fire!" shouted Constance. She aimed her flashlight at the spot where the creature had disappeared. It was like nothing had ever come through the hull in the first place.

Karam knelt down in front of Jagr. "Maybe we can get him to sickbay," he said, his voice breaking.

"Too late for that, I think," said Constance.

Bohannon kept her CBJ pointed at the hull. Constance aimed her own pistol at the same spot. How had the creature come through? And if it did it once...

A tentacle came through the hull from another spot, striking Bohannon on the front of her throat. She dropped her small weapon and gagged, reaching up with both hands to try and pull it off. At the end of the tentacle was a crooked finger that waved once in the air and then thrust itself into her neck. It came out the other side with an audible squish and a spray of red blood. Bohannon's body went instantly limp and Constance knew she had to be dead. The finger curled into a hook on the back of Bohannon's neck and dragged her up through the hull. The only thing on the other side was the vacuum of space. Constance felt her guts clench. How could this even be possible?

Karam stared after Bohannon with his mouth open and eyes wide. Constance gathered her wits. She touched Karam's shoulder. She spoke softly and clearly.

"Get Jagr, now. Toss his body down through the hatch. I don't want to leave him for that...thing."

Karam jerked as if coming out of a trance. "Hell, no!" he shouted. "The man's dead! I'm getting out of here!"

He dropped down to his stomach and crawled towards the opening, glancing up at the hull as he went, trying to stay as far away as he could in case the tentacle returned. He didn't have long to wait.

A tentacle dropped down through the hull directly above Karam. Instead of piercing him like it had Bohannon, it wrapped itself around his waist like it had done to Jagr. Karam screamed and reached back to Constance. She tried to grab his foot and pull him free but the tentacle was too fast. It yanked Karam into the air and through the hull plating above. His scream was instantly cut off as he disappeared.

Constance's heart pounded like a jackhammer. She had to get out of this killing ground. She was smaller than the others and could move faster. She ran towards the opening and the light from the bridge below. It looked like a beacon of safety. Just as she had almost reached it, a tentacle dropped down right in front of her face. She had just enough time to dive headfirst through the opening. She somehow caught the top rung of the ladder and wrapped both her arms around it, her legs flopping down the sides. She held on. The ladder wobbled but then steadied. She stood on a lower rung and looked up through the opening. The tentacle was still there, waving back and forth like a black, oily rope. Another tentacle had joined it. She waited until both tentacles had swung away before pulling the hatch closed. She spun its wheel to seal it off. She could hear the tentacles slapping against its metal from the other side. Her breath came in great gasps. Would it simply come through the iron hatch the way it had come through the Bryantonium hull? Why wouldn't it be able to do that?

She clutched the top rung of the ladder and waited for one minute, then two, then three, expecting that terrible thing to come through any moment. But it didn't. Eventually, the slapping noise from above faded away and it was quiet.

She stumbled down the ladder, her legs beginning to give way as the adrenaline left her. She tried to take off her body armor but was unable. She collapsed to the deck in a heap. Well, maybe Jelly Roll would come along and help her out. In fact, seeing Jelly Roll right now sounded like the most wonderful thing in the solar system.

She hugged herself tightly. How would they fight against something that could come through a Bryantonium hull from the vacuum of space? It had easily killed three of her boarding party and it had almost killed her. She had been mere inches from her own death.

She never wanted to be that close again.

24

SS JOHN W CAMPBELL JR

Aaron Ljungman had experienced a lot of frightening things during his time in space but nothing like this. He and the woman had fled down one dark corridor after another, turning left and right and left again, seemingly circling back the way they had come as if in a labyrinth, any moment expecting to run across another one of those creeping monsters.

But his fear came from much more than that.

A feeling of helpless dread permeated this ship. The walls themselves heaved and groaned as if they were about to change shape and swallow him whole. The decks and overheads did the same, making Aaron instinctively duck his head at random times, even though the overheads were at least two meters above his head. In the flickering beam of the woman's flashlight, no corner looked perfectly square, no angle was ninety degrees. It was almost like being in a funhouse back in Borås when he was a kid, or maybe in a spaceship made of putty. But the smell was the worst.

A strong body odor emanated from the woman up ahead but that was nothing compared to the stench of the air itself. All spaceships got pretty ripe after a while, no matter how sophisticated the filtration systems. And this was an old freighter which had probably never smelled like North Sea breezes in the first place. But the canned air of this ship was rank with something else, an odor that was mechanical, electrical, and biological. It reminded Aaron of stale grease, shorted-out wires, and dead animals all mixed together. And beneath that was another smell that he had no words for. It simply smelled alien.

The woman pulled up at yet another cockeyed junction. Aaron nearly ran into her. He thought he had been paying attention but found that he couldn't remember the last several turns, not that it would have done him much good.

She pointed her flashlight into his eyes. "You're not exactly a *babbelbekkie*, are you?"

"What?"

"You don't talk much."

He glanced back the way they had just come. "Do you think it's still following us?"

"The Gek monster?"

"Is that what it's called?"

She lowered the flashlight. "Good a naam as any. Not reptiel. Not fout. So why not Gek?"

Aaron Ljungman shook his head. Didn't they speak English in South Africa? At least he thought they did. Or maybe it was Dutch. Was there such a thing as Dutchlish? If this hadn't been such a tense moment, he might have laughed.

She looked into his eyes, evidently waiting for him to say something else. When he didn't, she said, "Why you no talk? I been lonely lonely for long time, loopin' round like a rat in a cage. Den finally, here come someone to help. But you don't talk. Are you Swedish?"

This time Aaron managed a chuckle and it diffused a little of his fear. This wasn't the first time he'd been accused of being a cold fish. And why not? He'd been living on the ice of Europa for four years. He'd grown up in Sweden, a place not known for overly gregarious men. But, like it or not, he would have to work with this woman. If he was going to rescue Erik and get them out of here, he needed to find out everything she could tell him. "I guess I'm kind of quiet," he mumbled. "Unless I know somebody."

She held out her hand. "That's mo better. Let's know each other. I'm Hansie Addington. But everyone calls me Gugu. So there. Now you know me. You can be my bra."

"Your bra?" stuttered Aaron, feeling his face flush.

She broke into raucous laughter and the sound echoed around the corridor.

"Yeah, Bra. That means male friend. Like...uh...Dude. Okay?"

"You're gonna have to speak English," said Aaron. "Everybody in the solar system speaks English."

She chuckled again. "I am speaking English. But maybe I should cut back on my *Afrikaans* slang. My mates on the *Campbell* got used to it. I guess I can't expect you to yet. But you will. In the meantime..." She held her head high and spoke like a dinner guest at Windsor Castle. "Is this oh so much better? From now on, I will speak proper English and we'll have a jolly good time, won't we then?" She waved her free hand with a flourish.

"That works," said Aaron, suddenly feeling much more comfortable than he ever thought he could in a situation like this.

"And what's your name?" she asked.

"Aaron. Aaron Ljungman. " He held out his own hand.

"So you are Swedish," she said as they shook hands.

"Guilty as charged." He was warming up to this woman. Her eyes were intelligent, sparkling a bright blue even through all the grime on her face.

"Let's have a bit of a rest and a snack, shall we?" said Gugu, still sounding like English royalty. She slid down onto the deck with her back to the wall. Aaron did the same and waited while she pulled some sort of biscuit from her backpack, along with a small canteen.

Aaron felt the wall move ever so slightly behind his back as if he were leaning up against a sleeping elephant. He pulled away and jumped to his feet.

"You'll get used to it," said Gugu with a wave of her hand. "It's mostly harmless. They've got some way to manipulate matter or at least some matter. But not everything. I've been able to wander all over the ship without them knowing I'm here. But they're learning. When they finish figuring us out, we're going to be in real drift sand."

Aaron sat back down. "Are you talking about those...Gek monsters?"

"No. Those are just their attack dogs. Wait 'til you see the ones pulling the strings."

Aaron shuddered. "So how did they get on board?"

"Can't be sure," said Gugu. "But I think I know. We picked up a load of Bryantonium ore from Titan Outpost after our trip to...well, never mind that. But we decided to stop at Titan on the way back in. Might as well get some metal to help pay for the voyage. The owners allowed us to do that, even though it wasn't the primary. All of us were supposed to get a percentage. This was a freighter after all. It was right after that when the weird things started."

"What kinds of things?" asked Aaron.

"Oh, little things at first. Computer systems acting afskilfer...um...what's the word?...acting flaky. Understand?"

Aaron nodded. He could relate to that from what had happened on *Trollslända*.

"Go on."

"Then we all started having dreams."

"What kinds of dreams?"

"Vreemd...um...weird. Vivid dreams, nightmares. Like they were really happening. About Gek monsters, but we didn't know that yet of course. We all thought it was because we'd been in space too long. Deep space. So we couldn't wait to get to Europa. Even down time on the ice sounded good."

Aaron nodded again. People had invented a surprising amount of recreational activities to do on a remote, icebound moon.

"So then one day I was with my bru...um...my boyfriend...havin' a jol...I mean a..." Gugu sighed. Even through the grime, Aaron could see her blush.

"I understand," he said.

"Oh. Okay then. So we suddenly heard this piercing noise from up on the bridge, and some screaming. My boyfriend was Head of Security. He put on his pants and raced out the door. The next time I saw him..."

Gugu swallowed hard. Clearly, she was struggling to get the words out and Aaron knew enough to not press her. She continued softly. "After a while, I crept out of my room. I was bang afraid by now because of all the weird noises. I peeked around a corner near the bridge and there was my bru on the deck. One of them things was on top of him like I had been a few minutes before. Only they weren't havin' a jol. The thing had its tentacles all up inside my bru's ears and nose, slidin' in and out, in and out. I don't think my bru was dead yet because his legs were twitching like from an electric shock and his eyes were open wide. Maybe I could have done something. But I was just too geskok...too...too..."

Aaron put his hand on Gugu's arm. "I know," he said. "You don't have to explain."

"I suppose not," she muttered. "But I ran away. I have been running from those things ever since. But just like them, I been learning everything I can. Everything. I think we can beat them."

"What was your job on the ship?" asked Aaron.

"Weapons Officer. And I would like to have my job back."

"Can I ask you something else?"

"Ja."

"I came aboard to rescue a friend of mine. His name is Erik. I saw him back in that big room when I first came aboard. Have you seen him?"

She paused and pursed her grimy lips. "My crew is all dead. I saw their bodies piled up in the airlock a few days after all of this happened. The next time I looked the bodies were gone. As to your friend, no. I never saw him. I thought I was the only human left alive here. I couldn't even find my pet cat, Skattebol. I guess they got her too."

Aaron got a sinking feeling in the pit of his stomach. "But Erik talked to me," he muttered. "He warned me. Otherwise one of those things would have gotten me too."

"Then he must be alive," said Gugu. "And at least a little bit human."

"So what do we do now?"

"We'll have to do a lot of twists and turns. We have to get some more food and I'd love to be able to grab a shower. But eventually, we'll be heading for engineering. They'll be hanging around there. And not just the Gek monsters. But now that there are two of us, maybe we can snotklap 'em."

By the way, she pronounced the word, Aaron didn't need a translation.

25

SHUTTLE

The shuttle's head was located in the little ship's smallest space but it was private. Oscar looked at himself in the mirror and, like so many times before, he remembered his grandfather. And with the remembering, one of his grandfather's many sayings ran through his head.

"If you're real, and always stay true to yourself, you can go anywhere."

That had been one of the old man's favorite subjects during the countless times they went fishing together when Oscar was a boy in South Carolina. "People don't expect anybody to be real any longer. Everyone wants to be somebody else besides who they really are. So they end up faking themselves out without even knowing it. Don't ever do that, Son. Don't be a fake. Always be true to yourself."

"Yes, Sir," said Oscar, standing in the boat and making another cast with his fishing pole.

"And part of that is not telling lies."

"Uh huh."

"But you told a lie today, didn't you, Son? At school."

His grandfather stood in the boat's stern and used a long pole to slowly propel the boat through low coastal grasses as the tide retreated. "And you told a lie to a girl. That's never a good idea."

Oscar finished reeling in his line. He double checked his lure. "They're not biting today. Maybe I should change this artificial lure to a different one. The redfish don't seem to want it at all."

"So, you think it's the lure and not the fisherman who's the problem," said his grandfather.

Along the shallows, a snowy egret flapped its graceful, white wings and looked for the best place to fish. The bird hunted much smaller fish and wouldn't wade into the water any deeper than he could stand in. All the birds of the low coast had their own techniques to catch fish. Some, like egrets, waited for the tide to retreat and found the tiny fish that the water left behind. Brown pelicans liked to fly in small squadrons above the incoming waves so they could spot fish from up there. There were also deep divers like the masked booby, who weren't afraid to plunge into the sea to catch fish. Oscar had always thought 'booby' was a strange name for a bird and sometimes it made him blush when his grandfather talked about them and...

Oscar turned on the water in the shuttle's head and washed his hands. God, he missed that old man so much. He'd pay a hundred times more money than he would make from Molly's father to have one more day of fishing with his grandfather.

Except for his bunk, the head was the only place in the little spacecraft where he could get away from Molly and Tormod, the only place where he could think. He splashed some water on his face. It tasted stale on his lips. How many times had the water been recycled over the years? A hundred? A thousand? A million? The water had lost its crispness, its bite over time. Maybe the same thing had happened to him. He'd been away for too long. He missed the crispness of the sea. He missed its salty taste. When this was over, he would return to Earth and go back to Mitchellville. He still owned his grandfather's house. He would buy another boat and reclaim the salt he lacked in his veins out here in space.

But first, he had to finish the task he was involved in now. And that meant Molly. He didn't know if he had the strength to face her again. She was waiting on him right now outside the head. She wasn't happy, and he was sure she was getting ready to yell at him again for another of his many faults. He looked up at the mirror once more and set his lips into a grim line. He made up his mind that he wouldn't kill her. He would get her back home to her father no matter how much more foolishness she got them all into. What kind of bird was Molly anyhow? Birds didn't act like fools. They never acted out of anger or pride. No, he had never come across a bird like Molly before.

And what about the boy? What about Tormod? They should never have taken him along. Oscar needed to get him home again. That's what his grandfather would've done. Get the boy back to Ganymede, back to the O'Neils, the people who missed him. It was the right thing to do. But how was he going to do that? The whole clan was surely up in arms and would be waiting for Oscar with guns blazing.

He had come up against a lot of fighters over the years, but Molly had proved to be the most tenacious opponent he ever faced. He thought he had the upper hand when he forced her to tell him what she knew about project Lapetus. That should have been a victory for him. But after she had told him, she turned his victory on its head. Like always, she wouldn't listen to his logic and reasoning. She insisted that when they boarded the *Campbell* they would do it her way. She knew the codes to get them on, she had the access key, and she would be the first to set foot on the other ship without knowing what was over there waiting for them. When he continued to threaten her with his gun, she practically laughed in his face. Oscar had won a couple rounds but was losing this fight. All of the judges' cards would be unanimously against him at the end. Unless he could throw a knockout punch. And now, instead of sitting in his corner, he had retreated to the head for a much-needed timeout between rounds.

"Why did you lie to that girl in your class?" asked his Grandfather. He kept the pole down this time so it firmly planted itself in the sand and the boat stopped.

When the boat steadied, Oscar made a perfect cast out into deeper water. "I don't know why. I guess I just wanted to impress her. To show her I'm stronger than anybody else in the school. So I told her the guy tried to take my lunch money."

"But he didn't."

"No, Sir."

"But you got into a fight anyhow. A fight you started."

"Yes, Sir."

"And that's why the teacher sent you to the principal's office?"

Oscar had never lied to his grandfather and he wasn't about to start now. He had lied to his father and his mother but not to this man. "Yes, Sir."

Oscar pulled in a striped bass and set the pole back inside the boat. He looked up at the sky. The sun would be down in an hour and it was almost time for them to head back home. A few clouds were blowing towards shore so there might be some rain later in the evening.

"So who was he?" asked his grandfather.

"Brian Dudley," said Oscar defensively. "He's the biggest boy in our class. I gave him a bloody nose." He wanted to justify what he did but instead, he told the truth. "All the girls like him. I thought if I fought him and won, a few of the girls might like me."

"So you got into a fight with that boy just to impress the girls? Did it work?"

"No, Sir. It got worse. The girls were all mad at me and wouldn't speak to me for the rest of the day. I almost don't want to go back to school on Monday morning. Everyone is mad at me. Mom grounded me. I only got out of the house because I promised Grandma I'd go to church with her in the morning."

"Your mother's no fool. She guessed the two of us would go fishing after lunch and maybe she hoped you might talk to me about your fight." He walked back and started the boat's engine. "Those girls might be mad at you for a long time, but you'll make it better eventually. As long as you don't pretend you're something else. Something you're not. Girls have a built in truth-detector. Maybe they always expect boys to lie to them, I don't know. But I do know you'll find calmer waters with them if you're truthful. Besides, do you really want the kind of girl who only likes you because you can fight?"

Molly knocked on the door of the head again. Oscar knew he needed to go out there and confront her. He would listen to her arguments no matter how much pain she brought to his ears. And he'd find a way to win the fight. He slid open the small door. He could barely squeeze his large shoulders through the opening. She was standing there with her hands on her hips, even angrier than when he had gone in.

Molly's mouth twisted into a grim line as she launched another verbal assault. "I just don't know why you're not listening to me. I have the codes and the access key. We can get onto the *Campbell*. I'm smaller and faster than a big lug like you. We can find out what happened over there. But we're going to do it the right way. My way."

Oscar eased closer. When he was in reach, he moved his right arm around her lower back. Before she could react, he bent down and gave her a kiss. Molly's eyes opened wide in surprise. She pushed against his chest with both hands. He took a step back and she punched him in the gut. Oscar hadn't had time to flex his abdominal so he let out a small groan. She quickly grabbed his shirt and pulled him closer. This time, instead of punching him she planted a kiss of her own on Oscar's lips. Now it was his turn to look surprised. The small woman had won another round. Maybe she had just won the whole fight. The judges wouldn't have to look at their score cards for this one.

But somehow, Oscar suddenly wasn't too upset from losing to a featherweight.

26

HSWMS TROLLSLÄNDA

Not once in her life had Jenny Broberg ever imagined she would find herself in command of a warship, much less a newly reconfigured one with a top secret weapon on board. She was much too sensible a person to even dream up such a crazy idea. The most daring thing she had ever done while growing up in Örnsköldsvik was to sneak into the Forsberg Ice Complex with a boyfriend one night for an after-closing skate. Yes, she was an engineer with a specialty in weapons tech on Europa Station. But when was the last time there had been a battle on Europa? Before she had been born.

Most of the weapons techs on spaceships these days, Swedish ships, Russian ships, Chinese ships, South African ships, were women. Back on Earth, women flocked to science and engineering classes at University. They had proved themselves to be the most even-tempered, which was good when dealing with technology that could blow things up. No one wanted someone who had a tendency to turn a routine disagreement into a pissing contest. It was only the Americans who clung to the idea that anyone with a big gun should be a cowboy.

So she was sensible, calm, and as stable as a Lapland glacier. So why had she helped Aaron Ljungman steal *Trollslända* away from Europa Station? Was it because the two of them had slept together? Maybe. Or was it because she was so sick of the layers and layers of bureaucracy she had to deal with every day, with orders coming from 600 million kilometers away? By the time Stockholm would have gotten around to approving a rescue of Erik Juergenson, he would have been space dust. So she had left her comfort zone and jumped. And now, with Aaron taking the cutter and disappearing onto the black ship, she was sitting in the captain's chair. The ultimate irony was that she wasn't in control at all. She was completely helpless because the black ship simply wouldn't let them go. It was pulling them in, closer and closer. And now they were only about a kilometer away. Once more she called down to engineering.

"Herko...Heidi, is there anything you can do? Anything at all? In about five minutes we're going to be swallowed up by that ship over there." For some reason, calling the engineer by her first name seemed like the right thing to do under the circumstances. This was a pirated ship after all.

"Only yust one ting I can tink of," answered Herko.

"For Odin's sake, what?"

"Vell, I can reverse the polarity on da Dora Yenerator."

"And what would that do?"

"I tink it might fool vatever is controlling us. At least long enough for us to get outa here. But den again it could make our power system go kaput."

"How long will it take you to do it?"

"Oh...tree seconds I tink."

"Why didn't you tell me this before? Do it!"

Maybe there were times when you actually needed to act like an American cowboy...

"But if da power goes out, den..."

"Do it!"

Broberg had screamed out the last order. Now she literally held her breath. On her left, Rasmussen had his eyes glued to the view screen. On her right, Renberg was gazing down at the life support controls. If this did fry the power, how long could they last? Well, anything was better than getting swallowed up by that ship. She expected that any moment the ghastly mouth would open up on its hull.

The lights on the bridge blinked off, thrusting them into complete blackness and total silence as fans stopped humming and generators stopped working. Broberg let out her breath in a gasp. All she could do was sit rock still in the darkness and hope. Moments ago she had felt helpless. Now she was blind as well. The artificial gravity had switched off and she grabbed the arm of her chair to keep from floating towards the overhead. Suddenly she flopped down again and the lights came back on.

"It worked!" shouted Renberg. He was tapping his console. "It's responding! I think we're free!"

Broberg looked down at her own controls. Moments ago, before the power had gone off, all of the lights had been frozen, the way they had been since before Aaron left. But now they were blinking, waiting for her to push something. "Hold on!" she shouted. "We're getting out of here!"

It took her a few maddening seconds to figure out how to throw *Trollslända* in reverse and goose the throttle. But goose she did and the warship lurched backward. The black ship was fading into the distance. There were cheers from Renberg and Rasmussen. She called down to engineering.

"Nice work, Heidi! I'm going to spin us around and point us towards Europa. Give me everything you've got. We're heading home. Then we're coming back with a whole fleet of warships. Let's see what that bastard ship will do when..."

Before she could turn the ship around, *Trollslända* stopped dead in its tracks as if it had just hit a wall, throwing her back against her chair. She gaped down at her console. It was frozen again. She pressed her fingers down hard on one light after another. Nothing. Finally, she pounded her fists on the console in frustration. "No, no, no," she said, feeling like she wanted to cry. But what good would that do?

Trollslända began to move forward towards the *Campbell*, slowly at first but then accelerating. She could only watch helplessly as the black ship grew larger on the viewscreen. This time they were moving much faster, as if the black ship was angry they had tried to escape and was yanking them through space in a temper tantrum. Much quicker than it should have been possible, they were hurtling just seconds away from impact.

"We're going to hit!" shouted Rasmussen.

Broberg wanted to call down to warn Herko but there was no time. The three of them on the bridge held tightly to the arms of their chairs. There was a shriek of metal as they crashed into the *Campbell*. Broberg was thrown forward, her face smashing down onto her console. The air was littered with flying objects and then they were upside down and sideways and right side up, like on a carnival ride. Broberg continued to hang on, even though she could feel blood running down her forehead. Everything was jumbled, but it felt to her that *Trollslända* was bouncing and rolling across the hull of the massive freighter like a pebble skipping on water. At any moment she expected them to get swallowed up by that gigantic mouth, even though she hadn't seen it on the view screen before the crash.

Suddenly all motion stopped. They were hanging in a sideways position. Objects clattered to the deck. That meant that the artificial gravity was still working. Broberg turned her head to the side and gaped at the view screen. It was black. Not black as if it had stopped working, but black as if they were plastered against the hull of the *Campbell*. Within the blackness, there were subtle, detectable variations. She saw tiny green and yellow lights. There was something else too. Something moving. It looked like...well...slitherings.

And then *Trollslända* thrust away from the other ship as if shot out of a cannon, or maybe like it was being spit out of a monster's mouth because they had tasted bad. *Trollslända* turned over and over like a spinning top. Broberg felt her stomach revolt and she was afraid she was going to throw up. But then the spinning slowed. Finally, it stopped. This time they were upright.

She heard breathing from her left and right. "Everyone okay?" she asked.

"I think so," muttered Rasmussen.

"Me too," said Renberg.

She called down to engineering. "Herko? You okay down there?"

It took a moment but an answer came. "Ja, I tink so. A bit black and blue."

Broberg felt her forehead. There was a large bump there but the blood running down the side of her face was only a trickle. "What just happened? Did we get swallowed up?"

"I don't think so," said Rasmussen. "Look at the view screen."

Broberg gazed up and saw the black ship, just like before. It was hanging in space maybe five kilometers away. But there was something very different. Something very wrong.

"Where are the stars?" asked Renberg.

"I don't know," answered Broberg. Behind the black ship, it was as if someone had covered the entire universe with black crepe paper, an even deeper black than the hull of the Campbell.

"Where are we?" asked Rasmussen.

"I have no idea," answered Broberg. "Let me have a look around if I can." She eased her joystick to the left and heard *Trollslända's* impulse engines kick in. The black ship glided to the right and off the screen. Within a few moments, a second ship came into view from their left.

"There!" said Renberg.

Broberg centered the joystick and the vessel stopped in the center of the view screen. It looked like an American privateer. She felt a surge of optimism. It looked like they weren't alone out here.

She keyed her mike. "American ship, this is the Swedish ship *Trollslända*. Do you copy?"

There was no answer.

She tried again. "American ship, do you read me?"

Still nothing.

Her hopes sank. Whatever ship that was, their radio wasn't working. Or maybe there was nobody on the bridge. Nobody alive.

"Maybe I can finally break us free," muttered Broberg. She pushed her joystick forward. The main engines kicked in, but the image of the American ship didn't change on the screen. She switched to impulse and tried again to move them forward. No change. She moved the joystick to the left and this time the American ship moved to the right and off the edge of the screen. Within a few moments, the black ship reappeared. She watched it glide across the screen until it was gone. Then the American ship reappeared.

After experimenting several more times, Broberg ground her teeth in frustration. They were still trapped, only this time they were in an inky void between the black ship and a silent, American privateer. And all they could do was spin in circles.

27

SENATOR ALAN K SIMPSON

Fire burns everything. It burned as far as Captain Martin could see. Everywhere he turned, he saw flames. He fell to his knees. He felt the heat as the flames got closer. He was going to burn. He was trapped and enclosed and he was going to die. He couldn't stay here any longer. He had to get to his feet.

Martin wasn't on the *Simpson* any longer. He was on Earth. He knew this place because he had lived here once. Maybe this was his home? But not everything was right. Even in the fire he could tell there were many things wrong. His grandmother's shabby white house was there but it was in the wrong place. Not the wrong neighborhood but the wrong state. The house was supposed to be in Spokane, Washington, but instead it sat in the middle of an Air Force base runway in Colorado. He knew both of those places from different times in his life but neither one of them existed any longer. His grandmother's house had been torn down when he was twelve years old, bulldozed when the interstate highway came through the neighborhood she had lived in all of her life.

The fire burned closer. His eyes watered from the smoke. He got to his feet. The heat from the fire seared the skin of his face. All he could do was run towards his grandmother's house.

The thunder of a jet engine made the ground shake beneath his feet. He almost fell down. A fighter jet was approaching from behind. It couldn't land here. Martin looked back, puzzled. Why couldn't the pilot see that his grandmother's house was blocking the runway? The jet aircraft screamed right over Martin's head. He reached up with both hands to cover his ears. At the last second the jet aborted, its landing gear barely missing the house. Martin lost sight of the plane as it flew over the flames. He continued running towards the house. He was almost there.

Martin had been one of the few naval officers stationed with the Air Force's 460th Space Command in Colorado. He had been a lieutenant junior grade at Buckley Air Force Base. Both the Navy and Air Force had worked together from the suburbs of Denver to oversee the whole solar system. Monitors inside the base's large white surveillance domes detected spaceships that ventured out to the distant planets and beyond, to man's furthest travels.

But that base was no longer there. It was dismantled years ago when Space Command relocated to Houston. The last time Martin had been there, Denver's suburbs had swallowed up the abandoned base and replaced it with luxury homes and golf courses.

Martin reached the front door of his grandmother's house. He was surprised to find it unlocked. His grandmother always had multiple locks on the door and even with a key it had always taken him a long time to get inside. So this couldn't really be her house. And it couldn't really be the military base he had been stationed at so many years ago.

But his grandmother was waiting for him when he came through the door. She was holding out a big plate of cookies. They were chocolate chip cookies and the whole house smelled of them. Such a pleasant smell. This was a great place to be. His grandmother smiled. This was wonderful. This was great. He reached out his hand and took one of the cookies. It was still warm. He popped it into his mouth. It was perfect. The rest of the cookies on the plate looked like they were perfect too. Martin couldn't help himself and he grabbed another one. The woman in front of him continued to simply smile, not saying anything at all. She was the perfect grandmother. But not the one he remembered.

Martin's grandmother's house had been one block away from his elementary school. After school, he would go there and wait for his mom to pick him up after work. But he rarely went into the house because his grandmother was usually in her garage. Before Martin had been born, she had changed her garage into an art studio. She would paint all day in there while she watched her soap operas on AmericaNet. The room always smelled of paint, turpentine, and stale cigarettes. Martin never remembered her making him cookies. Instead, he used to go to her refrigerator and pull out a package of bologna. Then he'd grab a couple of slices of white bread from the counter and make himself a snack. There was always a shelf full of Dr. Peppers in the small fridge in her art studio. He'd take one to go along with the sandwich. While he ate, he usually watched her paint with oils and brushes. She would mix the paint on the palette with a small spackling knife until she found just the right color. Martin couldn't remember a time when they spoke while she was painting. It wasn't because she didn't love him, but because the two of them had their own rhythm and needed few words. He would wait quietly for her to finish the area of canvas she had been working on that day. It was comfortable. They simply liked to be in each other's company.

His grandmother had died many years ago. He wished he owned more of her paintings. His mother sold them as part of her estate after the funeral. Over the past few years he had purchased a few. They had gone up in value but money was never the point. He just wanted them because his grandmother had done them. He had an art agent on Earth who hunted them over the net, but it had been a year since he had last acquired one.

And now this woman...the woman who stood in front of him, had all of his grandmother's features. But it wasn't her. Martin reached for his third cookie and looked around the rest of the house. Looking out the window he could no longer could see the fire that had chased him inside this safe place of his dreams. There was no Air Force base, no runway. There were only quiet streets and trees like back in Spokane. A breeze through the window was filled with a rich pine scent. But the woman in front of him wasn't the woman he remembered...

She dropped the plate of cookies and it fell to the floor with a crash. The woman attacked him. She was lightning fast and before he could defend himself she wrapped both of her hands around his throat. She was surprisingly strong for an old woman and Martin couldn't break free of her grip. He sensed that he had only seconds before she broke his neck. She smiled at him as she choked him and her eyes gleamed. It seemed as if she would take pleasure in killing him.

A tentacle came out of her mouth. It was the same tentacle that had attacked him on the bridge. The one that had plucked out his eye. He closed one eye and then the other. He had two eyes here. But on his ship, his eye had been violently torn out of its socket. Where was he now? A dream? A nightmare? It didn't matter because he needed to get away. The tentacle caught him. Its tip bore through his lips and started to pry his teeth apart. He tried to clench them tight but his jaw wasn't strong enough to keep the tentacle out. He could feel one of his front teeth break. And then another. The tentacle was going to force itself into his mouth. There was nothing he could do. Blood spilled down his chin along with bits of broken teeth. He wanted to scream but no sound escaped his mouth. The pain was simply too great. He wouldn't be able to endure this for long. He would pass out soon.

The tentacle bored further into his mouth and started to make its way down his throat. He began to gag. His grandmother wasn't going to kill him with her hands, she was going to suffocate him with her tentacle. He felt it slide down his throat and into his lungs. He pulled at it with both his hands. At first, it continued to descend, but soon he started to win the fight. He pulled on the tentacle as hard as he could while trying to breathe. It started to retreat so he grabbed hold of another section and continued to pull. It felt like forever but eventually Martin got it out of his throat and free of his mouth. The tentacle flopped around wildly, trying to make its way back in.

He would have to kill the ghastly thing. And to do that, he would have to kill his grandmother.

He kicked the old woman with his right foot. At first, she didn't budge. But he kicked her again, screaming in revulsion. She seemed to move a little as the tentacle flailed in front of her face. He kicked and kicked and then began pummeling her with his fists. Her face cracked like a mirror and disappeared. He found himself still holding onto the tentacle, which now wasn't attached to anything. He gripped it tightly as it flailed, knowing he couldn't let go and allow it to find its way back into his mouth. He needed to keep kicking. To keep on fighting...

The top of the AutoMed shattered, sending shards flying around the medical bay. Martin sat up. His head felt like it was full of marshmallows but things began to clear up. He let out a sigh of relief. He was back on the *Simpson*. The place where he had lost his eye. The tentacle he had been holding onto was simply a long respirator tube. There was no tentacle. And no grandmother.

He reached a hand to his mouth. The pain he felt there was no dream. Had he dreamt about breaking his teeth? He spat. Blood went everywhere and trickled down the front of his medical gown. He must have broken some teeth when he ripped the respirator tube from his throat. He ran his tongue across his lips and found that there was a gap where his two front teeth should have been. He grimaced, feeling the throb in his mouth. And what about his eye, the one he had lost? Was it still gone? Martin reached up. There was a hole where it should have been, just like before.

The pain. The pain was excruciating. He would have to clean up his mouth as best as he could without the help of the broken AutoMed. Afterward, he would find something for the pain. But for now, he needed to go and find out what was happening with his ship. He was still committed to saving his crew, even if he had to lose a few more teeth. Or even his other eye.

28

SENATOR ALAN K SIMPSON

Jelly Roll exited the head after he had thoroughly washed his hands. Things might be falling apart on the *Simpson*, but that didn't make him a barbarian. He always did everything he could to help out; he cooked, he cleaned, and he even acted as the ship's morale officer when needed. And lately, one of the things the ship had needed very badly was a morale officer. Things had been spinning out of control, especially in the past couple hours, but that didn't mean he needed to panic.

Three of his crew mates were dead. Jagr, Karam, and Bohannon had been slaughtered by an alien. There was blood everywhere on the bridge, red human blood and black alien blood, both having flowed like a river down through the hatch while Lt. Constance and her party were up there battling the monsters. Jelly Roll didn't know when he would find the time to clean up all that gore.

Jelly Roll and Michelson had come running when Lt. Constance finally managed to radio from the bridge after the whole gruesome battle was over. They'd taken her back to her cabin. She was in shock. He hoped she was getting some sleep down there, but peace for her would be hard to come by after the violent deaths of her team. Undoubtedly, she would be blaming herself.

And then there was Captain Martin. He was still down in sickbay inside the AutoMed after one of those alien tentacle things had plucked out his eye. Which meant that no one was currently on the bridge. But what difference did that make? They were still trapped in a void of space along with the old-Earth freighter, *John W. Campbell Jr.* And things were only getting worse. The tentacled alien that had killed three crew members was still on board. From what Lt. Constance had told them, it would be back. They might be safe for the moment, but, without a doubt, it meant to kill them all. Maybe that's what had happened to the crew of the *Campbell*. What had they stumbled upon? He doubted any of them were still alive over there.

Jelly Roll pulled on the ends of his sleeves and buttoned his white chef's jacket. He had found a crisp, clean one in his locker. He wanted to look his best for the meeting he had called in the mess. There were still people alive on his ship, and the cook had decided he wouldn't lose anybody else to that alien monster. It was time for him to step up. His crew would need him if they were going to survive.

He dug deep down into his foot locker, removing most of its contents. He pried open a false bottom. He removed the gold envelope he kept there, the one he always had with him wherever his assignments took him. He never had the need to open it before today, because a situation like this had never happened. Sure, he had seen his share of dangers over the years, but nothing like this.

He turned the shiny, gold envelope over in his large, chubby hands. On the front, the Party's symbol was emblazoned, a black stone eagle within a red circle. On interplanetary ships, there was very little need for printed paper. Personal space was at a premium, and crew members had tablets assigned to them with all the information they needed. So real, old-fashioned envelopes were a rarity, and this one was striking in its simplicity and form. It was beautiful. Jelly Roll hated the fact that he would have to tear it open. But he needed the authorization it gave him.

Michaelson was Third Mate. He should have been next in the chain of command. But conditions had spiraled out of control and he clearly wasn't up to the task. Jelly Roll didn't know if he himself was either. However, that didn't matter. He was an officer of The Party and The Party never made mistakes. Never. It was rare for a Political Officer to have to open the gold envelope. But ultimately, it was there for a reason.

When Jelly Roll walked into the mess, Michaelson and engineer Silas Onion were already waiting for him, sitting at the table where he usually chopped vegetables and prepared meals. Their faces looked drawn and stark in the harsh, bright light from the hanging overhead lamp. He imagined that his own face must look the same way. Losing three crew members had been an excellent way to chase his normal jolliness away. Now there would be a completely different Jelly Roll.

It was time for him to take over.

Michaelson was scrolling through screens on his tablet, reviewing the condition of the systems on the ship. Onion looked on. The two men had evidently been discussing strategies for trying to get away from the *Campbell.*

Jelly Roll carefully laid the gold envelope on the table and cleared his throat. He felt his heart pound in his chest. Every crew member would know what that envelope meant. What would these two men think, especially Michaelson? But, to his surprise, Michaelson took one look at it and went back to what he had been doing. Onion just looked into Jelly Roll's eyes and took another sip of coffee out of his favorite mug. His expression seemed to say, "Well?" No one spoke for several moments.

Finally, Jelly Roll cleared his throat again and said, with as much confidence as he could muster, "Under special orders, and due to circumstances, I just wanted you to know that The Party gives me the authority to take command of the *Simpson.*"

Onion glanced over at Michaelson, who was still scrolling through pages on his tablet. Then he looked back up at the cook. "No shit," he said.

"What?" asked Jelly Roll.

"It means we knew you were the sodding political dick on board the ship. Who else could it have been? Any spacer who has served more than ten minutes out here knows the Party always plants a P.O. on privateers. They like Earth ships to keep the solar system safe. To keep things running as smooth as a baby's bottom. But it makes their sphincters clench to think of all that fire power not under their direct control. The Party isn't dumb. They don't trust us. So they put P.O.'s on board. Whenever we leave for a mission, we try and guess who it is. We knew right away that it had to be you."

"Why?"

"Because it wasn't any of us."

"Oh."

Jelly Roll picked the envelope up and turned it over in his hands. "So I don't need to open this for you?"

"Not unless you really want to," said Onion. He looked at Michaelson. "Does he need to open it for you?"

Michaelson glanced up from his tablet. "Nope. Now that the formalities are over, can we finally talk about getting the *Homer* out of here?"

"I guess," said Jelly Roll. "Do you have something in mind?"

"We've come up with a plan," said Onion. "We think we know what kind of black, gooey shit we're stuck in. What did you call it, M?"

Jelly Roll grimaced. *M?* How long had these two been working together?

"I think this blackness, this *void*, is a bubble," said Michaelson. "A plasma bubble created by the *Campbell's* engines."

"Which means that son of a space freighter whore has something a lot better than standard engines under its hood," chimed Onion. "It's like the hotrod I used to tool around in back in Texas when I was full of piss and vinegar. It ain't pretty to look at, but it must have a shitload of horses, more than any other ship in the solar system. Otherwise, it wouldn't have been able to trap us in this damn fly paper."

Michaelson continued, "The curious thing is, we seem to be acting as an anchor to *them*. As long as they're holding us here, it seems like they can't hardly move either. To keep us in this bubble must be taking a whole lot of power and has to be overloading their engines. I don't know who's running things over there, but they don't seem care about the condition of their equipment."

"What does that mean?" asked Jelly Roll, trying to keep up.

Onion said, "No matter what kind of technology they have, if they keep overloading their engines, eventually they're going to explode, sending alien tentacles flying through the solar system like shit from an outhouse in a tornado. We don't want to be anywhere near them when that happens. So I suggest we take our hands off our peckers and get out of here. The sooner the better."

Both men looked at Jelly Roll. They were waiting for him to reply, as if they had already accepted his authority. "From the way you're talking, I imagine you two already have a plan worked up," he said. He tapped the gold envelope against his palm, a little disappointed in his crewmates for not wanting to see what was inside.

"We do have a plan," said Onion, "but we need a few hours. And I sure could use another pair of hands. Can you get Constance down to engineering? Yeah, she's a female. And her hands aren't exactly like the hide on a rhino's ass. But she knows my engines. I'm surprised she ended up being a bridge jockey in the first place. I can spot a good engineer from miles away, and she's a good one. In a few years she could have even taken my place."

"Well," said Jelly Roll, "she's pretty beat up. But under the circumstances, I'll bet she could help. Maybe she'd even welcome a little extra work right now."

Jelly Roll could tell from their body language that they were anxious to get back to work. And he was relieved that there was actually a plan. But somehow, being in charge of the ship didn't feel any different than it had felt when he was just the cook. Before he turned to head up to the bridge, he asked, "Are you *sure* you don't want me to show you what's inside the gold envelope?"

Neither man replied.

29

SHUTTLE

Molly hated distractions, and Oscar was a big one. Her life would have been so much simpler if the fighter hadn't come and 'rescued' her on Ganymede. She was frustrated with her father for sending the big man in the first place. She hadn't needed rescue. She'd planned her own escape from the O'Neil clan to the last detail. She'd known her exact location within Brahe Station on Ganymede. It was the place where the clan held all of their hostages. Why hadn't her father learned to simply trust her to take care of herself?

The three of them were on the shuttle's bridge. She and Oscar sat side by side while Tormod kept busy in the captain's chair. Oscar had his laptop open and was surfing SpaceNet yet again, trying to find more information about the *Campbell*. He wouldn't find it. The Salome Corporation had long ago erased any recent information about that ship, as hard as that was to do. But the shadowy company had very long tentacles indeed. She'd told Oscar that several times, but here he was, looking again. Most of the important documents about the *Campbell* were locked away in company vaults at their headquarters on Earth. Molly hadn't seen them herself but she knew they were there. The *Campbell* was why she had come out to this part of the solar system in the first place. Her plan to get herself to the ship had been well thought out, although she hadn't expected to get taken hostage by the O'Neils. But she was almost to the *Campbell* now. And even she had to admit she needed more information.

Molly glanced at Tormod. The teen was a capable pilot, and she had chosen wisely when she had picked him out of all the O'Neils on Brahe to help her escape. He'd gotten them away and had done most of the piloting. Of course, she'd lied to him. She'd gotten to know him even before she had been taken hostage. He had been a lonely misfit on Brahe. It didn't take her long to convince him she was his half-sister. And now she felt guilty about that. She would tell him the truth when she had a chance. They might not be related, but she'd grown close to him, and even wished he *was* her little brother.

She sipped from the cup of tea she'd made herself, but it had grown cold. She set it down on the deck. She'd been so focused on getting to the *Campbell*, even if it meant she'd have to hurt somebody along the way. But now, she wasn't the same person who had boarded the shuttle. Even after a just a handful of days, she was having strong feelings for the two men with her, Tormod as a younger brother, and Oscar...was she having strong feelings for Oscar? Yes. She sighed. Her life had gotten way too complicated.

Oscar cleared his throat and looked at her. Clearly, he wanted to say something, but didn't. Now he looked away.

"What?" asked Molly.

"Nothing," he mumbled.

Molly hadn't known Oscar for very long, but she was able to read his emotions. Despite his physical strength, he was an easy man to figure out. Was he getting ready to lie to her? Could she love a man who lied to her? "You might as well spit it out," she said.

Oscar looked up at the overhead and then back at her. "Okay," he said. "You were right. I didn't find anything else about the *Campbell*."

She waited. "And?"

"And...I think that's the point."

"What do you mean?"

"I didn't find out *anything*. There's nothing out there after a certain date. There's information about every other ship that made it as far as Saturn. But not this one. As far as SpaceNet is concerned, the *Campbell* no longer exists. The ship owned by your father. His company. And I think I know why."

Molly gaped at him. Did she really care about this man? Or did she care more about what he knew, or what he might be able to do for her? Was he going to tell her a lie to keep her away from the *Campbell?* She had grown up around too many liars, people who were loyal to her father, more worried about their salaries or their next promotion. None of them had cared about her. So she'd learned to be a good liar, but she'd spent most of her life with even better ones. "Go on," she said.

"Whoever erased the information about the *Campbell* did too good of a job. They got rid of too much information."

"I know that. So what?"

"Look. Ships go back and forth to Saturn all the time. But never any further. The Salome Corporation has a base on Titan. Even the Party has bases on the other side of that same moon. The EU has a base on the smaller moon, Tethys. But no one goes beyond. There's no mention of any ship going to Neptune or Uranus or even to Pluto. It's the nature of people to push boundaries, but this is one boundary that hasn't been pushed. Not in ten years. In the last mention of the *Campbell*, they were headed out past Saturn. And then nothing. Does that make any sense to you?"

Molly pursed her lips. "Well, something must be stopping ships from going further. But if there's some sort of barrier, I would think we'd have heard about it by now. "

"Not necessarily. There are a lot of factions out here and none of them like to show their cards, especially after the revolts on the inner planets. If the *Campbell* made it out there, and now they're back, who knows what they came across?" His eyes flashed. "Who knows what they brought *back?* Maybe we should turn around. Go back to Jupiter. We don't need to return to Ganymede. We could hang out with the Swedes on Europa instead. Maybe they'll even buy this shuttle from us. Nobody likes the O'Neils. Besides, there are only three of us on this tiny shuttle and who knows what we'll be up against? Let's not go any closer to that ship."

Molly felt a fluttering in her stomach. This was a big, strong man who had been through a lot of fights on different moons and planets. But he was clearly spooked. And now he was spooking her. "But I need to know what's happened to my father's ship. I owe it to him. Besides, if we go to Europa, my father might not pay you. You'll have traveled all this way for nothing."

Oscar nodded. "I've thought of that. But I'd rather lose out on that money than be dead."

"I see it!" shouted Tormod. "There's your ship!" Oscar and Molly glanced over. He was grinning at them like a little boy who has just completed a sand castle. "It's been a speck on my view screen for a little while, but now it's big enough to see for sure. It's right there. I told you I could get you here! "

Molly looked out the shuttle's cockpit window and, sure enough, there was the freighter, growing ever larger. After such a long time, and after so many detours and complicated twists and turns, she had finally found the *Campbell*. She had done it. She had to breathe. Had she taken a breath? She couldn't tell. And she was no longer spooked. "I have to do this," she said to Oscar. "My father needs to know."

"Would your father risk his life for you?" asked Oscar.

Molly knew the answer to that one.

30

SHUTTLE

Tomod said, "That's weird."

"What's weird?" asked Molly.

"Look out the cockpit window. What do you see?"

She looked. "I see the *John W. Campbell*. It's right there. What are we, maybe ten kilometers away?"

"Seven," replied Tormod. "Now look at my view screen."

"What are those other two shapes?" asked Molly.

"That's what I'd like to know." Taking up most of the view screen was the huge, black freighter. But in the top left and right corners of the screen were two dark silhouettes, phasing in and out in flashes of green.

Suddenly, Tormod let out a hearty laugh. "Well, what do ya' know? Looks like we've arrived late at the church's potluck dinner on a Saturday night. Everyone else is already sitting in the chairs nearest the priest so I don't know how close we can get."

"What the hell are you talking about?" asked Molly.

"See those two silhouettes there, the ones that keep blinking on and off? Those are two spaceships. From their shape, I'd guess that the one on the left, the one in the shape of a dragonfly, is a Swedish warship. The other looks like an American privateer."

"But why can't we see them out the window?"

Tormod turned to face them. "Bodean Crockabilly!"

"What?" both Molly and Oscar blurted out at the same time.

"Bodean Crockabilly. He was at Brahe last year. We all thought he was just a huckster. He sure looked the part, anyway, bow tie, white shoes, like a traveling salesman in one of those old movies on SpaceNet. But somehow he convinced Grandpa O'Neil to buy this new, top secret sensing device. He went on and on about how it could penetrate subspace interference and quantum holes and all kinds of other things no one had ever heard of. But since there have been rumors about the South Africans experimenting with a plasma cloaking device, it seemed to Grandpa that it might be sort of an insurance policy. And no one on Brahe disagrees with Grandpa O'Neil. So we spent a bunch of credits to get it installed in all of our ships, including shuttles. And look! It works!"

They gazed at the view screen and watched the images phase in and out for a few moments. "But what are those two other ships doing there?" asked Molly. She felt slightly sick to her stomach at the thought that others had beaten her to the *Campbell*.

"I don't know," said Tormod. "But we better step carefully. Ships like that could easily blow us out of space if they want. I recommend we don't piss anyone off."

Molly stood up. "Can you tell if either one of them has boarded the *Campbell*?"

Tormod squinted to get a better look. Then he pushed a couple of buttons on his control panel. "I doubt they have. It looks like they're both stuck there next to the *Campbell*. According to my scans, both ships are running on minimum power. They have life support and a few other systems, but no engines or weapons. Those ships are as dead as Lazarus before Jesus got a chance to get to the party."

Molly took a deep breath and smiled.

Oscar asked, "What are you so happy about?"

Molly turned to look down at him. "Have you ever heard of Tesla, Edison, Fulton, or the Wright Brothers?"

Oscar didn't like anyone talking down to him, especially a woman whom he had kissed about an hour ago. "Of course," he answered testily. "But what's that got to do with anything?"

"They were all great inventors. History will remember them forever. My next question; had you ever heard of my father, Duncan Mackintosh, before he hired you?"

Oscar paused for a heartbeat. "No."

Molly continued. "Before long, everyone will have heard that name. What you see is the *John W. Campbell Jr.* It might be the first manned ship to have left the solar system. It might have even made it as far as Alpha Centauri. That was its destination. It was supposed to go to our nearest star and return. It was gone quite a while. Now it's finally back. My father built the engines that made the journey happen. It's a completely new technology, as revolutionary as the light bulb when Edison first came up with it."

The other two stared out the cockpit window with new eyes. "But no one's heard from the crew. Is there anyone still alive on that ship?" asked Oscar.

"That's one of the things I'm here to find out," said Molly.

"That's all fine and good," replied Oscar, "but those other two ships are dead in the water. Won't the same thing happen to us if we get any closer?"

Molly laughed. " The whole solar system is going to want this. Any company or government would steal his engine design in a heartbeat. It happens all the time. So it's obvious to me what happened to those two ships. My father would have built in safeguards. He must have come up with a dampening field to disable those other ships. As soon as the *Campbell* gets far enough away they'll go back to normal. Once we get on board, we'll take the *Campbell* out of here and we'll be on our way back to my father. Think of the ransom he'll pay you for this!"

Oscar stared through the cockpit window at the huge, black ship and shook his head. "It sounds too easy. Besides, how are we even going to get on board?"

Molly reached into her pocket and produced a small thumb drive. "I have the key!"

She handed the device to Tormod. "Please plug this into the nav-computer. It should take us to the docking port on the starboard side of the *Campbell*. Then all we have to do is knock on the door politely and they'll open up for us."

"Cool," said Tormod. He took the thumb drive, fumbling it once in his excitement. He plugged it into the computer. Immediately, the shuttle's thrusters took over. Looking out the window, they watched the huge, black freighter grow larger until it blocked out their entire view, like a moon totally eclipsing a sun. They watched the rest of the approach on the view screen, seeing the *Campbell's* starboard hull coming closer and closer. Tormod raised his arms in the air and gave a delighted laugh. "I love this! Automatic docking!"

Tormod stood up and made his way to the docking hatch.

Oscar and Molly followed. Within a few minutes, there was a bump as the shuttle connected with the huge freighter. The three of them stumbled for a moment. Tormod stood in the doorway of the hatch and the light over his head turned green to let them know the two ships were securely connected.

Molly said, "See, I told you I had things all figured out."

Tormod began to turn the wheel which would open the hatch.

"I think we should wait a few minutes," said Oscar. "At least let me go back and grab the pistol from out of my duffel bag."

"We've been in this little tin can long enough," muttered Tormod. He continued to turn the wheel. There was a hissing noise and the hatch swung open, letting in a gust of stale air. No, stale wasn't the right word. The air was foul. The temperature in the shuttle dropped ten degrees. On the other side of the door, a dark corridor angled off to the left.

Oscar spoke more harshly. "I said wait! Don't go over there until I get my pistol."

Molly walked up to Tormod and put her hand on his shoulder. "Oscar's right. Why can't we wait a few more minutes? You've done a great job. You got us all the way here. I couldn't have gotten this far without you."

Tormod turned towards Molly. "The O'Neils have a motto. 'Family does for family.' You're my sister. Of course, I helped you get here."

Molly pursed her lips for a moment. Then she smiled. "You're right. I couldn't have asked for a better little brother than you."

"Don't do anything until I get back. Don't move!" said Oscar firmly. But as he turned to head for his bunk, they all heard the sound from the dark corridor on the other side of the hatch. It was like knives scraping against a chalkboard. Oscar whirled and shouted, "Close the hatch! Now!"

But it was too late.

A large tentacle slithered through the opening.

Tormod immediately stepped forward to protect Molly. But he never had a chance. The tentacle pierced him through the center of his chest so hard that it pushed him into Molly, knocking them both down to the deck with the boy on his back on top of her. Oscar raced forward and grabbed Molly's arm, pulling as hard as he could. Tormod's blood was already covering her mid-section. Tormod coughed up some blood and let out a pitiful scream, like a dog that has just been run over by a truck. And then he went silent and still.

Several more tentacles moved in. At the end of the thickest one was a triangular head. Oscar kicked Tormod's body off Molly and pulled her to her feet as fast as he could. He put himself between her and the waving tentacles. "Go get my pistol! It's in my bag!" he shouted.

Molly blinked, feeling herself starting to freeze up in shock. But that only lasted for a second.

The last thing Molly saw before she turned to run for Oscar's pistol was the big fighter rocking off his heels and up onto his toes, standing tall with his fists in the air, bobbing and weaving with all the dexterity of a seasoned fighter. "Come on, you son of a bitch," she heard Oscar grunt as the tentacles waved and the triangular head reared up, yellow eyes blinking.

31

SHUTTLE

There had been moments in Oscar Gunn's life when death had stared him in the face. He knew the feeling well and he wasn't afraid. He didn't have the slightest desire to run away. He was a fighter and he wanted to fight. He had made up his mind. Something was going to die and it wasn't going to be him. He hadn't been able to protect Tormod but he would fight for Molly. Besides, something deep inside told him he wasn't going to die today. And he wasn't going to let Molly die either.

He stared down the thing with the triangular head, looking straight into its blinking, yellow eyes. Rocking on his feet, he bobbed and weaved, dodging tentacles trying to get at him from the side. But he never stopped focusing on those eyes. And then, the way he had done so many times before in his career, he struck, lashing out with his right foot and smacking the triangular head with all his might. He heard a shriek, high pitched and terrible. The sound was loud enough to make Oscar close his eyes. When he opened them, the creature was gone.

Oscar blinked. Was it going to be that easy? He gaped at the open hatch and the dark corridor beyond. Had the thing slithered away in the instant he closed his eyes? He stood there, still bobbing and weaving, breathing heavily. But it was quiet in the hatchway. He dropped his hands. This couldn't be over. He waited a few more moments but nothing else happened.

He looked down at the body of Tormod. He needed to move it away from the door and then close the hatch. He wanted to show Tormod respect, now that he was dead. He had learned respect for the dead when he was growing up. He knelt beside the boy and said a little prayer with his eyes open, still watching the open hatch. He hadn't prayed in a very long time, not since he was a boy, but it seemed like the right thing to do.

Something stopped his prayer before it was finished. It wasn't the ear-piercing shriek, but the scraping they had heard before the tentacle had come for Tormod, a sound like a knife scratching against a blackboard. The creature was coming back and maybe it was bringing friends....

"I'm here." The voice was Molly's. She stood behind him, holding his pistol and pointing it at the open hatchway.

Oscar knew it was too late to close the hatch. There wasn't much space for them to retreat, but they stood back as far as they could. Along the deck, a single tentacle writhed slowly around the corner.

Oscar put his hand up to let Molly know not to shoot yet. She nodded, continuing to hold the pistol in steady hands.

The tentacle crawled over to Tormod's body, which was lying on its back. Slowly, the tip of the tentacle inserted itself back into the hole in the chest where it had first pierced the boy. To Oscar's surprise and revulsion, Tormod's left arm began to twitch. Then both arms. His legs moved several times and then began to shake, the way someone's legs shake in bed during a dream about running. Soon both arms and legs moved in tandem as if Tormod was doing bicycles in the gym.

Molly made a disgusted, grunting sound deep in her throat. Then she fired the pistol. The bullet entered the torso of the boy, but that didn't stop him from moving. Instead, Tormod slowly got to his feet like a wind-up toy.

Oscar's ears were ringing from the pistol shot. "Shoot him again!" he shouted, his own voice sounding muffled in his ears.

Molly did as she was told, emptying all the pistol's bullets into Tormod. But that didn't stop him. He simply smiled at them, blood dripping from his mouth.

Oscar gaped at this horror. What was going on? The abomination that had been Tormod didn't move any closer, even though the pistol was empty. It felt like a stalemate. Or was the Tormod-thing waiting for something else?

Oscar didn't have to kill time to find out. Just when he thought it couldn't get any weirder, something else came around the corner along the deck. At first, Oscar thought it was a black cat. Maybe it had been a cat at one time. Whatever it was, it wasn't a cat any longer. It had a large spider's head where it might have once had the head of a feline. It had an extra pair of legs sticking out of its side, and a small tentacle of its own protruding from its belly. All the limbs moved in unison as it made its jerky way along the deck.

"That's what happens when no one keeps an eye on the ship's cat," said Oscar. "They always manage to get themselves into trouble."

"What is that?" asked Molly.

"You tell me," said Oscar. "Quick! Go and find some more bullets. They're in the bottom of my bag."

"I don't think there are any left," she said. "I dumped everything on the floor when I got the pistol."

"You try to be neat and tidy..." muttered Oscar. "Well, find something else then. Maybe there's a toolbox. Anything we can use as a weapon."

Molly darted away. Oscar hoped she'd find something, but if not, he still had his fists and feet. The Tormod-thing kept looking at him with unblinking eyes, the tentacle sticking through the center of its chest, out the back, and along the deck into the corridor. It seemed like it was still waiting for something.

The spider-cat began to crawl up the tentacle. Halfway up, it seemed bored and stopped. Then its front and back legs flexed. It leaped into the air, all its appendages flailing, and landed on the back of Tormod's head, using its four cat claws and the two extra limbs to lock itself in place. Had Tormod still been alive, he might have screamed. But instead, he stood there impassively with that same, vacant smile pasted on his bloody face.

Oscar stepped to the side to get a better look. The tentacle coming from the spider-cats' belly was a miniature of the larger one sticking out of the Tormod-thing's back. It waved in the air once and then pierced the back of Tormod's head. Blood and brain spilled out and flowed down onto the deck. The Tormod-thing no longer smiled and the face went slack. The spider-cat throbbed on top of its head and the Tormod-thing's legs and arms twitched. Then it raised its arms to its waist. The fingers opened and closed several times. Then they settled into fists.

"Will these do?" asked Molly.

Oscar glanced back. Molly was holding up a small hammer, a screwdriver, and a propane torch used for soldering.

"Keep the hammer and torch and stay behind me," he said through clenched teeth. "I'm going to need your help but I don't want you getting hurt."

Oscar grabbed the screwdriver with his left hand. That meant his right hand was free. He always liked to have a free right hand in a fight.

The Tormod-thing began to speak through slack lips. It didn't sound like Tormod. "We will now pierce you," it said in a low, metallic growl. "And then you will be ours."

Oscar heard the propane torch come to life behind him and felt its heat. "Here, kitty, kitty, kitty," said Molly.

Before he stepped forward to throw the first punch, Oscar thought, This woman really has some issues. But I like her just the way she is.

32

SS JOHN W CAMPBELL JR

Aaron and Gugu heard the shrieking sound from somewhere far above their heads. In Aaron's imagination, it sounded like a pterodactyl, fighting a battle in some misty, prehistoric swamp. Even from far away, the sound poured ice water down his backbone. "What is that?" he asked.

"It's a Gek monster," answered Gugu. "That's the sound they make just before they attack. But I didn't think there was anyone else on board this ship. So who is it attacking?"

"Maybe they're attacking each other?" asked Aaron hopefully.

"We should be so lucky."

"So what should we do? Maybe it's one of your crew members."

She shook her head. "I told you. All of them are dead. I saw the bodies. Besides, this is a huge ship and that sounded really far away. Way too far to get there in time."

"But what if it's Erik?"

Gugu pursed her lips. "If what you told me is true, there's nothing we can do for your friend now."

Aaron felt his heart sink. The main reason he had piloted the cutter away from *Trollslända* was to come here and rescue Erik. But now he seemed to be involved in something much bigger.

They had pulled up to the entrance of one of hundreds of cargo bays on the huge freighter. In this part of the ship, recessed, blue safety lights were still working. Gugu turned off her flashlight. She pointed to the cargo bay. "There's the ore we picked up on Titan."

Aaron looked into the hold. Chunks of dull, purplish-grey Bryantonium ore was piled from deck to overhead, a familiar sight from his days working on Europa. Ever since it had been discovered by an American ship fifty years ago on Ceres, and named after a science-fiction writer from the last century, Bryantonium had become the most valuable metal in the solar system, used on virtually every hull on every spaceship. It was lighter than aluminum and stronger than diamonds and geologists weren't even sure why. There was something mysterious about its structure at the subatomic level. But when it was found on more dwarf planets and asteroids, it became indispensible to the solar system's economy. There was an ancient saying on Earth that said, "If you build a better mousetrap, the world will beat a path to your door." These days, that could be modified to say, "If you find a better metal, the whole solar system will line up to fill your bank accounts."

"Look at it closely," said Gugu. She handed him her flashlight.

Aaron switched it on and pointed it at the pile of ore. In the bright, white beam, he could more clearly see the characteristic flecks of violet that had given the ore its nickname of 'Purple Gold.' He'd seen it plenty of times when inspecting and taxing cargo holds of ships passing through Europa on the way to the inner planets. But this was different. "What is that?" he asked, instinctively backing away and bumping into the far wall of the corridor. The ore seemed to be moving, as if, instead of solid rock, it was infused with some sort of thick mucous.

"The Gek monsters love this stuff," said Gugu. "They want to have a jol with it. I think they're made out of it. They can phase right through it. And with most spaceships having Bryantonium hulls, well..."

Aaron swallowed hard. The ship he had pirated, *Trollslända*, had a Bryantonium hull. But not just that. It had gone through a complete makeover so it could become an elite warship. It had a top-secret weapon. New fixtures. Re-done decks, overheads, sinks, and water reclamation system. Swedish Space Fleet had spared no expense to re-fit their prized ship. In their usual, neat and efficient manner, they'd done most of those upgrades with Bryantonium. And Jenny Broberg was at the helm. When he had left the ship, *Trollslända* was being pulled towards the *Campbell*. Maybe it was her who the Gek monster had just been attacking...

"Are you okay?" asked Gugu.

Aaron gritted his teeth. He felt sweat running down his armpits. "I...think," he managed to sputter, "that there might be someone else for me to worry about. A woman. A crewmate. A..."

She reached out and touched his shoulder. "A lover?"

He shook his head. "No. Well, not exactly. Maybe."

She nodded. "So. We have something in common, you and I. I lost my bru. Now you've lost your..."

"Don't say that," barked Aaron. "You don't know that for sure."

She held up her hand. "Okay, okay. It's just, well, I don't know. Why don't we sit down here and have another rest, shall we?"

"Why?"

"I have something to tell you."

They sat down on the deck, Gugu with her back to the wall and Aaron bent forward so his back didn't touch. He clasped his hands around his knees.

"I just met you not long ago," said Gugu. "But we're stuck here together like seeds in a sausage tree pod. There's a good chance we won't make it. So we should be honest with each other, Ja?"

Aaron nodded, wondering what new revelation this woman was going to spill now.

"This ship, the *SS John W. Campbell Jr*, is not a freighter. Okay, it was built as a freighter. But it's really a pioneer. Duncan Mackintosh is the owner and that's the way he sold the idea to me. 'Join our crew and make more than money. Make history.' So I signed on. And we did make history. Big time.

"You might know this and you might not. Out beyond Saturn is a...curtain. Small craft, probes, and things, can go through it like there's nothing there and can make it to Uranus and Neptune and beyond. But larger ships, especially manned ships, come up against it and all their sensors and navigation systems go afskilfer. They get tossed around like small boats in a hurricane. If they try to ride it out they get smashed into space dust.

"So what is it? A black hole? No. But it's like someone put it there to keep us penned up in our own solar system. Like a lighthouse to warn us off the reef. But this lighthouse reaches out and throws boats back where they came from.

"Mackintosh studied this thing. All his company's freighters around Saturn took readings. So he said, 'Okay, it's not a black hole. But according to my calculations, it will act like one. If we could blast through fast enough, we'll end up in another part of the galaxy.' And he knew how to make a ship go faster than anyone ever has. His proton-fusion drive. It's on this ship. To try out that drive, he needed a honking, groot ship that wouldn't break apart with vibration."

She pulled out her canteen and took a sip. She offered some to Aaron but he waved her off. This was fascinating stuff.

"So we all signed on. It took some jaw grinding to say yes. But I studied ancient navigation in Universiteit. This reminded me of those old maps that said, 'Here there be dragons.' But I wanted to go anyway. So I did. And it worked. We made it through. There weren't no dragons, but looking back, I think we picked up something worse."

"Let me have some of that water," said Aaron. He reached out to take a gulp from Gugu's canteen. "Where did you end up?"

"I don't know," she answered. "There was no big vibration, no flashing lights. We fired up the new engines and blasted away from Saturn. We all held our breaths because this was where those other ships got snotklapped. But nothing happened. We blasted right through the...well...curtain. That's the best way I can describe it. Suddenly we were someplace else. The stars were all different. No planets nearby, at least according to our sensors. Our orders were clear. Take 360-degree videos of everything around us. Then hightail it back the way we came. When we got home, Salome Corporation would analyze the star configurations on our videos and figure out where we'd gone. And then they'd open up the universe."

She looked down. "We were in the middle of taking those videos when we felt the bump."

"Bump?"

"Ja. Big bump. Like another ship colliding with us. A ship as big as us maybe. But we couldn't see anything. And then, aweh! Another bump! Like a giant hand knocking to come inside. It echoed around the whole ship. I'm not an old gogo. None of us were. But bladdy hell, it was time to get out of there. So that's what we did. We pointed ourselves back and held our breaths again. Fired the engines. We went back through the curtain and Titan showed up on our view screen, right where we left it. We found out later that we'd been gone a lot longer than a few hours, so time was skewed. But we were back. And we had the videos to prove where we'd been. It was all supposed to stay a secret so we carried on like nothing had happened. We picked up the Bryantonium on Titan. And you know what happened next."

Aaron stared at her. This was quite a story and he didn't know if he should believe it or not. But it wasn't more improbable than anything else from the past week. He got to his feet and grunted. "Well, then," he said, "if we're going to snotklap those things, we'd better get going."

Gugu laughed at his use of her favorite slang word. She got to her feet and they headed down the corridor towards whatever was waiting for them ahead in the eerie blue light. From over their heads, in a far corner of the spaceship, the screeching, pterodactyl sound continued.

33

SENATOR ALAN K SIMPSON

Jelly Roll thought of his life. This wasn't supposed to happen. He was never meant to be in command of a spaceship. That's not how it usually worked. Sure, his status in the party had let him take over the *Simpson*. He was the Political Officer after all. But was he up to the job? Not really. He had been trained as a chef, although the Party had put him on board to ensure the crew wouldn't mutiny. The totalitarian American government kept a much tighter grip on their spaceships and privateers than the Russians, the Chinese, and even the Swedes. But what was the chance of revolution or mutiny even taking place these days? After the Mars wars, the nations had settled down. But America still made sure they had P.O.'s on every one of their ships because totalitarian governments never rested easy.

Old fighting ships like the *Simpson* were under the protection of the Letter of Marque, but in reality, they operated like old gunboats back on Earth during the beginning of the twentieth century. How had that Party hack explained it to him? He couldn't remember. With everything that had been going on these days, his brain felt like overcooked oatmeal.

After his meeting with Chief Onion and Michaelson, Onion had gone down to the engine room and Michaelson had gone to his quarters. Jelly Roll knew he should be up on the bridge, but instead, he was in his galley. He might be in command of this ship now, but his crew still needed to be fed. He actually chuckled to think that this might be the first time in history when an acting captain stayed away from the bridge so he could cook for his crew.

He rummaged around the freezer. There were enough stores in there to feed the remaining crew for sixth months. Since he had boarded this ship back in Earth orbit at the beginning of the mission, no one had gone hungry. He had made sure of that. He knew exactly how many pounds of beef, chicken, fish, and lamb were in there. He had a good memory, but he still kept inventory on his tablet. In space crew terms, the Homer had always been a 'good feeder.' Maybe an alien monster had been feeding on the crew lately, but that didn't mean the rest of them had to go hungry.

He squinted his eyes and noticed something. Then he smiled. The excitement of the last few days had caused him to forget a very important project. On the second shelf of the walk-in was a lump of dough wrapped in plastic. It was for the croissants he had started two nights ago. He took it out of the freezer and closed the door.

He took the lump to a good workspace in his galley and placed it on the countertop. It was frozen solid, but he knew he could soon warm it up to the right temperature just by kneading it in his chubby hands. Then the dough would be rolled out two more times.

After a few minutes of working it, his hands were numb with cold, but the dough was just about right. He took down his rolling pin from where it hung neatly on the wall. Then he gathered a bit of flour. Croissants were notoriously temperamental and didn't like to be handled too much. You couldn't over-flour them either because then you wouldn't get the layers you were hoping for. This job required a delicate touch, and at first, his cold fingers were clumsy. But then, the back and forth motion of his rolling pin smoothed things out nicely.

Jelly Roll began talking to himself like he usually did when all alone in his galley. He had never minded the sound of his own voice. Besides, there was no one else around to keep him company. The ship was eerily quiet with the small crew that was left.

The rule for the perfect croissant was to turn, roll, and fold it six times. This was never easy. Croissants always fought him during preparation. After he finished rolling, the protein of the dough would need time to relax. It might have to go back in the freezer. Or maybe it could go in the refrigerator. And rarely, oh so rarely, the proteins would be relaxed enough so he could work the dough right away. Sometimes Jelly Roll got lucky. But not tonight. Tonight it would have to go back in the freezer. Yes, making croissants was a slow process, but he knew if he was patient, it would be worth it. They would come out of his oven perfect, flaky and moist, with the exact right number of layers.

He closed the freezer door and rubbed his hands together. In a few hours, he would be able to cut the dough. Some of it would go into triangles to make crescent rolls. The rest would be cut into four-inch squares so he could make the special chocolate croissants that the crew loved. Hopefully, they would enjoy these, but they would never get the chance if he wasn't careful with his technique.

Of course, his baking gave him an idea; it always did. Working in the galley gave him time to think. Last year he had suggested to Captain Martin that he should try baking. But Martin hadn't listened. "Poor captain," muttered Jelly Roll. "I'll be down to check on you later. The AutoMed is doing its job, but everyone still needs a human touch. Maybe if you're awake, old Jelly Roll can bring you a croissant."

He wiped his hands with a towel and walked over to the com-box. He called engineering.

"What?" barked Silas Onion, sounding pissed off as usual.

"What's the status of the Campbell's engines?" asked Jelly Roll.

"Running strong like always. We're still stuck to that piece of shit like toilet paper on a shoe."

Jelly Roll paused for a heartbeat. "Will our engines be ready soon?"

The chief engineer grunted. "Not if I have to keep answering stupid questions. I can't do both, Jelly Roll....uh, Captain. Either I work on the engines or I talk to you. Which is more important right now?"

Jelly Roll had always been able to keep his patience with croissants. Now he would keep it with Silas Onion. "My apologies, Chief. When you're ready, I want you to fire them up. That should put extra strain on the Campbell. Maybe we can overload their engines."

The chief quickly corrected him. "We can't escape. We could never generate enough power to break out of a plasma bubble."

"I know, Chief. You told me that already. But what if we make them max out their engines trying to keep us in place? Wouldn't they overheat? Wouldn't they have to shut down? Then we could just float away or use our thrusters to break free."

There was a pause at the other end of the com-box. "That might work," mumbled the chief.

Jelly Roll waited a few seconds. Then a few more. "Chief, are you still there?"

"Yeah, yeah. Of course, I'm still here. Do you think I was playing with my pecker? I was just thinking, that's all. Yes, we might be able to overload their engines. Enough so they blow themselves up like a donkey with a cork up its ass. And since we're so cozied up and close, that would probably blow us up too."

Jelly Roll sighed. "I don't know about you, Chief, but I'm getting tired of that ship picking us apart like a leftover turkey carcass at Thanksgiving. Sure, we might die. But we'll also die if we sit around here and do nothing. That monster is still aboard this ship. Or hanging around outside the hull; Constance said it can move right through. So what's going to stop it from getting to the rest of us?"

As he said this, Jelly Roll glanced up at the overhead and felt a shiver down his spine.

There was silence from the other end. Finally, a different voice came over the com. It was Lt. Constance. Jelly Roll was surprised and pleased to hear her. He had always liked this young woman. "The chief is tired of talking to you," she said. "He says he has work to do. He wanted me to tell you that our engines will be ready to fire up when they're ready, and that the longer he talks to you, the longer it's going to take. He also said that when they are ready, we're going to give them such a big whack on their scrotums that we'll hear them scream from all the way over here."

Jelly Roll laughed out loud. "Thanks, Constance. I know the two of you can handle this. I'll go get Michaelson and head up to the bridge. Just keep us posted."

34

SENATOR ALAN K SIMPSON

Captain Matthew Martin had escaped the AutoMed but not his nightmares.

The canvas was painted black. The painting was large and filled a section of wall in his grandmother's garage-studio. Layers and layers of black paint had been applied, almost like crude oil. What had his grandmother been thinking? Martin let his fingers slide over the canvas. The texture was rough, uneven, and sharp. He put his face closer. When his eyes focused, little black shards of glass stared back at him.

He had to touch them. The closer his hand got to the shards, the colder his fingers became. If he had given it any thought, he might have pulled back. But now, the cold canvas drew his hand forward. Begging him to touch it. Asking him to not look away. The painting had power over him. He simply had to obey.

Martin was young again, remembering tales of things so cold they could burn you the instant they came into contact with your skin. He was a boy, feeling the flesh on his fingertips get warmer as his hand got closer to the glass shards. But he still needed to touch them. His will pushed his fingers forward.

His right index finger touched first. He felt the pain immediately. That didn't matter because he wanted his whole hand to touch; he wanted to feel the canvas.

Blood spurted from his index finger. The painting was so sharp and so cold at the same time. His middle finger touched next and starting bleeding as well. The ring finger followed, then his pinky, and finally, his thumb. They all started to bleed on the canvas. While the canvas was sharp, it was also cold. His blood steamed as it leaked out, filling the air above his hand. The steam turned black as it mixed with the warmth of his blood.

He knew should pull his hand away. But suffering seemed more important than retreat. He needed to keep his hand where it was. He knew by touching this painting he could understand it. He had to do that to save himself. And save his grandmother. And maybe his ship.

The blood from his fingers could only travel so far. After it lost its warmth it began to freeze to the canvas. Thick streaks of red flowed down and finally froze on top of the black paint. It looked as if he had purposely placed them there. Maybe he was a deranged artist, not knowing how much blood he needed to shed for his masterpiece. Never knowing when to stop. Never knowing when a painting was finished.

Finally, he couldn't take the pain any longer. He had had enough. He needed his hand to come back to him. His blood had defiled the canvas. His fingertips no longer had the right to touch the painting. They had violated it. Yet, they wanted to stay. They wanted to continue to touch the sharp paint and bleed down the canvas, no matter how much pain.

At first, his fingers refused to pull away. Martin knew he had to make his will stronger than the hand. At first, the blood stuck to his fingertips, holding him there in an icy grip. He pulled with all his might and finally, one by one, he began to pry his fingers away.

He screamed as they peeled away from the canvas. The sound of his youthful cries filled the studio, but his grandmother didn't come to help. Each finger left skin and blood in its place. The canvas had claimed them and didn't want to give them back. It wanted his hand to join the picture and become an extension of the art. Martin's hand still belonged to him, but the painting didn't want to let it go.

He woke. The nightmare was over. He was standing in sickbay. A bloody handprint, his own, faced him from the medical cabinet in front of him. He had broken its glass and some of it was still in his hand. His grandmother's black canvas was no longer there.

Martin glanced around. He saw the AutoMed he had kicked apart. He saw the breathing tube he had taken from his own throat. It lay on the floor. None of that mattered though. He wanted to laugh like a maniac. He declared loudly to himself, "I know how to save my ship! We must become a part of them. It's the only way."

35

SS JOHN W CAMPBELL JR

Erik Juergenson could scarcely believe he was still alive. How long had it been? He had no idea. This was a nightmare he couldn't wake from. And like all the worst nightmares, this one went on and on and on.

It had begun when he was on board his reliable, workhorse of a spaceship, *Skalbagge*. He had docked with the *John W Campbell Jr*, which was floating free in space like a ghost ship on a still ocean. Erik moved his ship slowly in while docking, talking to the huge freighter like a lover. "Don't be shy, my little Älskare," he had said. "I'll be gentle."

He had always talked that way while docking. But when they had hooked up, he found the opposite of a lover. When the hatch opened, he shone his flashlight and saw a dark, slithering tentacle come through. Quick as a snake, it wrapped itself around his torso and carried him away screaming.

The next few minutes were a bewildering rush of images. It was like an out-of-control carnival ride as he was dragged down one dim corridor after another. His stomach lurched and his helmet flew off. He grasped the tentacle, trying in vain to free himself. There were recessed blue lights in the overhead, turning dizzily around as he tumbled and bounced. He thought he might pass out. Or maybe vomit up the pickled herring he had had for lunch on Europa.

But then the tentacle unwrapped itself and he was free. He pulled himself to his feet. The room was spinning like he had downed a whole bottle of Akvavit. But he gathered his wits and looked around.

He was on the bridge of a freighter, dimly lit in purple light. He knew it must be the bridge of *John W. Campbell Jr.* But what had that thing been which brought him here? He looked down at the deck. The tentacle was gone.

And then he saw who was sitting in the captain's chair. Or rather, what was sitting there. Or lying there. Or perched there. He couldn't really tell. There was another in a chair on its left. The creatures had large, bulbous heads and bulging eyes that rotated in some sort of thick liquid, like marbles in mucous. Their bodies were fat, lumpy, and asymmetrical, looking black in the purple light. Stuff moved within that blackness like slinking goo. Each creature had two stick-arms that waved like bare branches in a winter breeze. Pink fingers at the ends of each arm fanned out like lily pads. They had no legs, but instead, three thick tentacles protruded from the bottoms of their bodies.

The creature in the captain's chair focused one rheumy eye on Erik, while the other eye continued to rotate. An area beneath the eyes opened up like a gaping wound and a voice spoke, low and metallic. "We will know you."

"What are you?" said Erik in revulsion. Something crawled up his leg. He looked down in horror and saw that the tentacle had returned. No, that wasn't right. This tentacle was smaller, much thinner than the one that had carried him here. Before he could resist, it had wrapped itself around his neck. He reached up to try and pull it away. But by then it had forced itself past his clenched lips and into his mouth. Another went up his nose. He gagged and felt his eyes roll back in his head.

And then everything went black.

He came to. He was still lying on the bridge. There was a water bottle in front of his eyes, along with a plate of nutro chips. He sat up. It took a moment to remember what had happened. He ran his hands over his face. There was a cakey substance beneath his nose and mouth. He brushed it with his fingers and looked down apprehensively. Steeling up his courage, he tasted a little bit of it. Dried blood. His blood. Swallowing, he felt a shooting pain in his throat, like strep, only ten times worse.

"Erik."

This time the voice was coming from inside his head. He looked frantically around. The two bulbous creatures were still in their chairs, only this time, just one was facing him. The one in the captain's chair was turned around, pressing things on the control panel with its lily pad fingers. On the viewscreen was a ship, an American privateer. But there were no stars behind it. It simply hung in inky blackness like a trophy head on an ebony wall.

"What...are...you?" he rasped, but each word burned his throat like a hot poker.

"Eat," the voice in his head commanded. He decided he'd better not disobey. Breaking nutro chips into tiny bites, he swallowed gingerly and took small sips of water. And then a tentacle slithered around the corner and climbed up his leg. He tried to scream but the thing had already found its way inside his mouth.

Everything went black. Again.

How many times had it been now? He had lost count. First food. Then water. Then boredom.

Then...

Violation.

After yet one more agonizing episode, something different happened. Both creatures on the bridge faced away from him, bulbous heads inclined towards the view screen. The American privateer was gone and the stars had returned. There was a different ship up there now. It looked like a giant, gleaming dragonfly.

Trollslända.

Erik sat up. Every Swede on Europa knew that ship. It was the jewel of Swedish Space Fleet, and when Erik left Europa, they had almost finished its re-fit. Now, on the view screen, *Trollslända* fired. First torpedoes and then lasers. They bounced off the *Campbell* like space dust. And then a green net fired out of Trollslända's hull. Erik had never seen anything like that before. It hurtled towards the *Campbell* like a spreading spider web. When it hit, the *Campbell's* deck bucked and heaved, tipping Erik sideways. The viewscreen flashed sparkling emeralds. Things on it phased in and out like a meteor storm. The creatures in the chairs looked frantic, waving their stick arms and the one in the middle pressing lights on the control board seemingly at random. But then everything went still.

On the screen, *Trollslända* inched closer. Something detached itself like a shiny pebble from its hull and grew larger. Soon Erik recognized what it was.

Trollslända's cutter.

Erik felt his guts clench. One of his countrymen was coming over here, hoping to sneak in and board the *Campbell* to rescue him. It was the only explanation that made any sense.

Both continued to stare at the screen. Erik knew he had to get out of there and warn whoever was coming. Was it his friend Aaron Ljungman?

He heard rapid slithering in the corridor. It sounded like several of those tentacle creatures. Were they heading for the docking port? Of course. Where else would they be going? They would grab whoever came through the hatch, the way they had grabbed Erik.

He got to his feet and steadied himself. The creatures watching the screen seemed oblivious. He crept around the corner. In the blue recessed lighting, he could see three tentacle creatures moving away along the deck. He followed. He pursued them through countless twists and turns. Sometimes he had to run to keep up, but he managed to do it quietly. Finally, rounding a corner, he saw...

Borås.

He was standing on a bridge over a pond. It was the bridge near where he had grown up in western Sweden. Across the pond was...

Aaron Ljungman.

"No!" he shouted. "Stay away! It's not real!"

Something took out his feet and he fell. He got back up and waved his arms. "Don't come close! Run!"

A tentacle crawled up Erik's leg and into his nose and mouth.

Everything went black. Again.

He came to once more on the bridge. He tried to remember what had just happened. The last thing he had seen was Aaron running away. Had he escaped? He could only hope. Maybe he was wandering around the ship. This was a huge, cavernous freighter, after all. He could hide. Somehow, he had to get to his friend. For Erik had some things to tell him.

Yes, the creatures had violated his body and his mind. They knew way too much about him. By using fear, and with sinister abilities Erik had never heard of before, they had controlled him. They seemed omnipotent, all-powerful. But they weren't.

Sometimes, when the creatures picked his thoughts like seeds from a watermelon, he was partially aware of what was going on. That's when the picking had gone both ways. And now, Erik had some very important things to tell Aaron about them.

36

SHUTTLE

Oscar stepped back with his left foot. The fighter hoped the monster controlling Tormod's corpse would throw the first punch. He knew inexperienced fighters sometimes fell for this ruse. And it worked. The Tormod-thing swung hard with its right arm. Oscar simply had to continue to step backward to avoid it, and when the teen-thing overextended itself, he punched it in the ribs. His punch was solid, and he heard ribs crack as he made contact. Any man would have cried out in pain, but not this thing. It remained quiet, with no hint that it was even bothered.

He took another step back. He knew he would soon run out of room. He needed to keep dancing around to make the monster circle away from Molly. Just by the way that Tormod-thing moved, Oscar could tell that the spider-cat controlling it had never boxed. Besides, even if it did figure out how to fight, Oscar still had fifty pounds on it.

Punch after punch, Oscar kept landing hard shots into the thing's ribs. And with all the damage he was causing, the thing still hadn't landed any punches in return.

Molly stood by Oscar's side, watching and waiting patiently. She still held the propane torch, waiting for her turn to fry the monster. The Tormod-thing seemed to be ignoring her for now, intent to keep all of its focus on Oscar. The fighter knew that was another mistake. Molly wouldn't wait forever to strike because patience had never been her strong suit. But so far it hadn't been much of a fight. Oscar would keep on punishing the thing's body until it could no longer move. At least he thought so. It was not like he'd fought something like this before.

Suddenly the spider-cat let forth with a keening howl from the mouth within its strange head. Oscar resisted the urge to forget his defenses and cover his ears. When the howl was over, there was a familiar scraping sound from down the corridor inside the *Campbell*. Another tentacle was coming. Oscar should have known better than to think there wouldn't be more. Evidently, the spider-cat had called in reinforcements.

Another tentacle rushed in, triangular head seeking out a target. The tentacle joined in the fight, coiling itself back and snapping forward like a whip. Luckily, Oscar saw it coming. Using his long years of experience, he jumped out of its way without thinking and the tentacle shot past. He was safe for the moment. But Molly wasn't. She was feisty but she didn't have Oscar's training. The tentacle curled around her ankle and pulled her down. She let out a small cry and dropped the propane torch. The tentacle began to pull her towards the dim corridor of the *Campbell*. She turned over on her stomach and tried to grab onto something, but the deck was smooth. She looked up helplessly at Oscar.

The fighter tried to break away from the Tormod-thing but it wouldn't let him. The spider-cat suddenly became bold and, instead of trying to punch Oscar, it reached out to grasp him and wrestle him instead. Oscar stepped backward to protect himself, moving farther away from Molly. "Shit!" he cried. This wasn't good. He had to get to Molly before it was too late.

The spider-cat forced a dead, eerie smile onto Tormod's face. Things had quickly changed, and now it was in control of this fight. But Oscar gritted his teeth and said, "So, you wanna wrassle? Well, shitface, I'm from South Carolina. I've wrassled bigger, tougher rednecks than you." He opened up his stance. It had been a long time since he'd done this type of fighting, but to someone like Oscar, fighting had always been like riding a bicycle.

Molly screamed. The tentacle pulled her through the hatch and into the *Campbell*. Oscar knew he had to break free of this creature and do it quickly. But how?

The Tormod-thing gave Oscar an even bigger smile. With revulsion, Oscar realized it was the same, rat-faced smile the kid used to give him on Ganymede. Oscar had always hated that smile. He hit Tormod in the mouth with a rabbit punch, something he had always longed to do. The smile instantly left the kid's face. Oscar wished his aim had been better and that he had broken all of Tormod's front teeth.

"That hurt, didn't it?" he asked.

There were things Oscar had seen in his life that he had never wanted to see. What the spider-cat did to Tormod then, he hoped never to see again for the rest of his days. It ripped the boy's body open from neck to groin. Blood and guts burst out onto the deck, but, somehow, Tormod stayed on his feet, ready for action. The loss of his innards didn't seem to faze him a bit. Now Oscar could see there was something else inside of the boy's body. More tentacles. Each had a tiny, triangular head.

From inside of the *Campbell*, Oscar heard a woman's scream. He felt a pang of despair. Poor Molly. He hadn't been able to save her. He hated to lose. He hated being overmatched in a fight. But now, nothing mattered any longer. He was pissed.

Oscar didn't usually lose control in a fight. Recklessness had been trained out of him. But not this time. He rushed Tormod and tackled him. Both of them flew to the deck. Baby tentacles bit into his chest, but Oscar ignored the pain. He needed to finish this fight so he could go and kill the tentacle that had dragged Molly away. He wasn't going to let it violate her like this one had done to Tormod. They rolled around on the shuttle's deck, each trying to gain an advantage. Razor-sharp teeth ripped flesh off Oscar's chest.

But he still had one hand free. That gave him an advantage. He reached for the spider-cat's head. Its skull was smaller than a basketball so he could easily palm it like he used to do in high school. He gripped the top of the skull and using the extra leverage of Tormod's forehead, brutally pulled the spider's head from the body of the cat. Oscar figured that it didn't matter how tough the monster was, it couldn't fight without its head. He held it in the air, dripping black blood. That had been easier than he expected. For once, something had gone right. Tormod's body went limp. The little teeth stopped biting.

This fight was over. Oscar had won.

He felt a moment of exhilaration, the way he always did after a victory. But then he remembered.

Molly.

Completely drenched in Tormod's red blood and the black stuff that passed for blood in the creature, he got to his feet and stumbled his way to the hatch leading to the *Campbell*. What would he find there? What had happened to Molly? He was probably much too late to save her.

He ducked his head and moved around the corner into the dim corridor. What he saw there made him gasp. And then it made his heart leap. Molly was walking towards him. She smiled when she saw him. She wasn't as bloody as Oscar, but she was a mess. Grasped tightly in her right hand was a torn-off tentacle with a triangular head. The head was limp and drooping, yellow eyes now dull. She threw it down and shouted at it. "Fuck with me, Mr. Monster? You picked on the wrong girl today. I'm in a bad mood. Nobody fucks with me unless I say it's okay!"

Molly kicked the head and it splattered against the nearest bulkhead in a black splash. "Now you go back to hell and fuck your mother instead!"

Oscar grabbed Molly and hugged her. She looked like she needed a hug. A big one. And, if he had to admit it, he needed one too.

37

HSWMS TROLLSLÄNDA

Jenny Broberg stared gloomily at the view screen. The scene hadn't changed in hours and the American ship still hung there in space. All its lights were on, and Broberg's sensors showed that their life support was working fine. Occasionally, she even detected a slight surge from their engines. But no one had answered Rasmussen's hails. There could be a very good explanation for that, of course. They could all be dead.

"Hail them again, Peg."

Peggy Rasmussen groaned and put her head in her hands. "I think I've already hailed them a thousand times," she grunted.

"Humor me," answered Broberg.

On her right, Mats Renberg was deep into a game of solitaire on his tablet. Being stationed on an ice-bound moon like Europa sometimes got boring. But it was nothing like being trapped in a black void on a stolen warship, unable to do a thing. The American ship was as silent as a Norwegian farmer who hadn't been drinking. Besides that, there were no stars here, no planets, nothing. It was like being cooped up in a very dark graveyard with a corpse.

"Come in, Swedish warship. We hear you."

Broberg nearly fell off her chair. The voice had come through the com as clear as day. Rasmussen handed her the mic.

"Um, hello! American privateer, is that you?"

"Yes it is...um...that's affirmative," answered the voice. It sounded like someone who hadn't spent a lot of time in the communications class at the Academy.

"This is the Swedish ship *Trollslända*. We see you on our view screen. In fact, we've been seeing you for hours. You never answered our hails."

"Um, yes," answered the voice. "Sorry about that. There was no one on the bridge. Things have been kind of crazy over here."

"I understand. This is Jennifer Broberg, acting captain of *Trollslända*. Who am I speaking to?"

"I'm...um, they just call me Jelly Roll. I'm the acting captain here too. This is the Homer...I mean, the *Alan K. Simpson*."

"Well, I can't tell you how good it is to hear another human voice. I thought we were all alone out here. How long have you been trapped in this...whatever it is?"

"Since the Earth's moon was made of cheese."

"Come again?"

Jelly Roll chuckled. "Sorry. I was trying to be funny. I suppose I shouldn't do that under the circumstances. We've been here a couple of days at least. I kind of lost track."

Broberg chuckled to herself. She was already starting to like this guy. "That's affirmative. We've only been here for a few hours ourselves and it already seems like days. So why do they call you Jelly Roll?"

"I'm actually the cook. Or I was. Maybe I still am. I don't know. As I said, things have been crazy."

Broberg smiled. It was nice to have someone else to connect with, even if he didn't sound like he knew what he was doing either. "Do you know how to cook Swedish food? No one on Europa does it well, although they try. We're supposed to be a Swedish station but you'd never know it from the cafeteria."

"I studied a few dishes at the Academy but that was a long time ago. I remember making lutefisk, but it just about killed us when we tried to eat it. I must have screwed up."

This time Broberg laughed out loud. "You probably did it just right. That's a normal reaction when you eat lutefisk for the first time."

"Okay, that's good to know. Maybe I'll try it again when we get some codfish."

"I wouldn't recommend it. You should probably stick with meatballs. Anyway, how did your ship get caught in here? And more important, how do we get out of here?"

"Let me turn you over to Michaelson," said Jelly Roll. "He knows more about the technical stuff than I do."

There was a pause before another voice came over the com. Unlike Jelly Roll, this man's voice was official-sounding and flat. "This is Third Mate George Michaelson. What do you want to know?"

Broberg found herself wishing she was still talking with Jelly Roll. He was a guy she would like to meet in person one day. "Tell me what happened to you."

Michaelson filled her in on all the major things the *Simpson* had faced since it first approached the *Campbell*. He mainly concentrated on technical things, including the *Campbell's* hack into their computer systems, his theories about how they were able to control other ships, and his explanation of plasma bubbles. Most of it went over Broberg's head. Halfway through, Jelly Roll cut in.

"It's been nice talking with you, Captain Broberg. But I have to go down to my mess now and make dinner for my crew. I'll be in touch."

Broberg cursed to herself. Now it was just her and the nörd...the American geek. She immediately missed her new friend Jelly Roll. Her mind wandered as Michaelson went on and on and on.

"Are you there, *Trollslända*?"

Jenny blinked and keyed the mic. "Yes. Sorry. I think the signal died for a minute. What did you just say?"

"I said that if we work together, the power from both ships might be able to break us free."

"Oh. That's good. In fact, that sounds great. Just tell me what you want us to do."

"I'll know pretty soon," said Michaelson. "Chief Onion's working on it right now down in engineering. But first I want to ask you something."

"Fire away."

"Okay, that's affirmative. Do you have much Bryantonium on your ship, besides on the hull?"

Broberg thought for a moment. "Yes, I think so. In fact, I know we do. *Trollslända* just went through a major re-fit and everything is first class. These days, that means Bryantonium. We even have Bryantonium sinks and toilets. Sometimes Swedish Space Fleet goes a little overboard."

"Oh," answered Michaelson. This time his voice didn't sound flat.

"What's wrong?" asked Broberg.

"When the *Campbell* took control of your ship and sent you here, did you come into contact with it at any time? Actual contact where your hulls touched?"

Broberg felt a flicker of anxiety. "Yes. We actually rammed into them and were stuck against their hull like a magnet. That lasted for a few minutes and then they sent us into this black void. Why?"

Michaelson cleared his throat. Now his voice was the opposite of official-sounding. "Well, unfortunately, there are these creatures. Nasty little buggers. They already killed three of our crew. I don't think they can travel through space. But evidently, they can latch onto hulls like barnacles. And they go right through Bryantonium. So if you were pressed up against the *Campbell*..."

Broberg finished the thought and Europa ice water filled her veins. She gaped around the bridge at all the brand new fixtures, gleaming silver and purple. This whole ship was just plastered with Bryantonium.

She took a deep breath before speaking. "Mr. Michaelson. George. Tell me everything you know about those creatures."

38

HSWMS TROLLSLÄNDA

Jenny Broberg signed off after talking with Michaelson. Rasmussen sat on one side and Renberg on the other. They both stared at her intently.

"Did you both catch that whole conversation?" she asked.

They nodded, looking like school children who had just found out they did the wrong homework assignment.

"Okay, then," she said, wishing she sounded more authoritative. She was supposed to be the acting captain, but what were you supposed to say after finding out that tentacled creatures might be lurking outside the hull, waiting to burst through and slaughter everyone on board?

Perhaps Michaelson was delusional. That would be understandable, considering that they'd been trapped in this black void for days. But he hadn't sounded crazy, not at all. Through all the long years of space exploration and colonization, however, there had never been any serious reports of aliens. Yes, there were bound to be other civilizations in the vast universe. But at least in this solar system, humans had been the only game in town. And no manned ship had made it out of the solar system. But there had been rumors, especially in the past year. So all she could do was take Michaelson seriously.

"Mats, can you check the feed from the cameras outside our hull? I know it's probably just a precaution but..."

An muffled shriek came from below decks. It sounded like a massive water pump on Europa that has just lost its lubrication. All three of them bolted upright in their chairs. Broberg grabbed the mic and called down to engineering. "Herko, are you there? Come in please. What was that noise?"

"*För fan i helvete!*" shouted Herko through the speaker.

Broberg swallowed hard. She had never heard Heidi swear before, not even once.

"Heidi, what is it?"

"Get off uf me!" shouted Heidi in her Laplander accent. She grunted. Then there was a liquid squishing sound and the shrieking stopped. Just after that, the mic went dead.

"Heidi? Tell me what's happening down there."

Nothing.

"Heidi, come in. Answer please."

Still nothing.

"I should go down there," said Renberg.

"No!" shouted Broberg. She turned towards Rasmussen. "Seal the bridge!"

"Yes, Kapten," answered Rasmussen, all business now. She fumbled her hands across the control panel, searching for the right instrument tree. Like the rest of them on this pirate mission, she didn't have much experience on the bridge of a ship.

Trollslända was a Swedish warship, and that meant the bridge could be sealed off during combat. Even if the rest of the ship was destroyed, those on the bridge would find themselves in a sealed capsule, with its own life support and small compliment of weapons. Swedish Space Fleet had always put the lives of their crews above everything.

"Found it!" shouted Rasmussen in triumph. She pressed an amber-colored light. Immediately, there was a hissing sound from behind them as a metal barrier slid down smoothly from above, blocking them off from the hallway. They heard a few clicks and a rush of air as the sequence completed. And then it was quiet, with only the hum of the life support systems.

All three of them whirled around and stared at the metal barrier. "Are we safe?" whispered Rasmussen.

"I don't know," answered Broberg. The barrier was shiny silver. With purple flecks.

Something came through the barrier like liquid metal. Whip like, it slithered along the deck. A second one came through with an ear-piercing shriek that rattled their ears. It nearly paralyzed Broberg, the way a fire alarm stuns somebody in the middle of the night. But she jumped to her feet and backed into a corner, away from the creatures.

Renberg and Rasmussen still sat where they were, frozen in place, gripping the arms of their chairs with mouths open like beached bass.

"Get up!" shouted Broberg. But it was too late. One tentacle wrapped itself around Renberg's torso and the other around Rasmussen's. Triangular-shaped heads reared up in front of them, letting out twin shrieks.

Second tentacles branched off from each creature. At the ends were hooked fingers. They waved in the air for a long moment before striking, piercing both Renberg and Rasmussen in the center of their chests. Blood gushed down onto their laps. Their eyes glazed over and their mouths went slack. Quick as a flash, the tentacles dragged them out of their chairs and along the deck like rag dolls. When they reached the metal barrier, Broberg watched in amazement and horror as the tentacle things pulled them right through as if the barrier wasn't even there.

"Bloody Helvete!" gasped Broberg from where she cowered in the corner. Panic threatened to overtake her. What chance did she have against things like that? Every bone in her body wanted to collapse into a fetal position. Because those monsters would surely be back.

She glanced frantically around the bridge. Was there a weapon she could use? Nothing immediately came into view. There were so many shiny fixtures on this ship, gleaming trim along the walls, the floors, the overheads. All made of Bryantonium. Those things could get at her from anywhere.

She spotted something in the far corner.

It had been one of the great controversies of Swedish Space Fleet twenty years ago. The HR department lobbied to include something on every Swedish spaceship, even warships. When they first floated the proposal, old-timers mocked the idea. Broberg's own father even wrote a letter over SpaceNet complaining that the younger generation was getting soft. But it passed. And now every Swedish ship had one.

A sauna.

Trollslända's sauna was tucked neatly into a far corner of the bridge. It was state-of-the-art, perfect for a momentary getaway and R+R on long space voyages. It contained the latest bells and whistles, energy efficient heating, and soft, plush, sweat-proof cushions. There was even a one-person tub next to it for those who wanted to replicate Scandinavian tradition by staying in a sauna as long as you could stand it before jumping into ice water. It was supposed to be healthy.

But what caught Broberg's attention was the material they had used to make it. Finnish Spruce. Smooth, beige wood. Not Bryantonium. Would those things be able to come through it? Probably. But it was all she had.

She took one step towards the sauna before the tentacle returned. This time there was only one. Maybe the other one was doing something unspeakable to the bodies in the hallway.

The creature shrieked. It didn't almost paralyze her like before. She barely heard it as she tried to get to the sauna. The tentacle blocked her way. Glancing around, she saw a plastic case beneath the console, blue and yellow in the colors of the Swedish flag. When Aaron had pirated this ship from its dock on Europa, workmen had left a case of Akvavit on board. It wasn't a weapon, but it would have to do.

Broberg reached down and snapped off the cover. Twelve bottles gleamed up at her. She grabbed one and took a step towards the creature, brandishing the Akvavit like a club. When the tentacle raced forward, she threw the bottle down as hard as she could. It crashed on the deck and splattered glass and liquor all over the monster. It pulled back, triangular-shaped head waving back and forth, eyes dimming. It wasn't much of a diversion, but it gave her a moment. She grabbed three more bottles, tucking two under her arm and brandishing a third. She took two more steps towards the sauna when the tentacle came at her again. She smashed another bottle down in front of it. Again, it paused.

She had two more bottles and ten feet to go.

The creature shrieked again. Jenny shrieked right back. Not in fear, but in anger. She locked eyes with the triangular-shaped head and shouted, "For Odin's sake! Would you please shut up?"

Amazingly, the head pulled back. It was all the opening Jenny Broberg needed. She smashed another bottle down while shrieking and running sideways. When she got to the sauna, she lifted the latch and pulled open the door. She scooted inside.

But before the door closed all the way, she felt something tug on her ankle.

Screaming in revulsion, she brought the last bottle of Akvavit down onto the tentacle that was wrapping around her leg. The bottle shattered, leaving a large shard of glass sticking in her hand. She closed her hand around it and stabbed the tentacle, cutting the end of it away. Black liquid gushed onto the wood floor of the sauna, mixing with her own red blood from the cut on her hand. The tentacle pulled away. She kicked the door shut and the latch fell into place. A soft, amber light switched on over her head.

She leaned against the door and breathed for the first time in several minutes. The creature pushed against the door from the outside. But, amazingly enough, it didn't come through. It seemed incomprehensible that it could travel through the hardest metal in the solar system but not wood. Well, maybe whatever planet that thing had come from didn't have any trees.

Outside the sauna, the shrieking stopped. Had the thing gone away? Broberg wasn't about to open the door to find out. She sat down on one of the benches. She kicked at the piece of tentacle she had severed. It looked like gray blubber. Fortunately, it wasn't moving.

She began to shake as the adrenaline left her body. She hugged her knees tightly and tried not to think about what had happened to Renberg and Rasmussen. She pulled the shard of glass from her hand and wrapped the edge of her shirt around the wound. It would bleed for a while, but it hadn't hit an artery.

What would she do now? She was trapped here, undoubtedly alone, the only human being left alive on a ship trapped in a black void, somewhere in deep space.

The interior of the sauna smelled like fresh spruce. There was the cast iron pit filled with lava rocks. Overhead was an amber lamp, giving off a soothing glow. On the near wall was a thermometer. On the far wall was...

A radio.

They had thought of everything. A ship's captain would need to stay in touch, even in the sauna. But would it work?

She took the microphone down off its cradle. Feeling her heart race, she pushed the key and said breathlessly, "American ship. *Simpson*, please come in. This is *Trollslända*."

No reply. The black plastic of the microphone smelled brand new, right out of the box. They probably hadn't hooked it up yet. Even if it worked, would it call out to other ships in the area, or just to her own bridge?

"American ship, please come in. Michaelson, are you there? George, this is Jenny Broberg. Please answer."

The speaker crackled. "*Trollslända* I read you. This is Michaelson. Jenny, are you okay?"

She let out a huge sigh. "No, I'm not okay. You were right about those creatures. My crew is dead. But I think I'm safe for now. I'm in the sauna."

"You're taking a sauna?"

In spite of everything that had just happened, she chuckled. "The sauna is made out of wood, not Bryantonium. I don't think they can get me in here."

"Oh. That's good. And there's a radio in there?"

"Affirmative. Swedish Space Fleet thinks of everything."

"I guess so. Well, I'm glad you're alive."

"Thanks. So what do I do now?"

Michaelson paused. "Hold tight. We're working on some things over here. There has to be a way to combine the power of our ships. And maybe you just found out some valuable info. I'll be in touch. Stay close to your radio."

"Don't worry," said Broberg. "I'm not going anywhere."

39

SENATOR ALAN K SIMPSON

A second shouldn't be a minute. A minute shouldn't be an hour. And an hour shouldn't seem like a day. Time moved like a glacier for Jelly Roll. The cook had done everything he could in his mess. Dinner was ready to serve when the time came.

He had decided to cook something simple for the four crew members still doing their jobs. He had whipped up a simple chicken noodle soup, crusty bread, and basic apple-cinnamon cake. After all that had happened, a meal of old-fashioned comfort food was the best idea. Michaelson, Onion, and Constance could eat any time they got hungry tonight, and if Jelly Roll wasn't around, his crew was more than capable of feeding themselves. The croissant dough was back in the freezer and he would have them ready for tomorrow's breakfast. The hard part of the croissants was finished, and in the morning, he would only need to roll them out one last time and put them in the oven. Easy.

He knew he shouldn't have left the bridge, especially after making contact with the Swedish ship. After all, he was supposed to be the captain now. But somehow, that role didn't seem to fit in the most important place, which was inside his own head. Yes, he was the Political Officer, but he had started out as the cook, he'd been the cook, and well, he was still the cook. And now, with dinner ready, there was nothing left for him to do. Michaelson had the bridge and Jelly Roll just didn't have it in him to go back up there.

With a sigh, he decided he should go and check on Captain Martin in sick bay. He was in the capable hands of the AutoMed, so there really wasn't anything Jelly Roll could do. The first diagnosis by the machine said the injured man would be in its care for three days before it could release him. But in Jelly Roll's mind, the AutoMed was like an oven with a cake in it. Everything should be fine, but it was still a good idea to check on the cake from time to time.

He walked towards the sickbay. He had never understood why the designers of the Simpson had put it so far away, near the stern of the ship and engineering. Most of the crew's quarters were closer to the bow. Spaceship designers were evidently a strange breed. But then again, if they were to see the way Jelly Roll organized his kitchen, they'd probably think he was a lunatic. Spaceship engineers and cooks obviously didn't speak the same language, and that might be a good thing.

As he walked towards the stern, he passed Chief Onion's quarters. He was the only crew member who bunked this far back. He liked his privacy and didn't seem to mind being away from everyone else. And to be honest, no one minded that Onion was such a loner. He wasn't the easiest guy to get along with.

This was the old Marine section of the ship. It had been decades since there had been any Marines on board. These days, on privateers like the Simpson, the normal compliment included only a small squad of soldiers and their sergeant. The ship's three dead mercenaries, Jagr, Karam, and Bohannon, hadn't lived back here, preferring to bunk in more comfortable quarters in the bow.

Jelly Roll hadn't been down here in a while, except for a brief trip through to take the captain to the Automed. He noticed that things were very clean and tidy. In spite of his crusty personality, Chief Onion took as much pride in his living area as Jelly Roll did in his mess. Maybe that's why Martin brought the old engineer along on every mission. Even though Jelly Roll had only been captain for a few hours, he was beginning to understand that a captain needed to have faith in his crew. Chief Onion was meticulous if he was anything, and did his job very well. He must have brought peace of mind to Martin during all those long years in deep space.

Just as Jelly Roll reached the door to sickbay, a light bulb went off in his head. He suddenly realized why the medical facilities had been placed back here in the first place. They were directly across from the original Marine quarters. Maybe the designers weren't so strange after all. Marines had the most dangerous occupation, so they were far more likely to end up in sickbay. They would be more comfortable recuperating near their quarters. It seemed so obvious now, but it had never occurred to him. He had so much to learn about commanding a ship. He would never be able to fill Martin's shoes. What had the Party been thinking when they had chosen him as P.O.? Was he simply a last resort, a Hail Mary pass? He knew the answer to that one…

"Ahhhhhhhhhhhhhh!"

The scream came from further down the passageway. It morphed into a shriek that kept going on and on. He felt his heart skip a beat. He knew what was lurking on this ship, and what had already killed three crew members. The last thing he wanted to do was to go and see what that shriek was.

But he was in charge now.

Warily, he made his way down the passageway. After a dozen meters, he came around a corner and nearly bumped into Captain Martin, dressed in his Automed gown, his back to Jelly Roll, looking up at the overhead. The shriek was coming from him. Jelly Roll stopped in his tracks, expecting to see a tentacle wrapped around the captain's leg or something. But there was nothing there. He reached out and put a hand on the captain's shoulder. The shrieking immediately stopped.

"Captain," said Jelly Roll softly. "How did you get out of the AutoMed? It's okay. I'm here. I can help you. Let's get you back into sickbay."

"I know how to save my ship," came the captain's slurred reply. "I know how to save the Simpson."

Jelly Roll gently turned the captain around and gasped. Evidently, the Automed had not had enough time to do its work. The first thing Jelly Roll noticed was the blood covering Martin's mouth. Worse than the blood was the missing eye. Jelly Roll had seen it before when they'd taken Martin to sickbay, but the sight of the empty socket still made him shudder. The eye muscles remained, hanging loose like gristle on a roast. Beyond that was a gaping, dark cavity, making the captain resemble a zombie on one of those SpaceNet shows Jelly Roll liked to watch. It took all of his courage, but he still kept his hand on Martin's shoulder. He reached out with his other hand. "Come on, Captain. I need to get you back to sickbay. You're going to be okay. I'll take care of you."

Martin opened his mouth to speak. Jelly Roll flinched when he saw the top row of broken teeth, looking like ragged pegs. "You don't understand," lisped the captain. "It's Bryantonuim. They're attracted to it. I have to become one with the monster."

"What are you talking about?" asked Jelly Roll.

Martin pulled his arm away. "One with the monster," he repeated. His remaining eye looked glassy and far away and his head lolled. "One with the monster. Only way to save my ship."

Just then, Chief Onion and Lt. Constance raced around the corner. Lt.

Constance was brandishing a pistol. "What's going on down here?" she said. "What was that shriek?"

"Thank God you're here," said Jelly Roll. "He's freaking out. Help me get him back to sickbay."

"No shit, Sherlock," said Chief Onion. He came forward to help. Lt. Constance glanced up at the overhead, brandishing her pistol with both hands. She looked like she was going to turn and run at any moment.

When Onion grabbed the captain's elbow, he began to shriek again. But this time, in-between the screams, he said, "Come and get me, you bastards! What are you waiting for? I know you want me! I've seen the painting! I know what it means!"

Jelly Roll grabbed Martin's other elbow. "It's okay, Captain. We're all here. We can help."

But then the tentacle came down from above like a mad dog being called by its master.

Onion dove out of the way. Constance uttered screams of her own, even louder than Martin's, and stumbled backwards. She fell to the deck and cowered like a frightened little girl as her pistol clattered away.

Only Jelly Roll and Captain Martin remained standing. They were closest to the tentacle. A triangular head with flickering yellow eyes waved in front of them. Even though he hadn't been there during the fatal battle in the compartment above the bridge, Jelly Roll knew what those glistening eyes meant.

Death had come to take all four of them.

40

SENATOR ALAN K SIMPSON

Jelly Roll's heart thudded in his chest like a jackhammer. He was supposed to be in charge of the ship now. His job was to protect the crew – all of his crew. Constance had told him that these creatures were incredibly quick. He would never be able to protect everyone. Some of them would die today. Maybe all of them. But not if old Jelly Roll could help it.

The yellow eyes gazed at each of them in turn. Jelly Roll had only seen this creature for a few moments, but already he had a visceral feeling that was more than fear. He hated this thing. He had always looked for the best in people but this abomination was alien, and Jelly Roll sensed pure, malevolent evil emanating from it. It meant to kill each of them in turn as if that were its sole purpose for existing. But who would it strike first?

Jelly Roll stared boldly into its eyes. They stopped flickering and focused directly on him. He found himself frozen in place. He couldn't turn away. Suddenly, he got a sensation of floating, of being drawn closer and closer to those eyes, even though his feet weren't moving. He tried to pull back but his mind thrust him forward. He burst into a dimly-lit tube, like a covered water slide, scales moving along the sides like leather bat wings. Round and round and up and down he went. Then he was dumped clumsily onto the bridge of a ship he didn't recognize. A creature was sitting in the captain's chair, not a tentacle creature, but something else. Something hideous. It had waving stick-arms and huge, bulbous eyes. Jelly Roll was pulled towards those eyes. It was like being dragged towards a pulsating mound of mucous.

"I see you," said a low, metallic voice. "I know you. You are nothing."

Jelly Roll felt despair well up from deep inside of him. It was like being ridiculed by his father, the way it had happened so many times when he was a child. The ghastly, alien creature meant to control him. And it would be so easy to just let go...

"No!" he heard himself shout. "I'm not that child! Not anymore!"

The creature's mind pulled back. And then Jelly Roll sensed something else. Something impossible. The creature was...afraid of him.

And then he was back on the Simpson. The whole thing must have only taken a moment because Onion and Constance and Martin were still in their same positions. And Jelly Roll's feet were still firmly planted on the deck.

He suddenly felt deep affection for his shipmates, in stark contrast to the loathing he felt towards the tentacled creature and that thing on the bridge. His crew was human. He'd come to respect and even love them through the long months in deep space at such close quarters. In spite of their many flaws, Jelly Roll knew that, unlike these foul creatures, they were good.

Again, Jelly Roll stared into the tentacled creature's yellow eyes. This time he was defiant and able to block out the feelers that tried to break into his mind. The creature's eyes blinked in frustration. How long before it gave up on Jelly Roll and turned its attention to the others?

Constance stirred from where she had plopped down into a sitting position. With his peripheral vision, Jelly Roll saw her reach towards a hatch on her left. Her hand brushed against the mechanical wheel. Would she be able to get enough leverage to open it without standing up? Jelly Roll didn't think so.

But they were all still alive, at least for the moment. The little mind games the creature had subjected him to had delayed things. He and Onion might be able to do something. He met Constance's eyes and tried to tell her to stay put, to not make any sudden moves which would attract the creature. She blinked once and he thought she understood.

He and Onion would do this together. The chief engineer would know how to handle himself. If there was a way to get out of this, he would be the first to find it.

But what about Captain Martin? He was gaping at the creature with the eyes of a lunatic, no longer the strong and competent man Jelly Roll remembered. Because the monster had taken his eye and broken his teeth, Jelly Roll hoped he wouldn't do something stupid.

The tentacle twitched and the triangular head rotated away. Something caught Jelly Roll's eye. Something on the wall. A fire extinguisher. Could he reach it? Could he snatch it off the wall before the creature struck?

It slithered towards Constance like a crawling snake. It raised up and floated above her. She suddenly screamed at the top of her lungs. Then she clutched her knees tightly and began to cry like a little girl. "No, no, no!" she shouted. "Stay away from me! Don't kill me like you killed the others!"

"Hey!" blurted Captain Martin. "Leave her alone! Take me! I'm the one they want!"

The tentacle whirled around like a snapping whip.

Jelly Roll stepped over and tore open the brackets holding the fire extinguisher to the bulkhead. If not to spray, maybe it was heavy enough to smash the tentacle to pieces. As he pulled it down, he saw Constance begin to turn the hatch wheel.

The tentacle made a quick, stabbing thrust at Martin. He danced out of the way like a boxer. "Ha!" he laughed. "You're not supposed to try and kill me, you're supposed to take me!"

Constance finished spinning the wheel. Now all she needed to do was stand up and open the hatch...

Martin saw what she was doing. He leaned in towards the creature and waved his arms. "Come on! I'm here! And I'm injured! I'm not that fast!" He seemed to be actually enjoying himself and Jelly Roll saw a flash of the old familiar captain.

Constance pulled on the hatch and it flew open. The tentacle whirled around, but Constance had already crawled through. Chief Onion tried to follow, but he didn't move nearly as fast. Before he could make it to the hatch, the tentacle wrapped around his legs.

"Let go of me, you sodding shit shark!" shouted Onion. It was the last thing he ever said. The creature's deadly spear-tip reared back and thrust into Onion's chest, piercing a lung and smashing ribs. Onion made a gurgling sound and collapsed to the floor like a punctured balloon.

"No!" shouted Martin. He grabbed the tentacle with both hands and held on.

Jelly Roll brandished the fire extinguisher helplessly, waiting for a chance to strike the monster. He could have followed Constance through the hatch, but he wasn't going any place. He was going to beat this thing. He and Martin. Because, looking at the punctured body on the deck, he knew Chief Onion was dead.

Martin still had both hands around the tentacle, but it was thrashing around, trying to break free. Jelly Roll swung the bulky fire extinguisher at the creature's head but missed, making a loud clang against the deck.

Martin wrapped his arms and legs around the tentacle, hanging on with all his might. It bucked like a bronco. "I told you to take me," he said. "I told you."

Jelly Roll could only watch as the two became even more entwined. Up and down and side to side they wrestled. Finally, the creature's head moved into an exposed position.

He saw his chance. He slammed the extinguisher down onto the creature's head with a liquid thud. The creature collapsed to the floor and stopped moving.

From where he was still entangled, Martin began to laugh like a maniac. "You should have just taken me!" he shouted. "I told you but you wouldn't listen!"

Martin continued to laugh uproariously. In spite of what had just happened, Jelly Roll couldn't help himself. Feeling a rush of elation, he began to laugh along with the captain. He had killed that foul, evil creature with nothing more than a fire extinguisher. He had really done it. The humans had won.

The creature snapped its head up. It looked directly at Jelly Roll with unblinking, yellow eyes. Its tentacle tightened around Martin. Before Jelly Roll could do a thing, it had pulled Martin up into the air like a rag doll. The captain made painful gasping sounds as if the tentacle was forcing the life out of him. Because it probably was.

In one more blink of an eye, the creature and Martin had both disappeared through the Bryantonium overhead, leaving Jelly Roll standing in the passageway with only Silas Onion's lifeless body to keep him company.

41

SS JOHN W CAMPBELL JR

I lived in darkness and now the darkness lives in me.

Oscar read the words that had been painted in bright orange on the ship's dark bulkhead. Molly stood beside him, reading them as well. "What do you think it means?" she asked.

"I don't know," answered Oscar. His eyes moved up and down Molly's body. Since the battle with the creatures, he found he couldn't stop gazing at her just to make sure she was alright. She looked battered and bruised but at least she was still alive. And she had killed one of those tentacle creatures with her own bare hands. She might not be a professional fighter like Oscar, but she had the strongest, feistiest will he had ever seen. His grandmother would've called her a survivor. But if she was going to continue to survive on this dark, ominous ship, she would need him.

And he would need her too.

"Someone must have painted it after those creatures first got on board," said Molly.

"I guess," answered Oscar. "It gives me the creeps."

"Me too."

She brushed her hand against his. He liked to feel her warm, human touch, especially after what had just happened.

Oscar spent another moment looking at the graffiti. "Maybe whoever wrote this simply went crazy because those things killed off the rest of the crew. And maybe they only had a moment to write it before being slaughtered too."

As he peered ahead down the winding corridor, Oscar felt a deep chill in his bones. This huge, cavernous freighter evidently held mysteries and monsters in equal portions. After their battles with the creatures, everything had gone quiet, with only the soft hum of life support. Some emergency lights were still working in this section, giving off just enough dim, blue light for his eyes to see. There was a lingering odor of blood in the air, probably from Tormod, and underneath that, something else. Something foul. But the ship seemed dead. Oscar didn't buy that for a moment. It had to be just playing dead to lure them in, the biggest possum in the solar system. Or maybe the biggest spider, waiting for them to come into its lair.

"We're a long way from the engine room, said Molly. "It's on the opposite corner of the ship. I wish we could've docked closer to the stern."

"So do I," said Oscar. "Who knows what's waiting for us down these corridors? Are you sure you want to do this?"

"I need to do this," snapped Molly. "For my father. And for Tormod. We have to find out what's going on."

Oscar sighed. "Is it worth finding something out if it gets you killed in the process? Some mysteries should stay hidden. I don't know if I can keep on protecting you."

"I did just fine without you a few minutes ago."

"Ouch," answered Oscar.

Molly ran a hand through her sweaty, red hair. "Sorry. I didn't mean that. Until a few days ago, I didn't think I needed anyone's help. Not ever. I used people, just like I used you and Tormod. I only needed you to help me get here to this ship. But along the way, something happened. I started caring about both of you. Tormod's gone, but you're still here. You can go back to the shuttle if you need to. I'll understand. But I sure could use your help."

Oscar knew she hadn't been questioning his manhood or bravery. For the first time, she had opened up to him. He hoped it would last. "Lead on, oh Great One," he muttered.

Molly managed a brief chuckle. "Okay, then. Wait here." She went around the corner into the shuttle and returned a moment later with the propane torch she had dropped during the battle. "Stay behind me. This is a huge ship, and there isn't much rhyme or reason to the layout. I studied the schematics in my father's office before I left Earth. He wouldn't let me take along any diagrams because this was a top secret mission. But I'm pretty sure that engineering is this way. That's where we need to go first."

She whirled around and led them in the opposite direction, away from the smashed body of the creature she had killed. Oscar followed closely behind.

It was clear that no one had been in this section of the ship for a very long time. The air was stale and musty, and everything was covered with dust. Occasionally, a rat scurried by and raced ahead of them. It reminded Oscar of wandering through the haunted house in Mitchellville on Halloween when he was a kid. But here, instead of older kids and adults dressed as ghosts and vampires, they were likely to meet up with real monsters.

They passed a wall panel that flickered and flashed. It was probably a radio that had shorted out a long time ago. They thought about trying to test it to see if they could raise anybody on the bridge. But the last thing they wanted to do was call attention to themselves. Whoever or whatever had sent those creatures would know Oscar and Molly were wandering around. It was best not to tell them where.

"How many crew members were on this ship?" asked Oscar.

Molly didn't answer.

"Do you think they're all dead?"

Molly stopped and Oscar almost ran into her back. She turned her head and put a finger to her lips.

"What?" whispered Oscar. His voice sounded flat and muted. The dust was much heavier here. Evidently, no one had changed the environmental filters in this section for a very long time. The foul smell was stronger now.

Molly pointed straight ahead to where another corridor crossed their path. The dust on the deck was disturbed as if someone had just passed that way. Or rather, the tracks were curved, as if something had just slithered by.

Oscar stared at those tracks. What had made them? Another tentacle? Another spider-cat? In a moment he knew. He heard an unmistakable scraping noise in the distance, softly at first and then growing steadily louder. It was one of those tentacle things, coming from the left, closing in on them from the intersecting passageway.

Molly lit her propane torch. The blue flame hissed as it filled the passageway with extra light.

"Wait!" whispered Oscar. "Let's get out of here!"

But Molly only raised the index finger of her free hand. She wasn't going to retreat. She was going to try and ambush the thing as it came around the corner. She truly did have the feistiest will he ever saw. But this was crazy. Why fight another battle when they didn't have to? There must be plenty of different ways to get to the bridge. But Molly was just being Molly, and of course, he wouldn't leave her.

Oscar stepped forward to stand at Molly's side as the propane torch hissed and sputtered.

42

SS JOHN W CAMPBELL JR

Aaron Ljungman had just found out he was part of something bigger than he could have ever imagined. Oh sure, he had pirated *Trollslända* from its hangar on Europa to go after his friend Erik Juergenson. That in itself was a pretty big thing. He didn't have the temperament of a pirate, although he did sometimes fantasize about going back in time to become a Viking. But mainly he was a mild-mannered, Swedish bureaucrat working on Europa. Or he had been just a few days ago. And now? Well, now he was part of a terrifying tale that spanned galaxies.

"How far are we from the bridge?" he asked.

"Too far," muttered Gugu. "This is one groot ship. You'll think I'm crazy coo coo but I sure could use a stort."

"A what?" Gugu had lapsed into Afrikaans slang again.

Oh," she said, reverting to a proper British accent. "I'm ever so sorry. I must take a shower or my nose will refuse to work again for the rest of my life."

Aaron gaped at her. "You want to take a shower? Now?"

"Please," she said. "My quarters are just ahead. If we are going to snotklap the alien creatures and save mankind, I must clean up first. Really, I must."

Aaron couldn't believe it. Gugu had just told him her story, about how the *Campbell* was a very special ship, and how it had found a way to go through the curtain to another galaxy. And how it had unwittingly brought back those alien creatures. It had been an incredible tale, but it was the only explanation that made sense of everything. So yes, he believed her about that. But now she wanted to stop and take a shower? He found that really hard to believe. This woman truly had him befuddled.

"I know you think I'm a mompie, but it'll only take two shakes of lion's tail."

He cleared his throat. "English, please?"

"Oh. Ever so sorry. You wait here. I'll only be a minute. I just have to do this. I couldn't do it before because there was no one to keep a lookout. But now I have you!"

And then she was off down the corridor, racing ahead in the dim blue light as if that lion was chasing her. Or maybe a gek monster.

Within a few minutes, Aaron was waiting alone in the corridor outside Gugu's quarters. Evidently, on a huge freighter like this, some of the crew had their own showers because he could hear the water running in there and Gugu singing softly. It was a lilting melody with lyrics he couldn't understand. It was probably Afrikaans, not that he would know for sure. He didn't much like being a lookout. What if one of those tentacle things came around the corner?

He rocked back and forth on his feet, hands behind his back, looking down at the deck. As a red-blooded Scandinavian male, he found himself wondering what Gugu looked like in the shower. Even through all the sweat and grime, he had been able to tell that she was an attractive woman. And now she would be naked in there, just a few meters away. He was much too polite to open the door and peek in. But maybe...

"Aaron."

The voice had come from off to his right. Startled, his head snapped up and his heart skipped a beat. He nearly turned to run, either into Gugu's quarters to warn her, or back down the corridor just to get away. But then he saw who was standing there.

Erik. Erik Juergenson.

Aaron tried to say something but his mouth went dry. He blinked, thinking it was an apparition. After all, not long ago he had thought he was back in his hometown on Earth. But the longer he stared, the more sure he became. Improbably, his friend Erik, the one he had come aboard this ship to rescue, was right there in front of him.

Finally, Aaron managed to speak. "My God, Erik, is that you?"

His friend nodded. He stood there stiffly, as if suffering from back trouble. His eyes looked pained and it appeared that he was having trouble focusing. He still wore the clothes he had on the day he'd left Europa, but they were ragged, with dark brown stains that could have been blood. His nose was running as if he had a cold. A smell emanated from him, the same foul smell that Aaron had noticed when he first boarded this ship.

Swedes are not usually demonstrative. In most situations, even after a long ordeal, they would simply shake hands at a time like this. But not today. Aaron raced forward and hugged Erik hard. "My friend," he said. "I found you at last."

Erik pulled away. "I don't know how much time I have. You have to listen to me."

"What are you talking about?" asked Aaron. "You're with us now. Me and Gugu. We'll protect you."

"Listen!" barked Erik. "They know where I am. I was only able to get away because something was happening on the view screen. They'll come for me in a few minutes. They always do."

Aaron glanced around in apprehension. The only sound he heard was the shower running in Gugu's quarters and her lilting song. "Okay," he said. "Go on."

"They got inside my brain," said Erik. "You saw that happen when I was standing up on that beam and you thought we were back in Borås. Do you remember that?"

Aaron nodded.

"So you saw those small tentacles go up through my mouth and nose. That's how they tapped into my brain. And once they did it that way, they must have found the right frequency or something, because now they can do it whenever they want."

Aaron gaped at his friend as he thought of the ramifications. "Are they inside your head now?"

Erik shook his head. "No, it's not all the time. But I know they can find me. And they'll bring me back. They like to toy with me. But that's not important now. You have to listen to me. You have to." He grabbed Aaron's arm.

"Go ahead," said Aaron. "I'm listening."

Erik took a deep breath. "When they're inside my head, sometimes it goes both ways, and I can know things about them. Important things. First, they're afraid of us. I know that's hard to believe. But we're as alien to them as they are to us. And all those things they can do? Things like going through Bryantonium and manipulating matter? That's all new to them. This whole galaxy is new.

"Usually they kill us because they're scared. We're like wild animals to them. But they know we have emotions. That really scares them. Especially strong emotions. When I feel the worst, when I want to start crying, they back off. They don't know how to deal with that."

Erik's eyes welled up with tears and Aaron wanted to hug his friend again. But Erik wasn't finished.

"They're experimenting all the time. We have to stop them before they figure out everything about us. Because then we won't have a chance. They found the missiles on this ship. And they're already playing with the molecular structure of those. Who knows what they'll be able to do against us when they finish with that?"

Erik's words were coming faster and faster. Aaron wondered if these were the ravings of a lunatic, of someone who has been pushed beyond all boundaries. Somehow he didn't think so. Looking into his friend's eyes, he still saw the same old Erik underneath the fear.

"When this ship made it through to another galaxy, it entered their territory. They had a ship of their own back there. Bigger than this one. Much bigger. It bumped up against the *Campbell* and some of them climbed onto the hull. They have built in pressure suits or something that allows them to survive in space. From the hull, they passed right through the Bryantonium and came inside. And then they started making the tentacle things. They're still making them. But that's not all."

"What?" asked Aaron. He wondered how bad this was going to get.

"That other ship saw where this ship went. So now they know where we live. And their ships are roaming around that other galaxy like cockroaches."

Erik stopped talking and his eyes rolled back, showing the whites of his eyes.

"Erik? What's wrong?"

Clearly, Erik was struggling against something. His hands clenched into fists. Then his pupils wrenched themselves back into view. He glanced left and right as if rediscovering where he was. Then he focused on Aaron.

Behind the door, Gugu turned off the shower.

"They're coming," said Erik. "They're coming right now."

43

SS JOHN W CAMPBELL JR

Oscar's stomach felt like he had just gone ten rounds while balancing on the back of a raging bull. He didn't want to get into another fight. He wanted to be done with fighting. But one of those damned tentacle monsters was coming their way down the corridor to the left. Or maybe two or three. Perhaps they'd be followed by some other abomination. He'd already done battle with the most hideous creature he'd ever seen, that Tormod thing back on the shuttle. Just thinking about that made his stomach do flip flops. But still, he stood his ground next to Molly. He would try his best to protect her, even though he'd lost his appetite for battle.

Molly held the propane torch in the air, it's flickering, amber glow lighting up her red hair and the freckles on her face and neck. Her lips were pressed into a tight line. The scraping sound in the corridor got louder as the monster approached the junction. But then it abruptly stopped. Both he and Molly stared at the empty space, waiting for the creature to come into view. But it didn't.

Molly and Oscar looked at each other. "What's it doing?" he mouthed. She shrugged.

They heard a sound that could have been a groan, or a low growl from a large dog. And then the scraping resumed this time in a lower pitch. A large tentacle slithered into view. It was moving slow as molasses, crawling through the junction in front of them. Oscar glanced over at Molly, hoping against hope that she wouldn't charge forward and try to roast the thing with her torch. Blessedly, she didn't, seemingly content to just watch for now. Her face showed not the slightest ounce of fear and Oscar felt a surge of affection. She might have grown up wealthy, the rich heiress of the Salome Corporation, but she had the spirit of a junkyard dog. When it came right down to it, he'd rather fight one of those monsters than battle against Molly.

The tentacle stopped moving again.

Oscar could only see a small portion of it because the junction was narrow, and its body stretched across all of it. He hadn't seen the triangular head yet and it was hard for him to tell which part he was looking at. Was this near the head or the tail? Or was it right in the middle? That was the trouble with tubular shaped monsters. You could never tell which part could hurt you the most. With that Tormod thing, a whole cluster of tiny heads with sharp teeth had burst right out of its middle.

Molly tapped his shoulder. He leaned close so she could whisper. "The only way to engineering is straight ahead. We've got to get past that thing. I need to know what happened to my father's engines."

Oscar stared at the tentacle. It still hadn't moved. Evidently, neither Molly's whispering nor the light from the torch had disturbed it. It was the biggest one they'd seen yet, so maybe its head was far enough down the corridor so it didn't know they were there. But if they tried to jump over it...

"There has to be another way," whispered Oscar.

Molly shook her head. "I studied the layout of this ship for years. We're way down in the bowels, the narrowest part. That thing is blocking the only route."

"Why don't we just wait for it to move on?"

"It's probably waiting for its friends. We need to go now."

Oscar sighed. Things had never been easy with Molly, not since he first tried to 'rescue' her on Ganymede. And this wouldn't be easy either. He didn't care anything about the ship's engines but he cared about Molly. A few days ago he might have left her here and taken his chances with the shuttle. But everything had changed. "No time like the present," he whispered.

Oscar took the first step forward. He would stay in front this time and protect Molly the best he could. But she had other ideas. She was much smaller and faster. Before he could even blink, she was racing past him to leap over the tentacle. "Wait!" he whispered, but she was already on the other side, motioning for him to follow.

That's when everything seemed to go into slow motion. Molly had been like a gazelle, but when Oscar tried to jump over, his left foot caught the tentacle and scraped across. He landed on his right foot and nearly fell, but Molly grabbed his arm to steady him. He looked back. The tentacle started moving immediately, its purple body rippling. Something shot into the air from his left, the triangular head. It lunged at Oscar, missing his arm by mere centimeters. It shrieked like a banshee, and the entire tentacle began to twist and shake as it turned itself around in the narrow corridor.

"Run!" shouted Molly. She took off like a shot, racing down the corridor straight ahead. Oscar followed, but he had a hard time keeping up with her as the passageway twisted and turned. Behind them, Oscar heard the scraping sound, along with several more shrieks. The creature was gaining on them, banging off the sides of the corridor like a rushing wall of water.

Incongruously, Oscar thought of the story about two hunters trying to outrun a bear. One hunter shouts that they'll never make it, while the other says, "I don't have to outrun the bear, I only have to outrun you!" Well, if this particular bear caught up with Oscar, at least Molly would get away.

He rounded one more corner and saw Molly straight ahead, standing in front of an open bulkhead door, propane torch held up like a beacon. "Go! Go! Go!" she shouted, waving her free hand. Oscar stumbled through the opening with Molly following close behind. They both turned to see the monster slither around the corner like a fireman's hose. Molly dropped her torch and pulled on the heavy, iron bulkhead door with both hands. Oscar reached out to help and they managed to slam it shut with a loud clang. The creature rammed against it from the other side, knocking Molly to the deck. Oscar put his shoulder against it, pushing it closed again. He turned the bulkhead wheel as fast as he could, three times, then four. Finally, it was secure.

Molly got to her feet and they both stared at the thick, iron door, breathing heavily. The creature continued to ram it from the other side, but this was an old freighter. The iron used in its construction was thick. Nothing would get through that door unless it had a bomb.

"We made it," said Molly. She smiled at Oscar. He liked that smile. He hoped he'd be seeing it for a long, long time.

Maybe for many years.

"Ms. Mackintosh. We were hoping you could join us," said a clear, resonant, masculine voice from behind them.

They whirled around to see an alien standing in front of the engineering console. Its body was lumpy and soft-looking, like a steaming pile of mucous. It had large, bulbous eyes that rolled around in mucous beds, above a black slash of a mouth, and a head like a gray jack-o-lantern rotting and collapsing into itself.

"Actually, Ms. Mackintosh, we were hoping for your father. But we understand he is getting up in years. So we have concluded that his offspring is an acceptable proxy."

Oscar swallowed hard as he gaped at the ghastly looking creature. The only good news was that it didn't look deadly, like the tentacled creatures or the spider-cat. It looked soft and...well...vulnerable. But the voice that had spoken was not coming from this alien creature. It was coming from just behind it, somewhere in the shadows.

44

SENATOR ALAN K SIMPSON

The Simpson's crew had been devastated. Only three of them were still alive – Jelly Roll, Constance, and Michaelson. Jelly Roll had known they were all in trouble even before one of those tentacle things murdered Onion, but now life was even more precarious. And he was supposed to be in charge. Somehow, he had to get the ship free of that damned plasma bubble created by the *Campbell's* engines. But how were they supposed to do that? They were still trapped in a black void, and the remaining crew was like flies in a spider web, waiting to be devoured. Only instead of an eight-legged spider coming to get them, it would undoubtedly be something much worse.

Somehow they had to find a way to survive. No place on the ship seemed safe from those creatures. But there had to be somewhere they could go, someplace they could defend themselves. He had to think, but his mind was spinning out of control like a spaceship with no thrusters.

Too many of his crewmates – no, not just crewmates, his friends – had been slaughtered. Onion's death was the worst, for even though he had been a crusty, foul-mouthed, old veteran, he was the one who might have been able to figure all this out. Constance was Jelly Roll's next best hope, but she had had a breakdown, going from a confident, gutsy fighter to a whimpering mess. Evidently, all the violence and death and gore had simply become too much for her. She had escaped through the hatchway during the battle. Was she in engineering now? That was most likely, for it was right down the hallway. Maybe he could get Michaelson to come down from the bridge and the three of them could run the ship from there. Was that possible? He didn't know, but it was worth a try.

Jelly Roll reached towards the combox on the wall, but when his finger got close enough to push the button, he stopped. Something was bothering him. Constance had suffered a breakdown. Or had she? He thought he knew the second-in-command very well. She'd never shown any fear in all the time he'd known her. Even after what had happened to her, it had been so out of character for her to cower on the deck and whimper like a frightened little girl. " Something is rotten in Denmark," he said to himself. " I may only be the ship's cook, but a cook can always tell when something smells foul."

He headed for engineering. If Constance really was there, she would be alone. He would talk with her and try to figure out what was up.

When he got to engineering, the bulkhead door was locked. He tried to spin it open manually, but the huge wheel refused to budge. He tried to override the lock from the keypad, but nothing happened. From the other side of the door, he heard the hum of the ship's engines, increasing in pitch. Constance was in there doing something with them. But what?

Jelly Roll found the nearest combox and called Michaelson, who was still up on the bridge. Maybe he would know what was going on. After a few heartbeats, Michaelson answered.

"I tried calling down there several times but no one answered," he said. "I heard the commotion even from up here and was afraid all of you had been killed. Then I saw the power readouts from engineering so I knew at least one of you must still be alive and kicking. But whoever is in there isn't answering."

"We lost Onion," answered Jelly Roll. "And one of those monsters dragged the captain away so he must be dead too. That leaves only three of us."

"So that must be Constance in engineering," said Michaelson. "She's having some problems down there."

"What do you mean? What's going on?"

"She's overloading the main engines. She must be giving them full juice from the ship's reactor. If she doesn't power them down soon, either the reactor or the engines are going to explode."

Jelly Roll gritted his teeth. Why would Constance be doing that? "Can't you shut them down from the bridge?"

"Nope. She's bypassed bridge control."

Jelly Roll sputtered. "Maybe she's trying to break us free from that plasma bubble. Wasn't that what Chief Onion was trying to do?"

"Yes, it is. But if that's her intention, it's not working. I double checked the readings. I was hoping all that power might free us. But nothing's happening. We're still stuck in this bubble like a fly in amber. And we're overloading. Pretty soon everything's gonna blow."

"So how do we shut down the engines?" asked Jelly Roll, wiping a hand across his sweaty forehead. His life had been so much simpler when he was only the cook.

Michaelson never showed emotion and he didn't show any now. He simply answered in his usual flat voice, "Well, if we don't figure it out, we're going to end up as space dust."

"I understand," said Jelly Roll. "But I can't get into engineering. Constance has me locked out. Can you override the bulkhead door lock from up there?"

Michaelson didn't answer for a few moments. Jelly Roll felt the acid churning in his stomach like he had just eaten salsa made with Orange Habanero chilies. Most of the ship's crew was dead. And now it seemed that Constance was trying to finish the job. Had she gone completely out of her mind?

Finally, Michaelson answered. "Yes, I should be able to override the lock. But if she damaged the mechanism from the other side, we'll have no chance. Not ever."

"Well, let's hope she hasn't thought of that."

Jelly Roll moved to the door and waited. The bulkhead lock made a loud click. Evidently, Michaelson had been able to trip it from the bridge. On any other day, Jelly Roll might have smiled at this bit of good fortune, but not today, for he didn't know what he was going to find in engineering. He turned the wheel and this time it spun freely. He pushed open the door.

He eased his considerable bulk through the opening. It was hot inside and steam filled the compartment. The Simpson was trying to save itself, but Constance must have overridden many of the safety systems. Jelly Roll squinted into the steam and at first, he couldn't see anything. But as he made his way deeper into the compartment, he could just make out Constance perched in Chief Onion's chair. She was typing commands into a keyboard. Jelly Roll crept up gingerly and placed a hand on her shoulder. She flinched and spun around.

"What are you doing?" asked Jelly Roll softly.

Constance looked up at him and her eyes flashed. "I'm going to blow us to smithereens. And you're not gonna stop me."

"But why?" asked Jelly Roll.

"Don't you know there's a Revolution going on? You're the Political Officer, the face of the Party. The same Party that killed my brother by throwing him into Coffee Prison. You know the one. It's on Luna. He lasted two weeks there before hanging himself. Have you ever seen that place? My brother never had a chance. He was the opposite of me. He wasn't a fighter. He was a writer and all he knew about was words. He posted a couple of letters on SpaceNet and the Party locked him up. So this is for him." She turned and began to type more commands into the console.

Jelly Roll gaped at her back and tried to think of something to say. He touched her shoulder again. "Lieutenant...I never knew. I'm so sorry..."

She spun around and cut off his words, practically spitting out her reply. "Sorry won't bring my brother back."

The Habaneros in Jelly Roll's stomach began to do a hat dance. He knew he had to stay calm. He'd never be able to overpower Constance. He was much older and had eaten way too many croissants with melted butter. He spoke quietly, just loud enough for her to hear. "What was your brother's name?"

Constance blinked. The question seemed to catch her off guard. "Tom. His name was Tom. Why?"

"Let's say you do this. Will it bring Tom back?"

Constance sputtered. "Of course not...but..."

"Would Tom want you to kill yourself? Because that's what you'll be doing. And would he really want you to kill me? Do you want to kill me?" Jelly Roll felt rivers of sweat running down his forehead and into his eyes. God, it was hot and humid in here. But if she went through with this, it was about to get a whole lot hotter. And then it would get cold as deep space.

"You're the Political Officer," answered Constance. "On this ship, you're the Party. And destroying you, along with one of their pet ships, would strike a blow for freedom."

Jelly Roll brought his face up close to hers. She was sweating as well. "Constance...Helen. We've been together on this ship for a long time. We've been through some terrible things lately. But you have to believe me. I don't give a flying shit about politics or the Party. I never did. I'm just a cook. Somebody has to be the P.O. and they asked me. If I had turned them down, they would have found someone else and I would have been left on shore. In case you hadn't noticed, I'm getting up in years. There aren't a lot of ships that will take me these days. So I said yes. But I never thought I'd have to do anything – I mean, how many times does a P.O. even make themselves known? Who would have thought all of this was going to happen? And now you want to destroy everything instead of fighting the aliens? Don't you want revenge for what they did to your boarding party? And to Captain Martin?"

Constance stared at him for several long moments. Jelly Roll saw a softening in her eyes. At least he hoped so. "Look," he said. "Why don't you just shut down the engines? You're a very strong woman. When you cowered during that fight, I sensed that it was just an act. I knew you'd never scream like that. It's not in your character. I've always been proud of you. You've got more guts than anyone I know. I think of you as my...I don't know...my niece or something. You wouldn't want to kill your favorite uncle would you?"

The combox on the wall next to Onion's chair flashed. He reached over and pushed the button to open the connection.

"What's going on down there?" asked Michaelson.

"Everything is under control," answered Jelly Roll. He looked into Constance's eyes. "Isn't it Lieutenant?"

"Well, it better be," answered Michaelson. "Because we're going to blow up in about three minutes."

Jelly Roll answered as firmly as he could. "Lieutenant Constance is just about to shut things down. Isn't that right?"

"But...the Revolution," sputtered Constance.

"The Revolution can wait," said Jelly Roll. "We need to survive this. All three of us."

"Two minutes and forty-five seconds," said Michaelson.

Constance fidgeted, her eyes darting back and forth liked a trapped rat. Jelly Roll gritted his teeth as the seconds counted down. He didn't know a single damned thing about ship's engines. He was just a cook.

"One minute and twenty-five seconds," said Michaelson over the combox, and now even his normally flat voice sounded agitated.

Finally, Constance hung her head. Then she reached out and typed a few commands on the keyboard. Immediately, the pitch of the engines began to lower. "Everything...under...control," she muttered.

"The engines are winding down," said Michaelson. "It will take a while for them to cool, but they're in the safe zone now. Um, thank you, Lieutenant. Now maybe we'll live to see another day. If we're lucky."

There was a long moment of silence. Finally, Constance got to her feet and faced Jelly Roll, weaving like a drunk. Along with the sweat running down her face, there were tears. These looked real, not like the crocodile ones she had shed in the corridor with the monster. "I wanted to get revenge for Tom," she said, her voice breaking.

"First let's get revenge against the monsters," answered Jelly Roll. "Then we'll see what we can do to the Party. Maybe I can even help."

She threw her arms around him in a bear hug. "I'm so sorry...Uncle."

Jelly Roll felt a rush of emotion and relief. "Uncle Jelly Roll. I like the sound of that."

Michaelson's voice interrupted them. "That's all warm and fuzzy but we've still got work to do. We have to figure out how to keep those monsters away. They can change the molecular makeup of Bryantonium. Anywhere our hull is lined with it, they can come through. But you're down in engineering where there are a few inches of iron surrounding you. So you're in the safest place on the ship right now. I'm on my way. We've got coms down there so maybe we can somehow work together with the Swedish ship and blast the *Campbell* to bits so we can get the hell out of here."

Jelly Roll hadn't quite gotten all of that because with all the adrenaline leaving his body, he had begun to tremble. But still, he allowed himself a brief smile. For whatever Michaelson had gone on about, it sounded like something he hadn't experienced for a while. It had sounded like hope.

45

SS JOHN W CAMPBELL JR

Aaron Ljungman felt his heart pound like a Swedish pulse drill boring through the ice on Europa. After all he had been through, and all the chances he had taken to get aboard this ship, he had finally found his friend Erik Juergenson. And now Erik was standing in front of him like a deflated balloon, clearly resigned to getting dragged away again by one of those creatures. Aaron heard one of them shriek as it scraped along the corridor to the left. And even worse, he heard a second one coming from further away on the right. When he first snuck aboard this ship, he had watched one of those ghastly things slither up Erik's body, forcing its tentacles into his mouth and nostrils. His own nostrils twitched as he thought of what that would feel like, and he unconsciously gagged. And now, two more were coming.

"What should I do?" pleaded Aaron, his voice breaking. But his friend didn't answer. Aaron looked around frantically. How could he help his friend, the one he had come so far to rescue? He had no weapons. He couldn't put himself between Erik and the creatures because they were coming from both directions. And he really didn't know anything about them.

But there was someone who did.

He turned and pounded on the door to Gugu's quarters. "Help!" he shouted.

The door flew open and Gugu stood tall in front of him. Naked.

"What is it?" she asked.

Aaron was caught between his innate, Swedish politeness and his sense of urgency. He yielded to both by looking down at the deck while blurting out, "I found my friend! But two of those things are coming right now!"

Aaron didn't see Gugu's expression because he was looking down at his feet. But an image had burned itself into his brain. He'd gotten a glimpse of her. Actually, he'd gotten an eyeful. She was a very attractive woman. After her shower, her dark hair was flowing long and wet onto smooth, proud shoulders. Her body was tight as if she'd been working out lately. She had full, ripe breasts. Between her legs was a patch of hair the same dark color as on her head. But above that, her stomach had a slight bulge, a tight, rounded swelling. It wasn't a pot belly, for there didn't seem to be an ounce of fat anywhere else. Did that mean that she was...

"For God's sake, look at me!" shouted Gugu.

Aaron forced his gaze upwards, again taking in the view before focusing on her eyes.

"I know I'm naak. Don't look if it bothers you! It's not going to matter if we're all dead in a few seconds!"

"Do you have a weapon in your quarters?" asked Aaron.

"No time for that."

Behind them, one of the creatures arrived at the junction with an ear-piercing shriek. As Aaron and Gugu watched helplessly, it wrapped itself around Erik's legs and small tentacles mechanically climbed up his torso and thrust themselves into his mouth and nose. Seeing this happen close up was even more ghastly than when Aaron had seen it from a distance.

"Erik!" shouted Aaron helplessly.

But Erik's eyes had already rolled back in his head. He was pulled down onto his back and dragged away down the corridor to the left. Aaron instinctively stepped forward, intending to follow, to try and do...something.

Gugu grabbed his shoulder. She pushed him back out of the way just as a second creature slithered into the junction. This one wasn't shrieking, but simply came around the corner and stopped. Gugu stood stiffly between the creature and Erik. The muscles of her naked back tensed but she didn't move. Slowly, relentlessly, a triangular head with blinking yellow eyes reared up in front of her, waving in the air like a cobra, seemingly hypnotizing Gugu. Aaron watched in fascination. How would she fight it? She had no weapon. She wasn't even wearing any clothes, and water still dripped down her bare legs from the shower.

Aaron knew he had to do something. A beautiful, naked woman was in peril. He stepped around her, intending to put himself between her and the creature, even though they were too close to each other and there wasn't enough room.

Then Gugu started crying.

At first, it was just a few sniffles. Then her bare shoulders began to shudder and soon her sobs turned into wails. Tears ran down her face like water. "My baby!" she screamed. She put her hands over the slight bulge on her stomach. "Can't you see I'm going to have a baby? If you kill me, you'll kill my baba!"

The triangular head paused. It seemed to be taken aback. Gugu bent down, moving her face inches from the yellow eyes. "I've always wanted to have a baba," said Gugu through her sobs.

By now, her sobs had increased until Aaron thought she might collapse into a heap on the deck.

He felt paralyzed. What was he supposed to do now? There was a weeping, naked woman right in front of him and the triangular head was mere inches from her face. If he moved, even in the slightest, it might strike.

But it was Gugu who struck first. Quick as a snake, her arms shot forward and wrapped her hands around the creature's purple, leathery neck. She squeezed tightly, no longer crying, as if someone had simply turned the faucet off. She grunted through clenched teeth and hung on, shaking the creature's head back and forth like a dog with a captured rabbit. Tentacles flew in all directions, some of them trying to latch onto her legs and midsection. But she squeezed even tighter, her knuckles turning white, biceps bulging. The creature let out a gurgling sound like Gugu had pushed its head under water. And then the noise stopped as Gugu ripped the head from the body.

She stood there triumphantly, holding two separate pieces in the air, black liquid dripping from the ends of each, along with random sparks coming from bits of purplish metal. The eyes in the severed head went from yellow to filmy white. Along the floor, the tangle of tentacles shuddered a few last times before going still.

"I snotklapped it," said Gugu breathlessly.

"You sure did," answered Aaron in amazement. "But how? One minute you were standing there crying and the next..."

"It's the emotion," said Gugu. "They haat that. They can't stand it. I don't think they have any emotions where they come from. Except maybe rage. They're good at that one. But as to all the rest, they don't understand them." She looked up into Aaron's eyes and smirked. "They don't have emotions where you come from either, do they?"

Aaron tried to think of a reply but simply sputtered. Then he gathered his wits and said, "But how can you just turn your emotions on and off like that?"

Gugu chuckled. "I'm a woman. Our emotions change like the wind on the savanna. Especially when we're pregnant. I don't suppose you get that. You're a man. A Swedish man at that. Emotions are a foreign language to you. But I suggest you learn them pretty soon because they just might save your life."

As Aaron stood there gaping at Gugu, standing among the wreckage of the tentacle creature, he began to feel some kind of emotion. Was lust an emotion? He didn't know for sure. But he was sure about one thing. She was beautiful. And she was still naked.

46

PARIS

It took longer to come back to reality than Martin thought it would. Afraid of what he was going to see, he refused to open his eyes. The longer he could keep his eyes shut, the longer it would take him to return to the nightmare that had been his reality in the last few days. If he did open his eyes, that meant he was still alive. He wasn't sure he wanted that.

"Captain, you can wake up now. I promise I won't let anything happen to you," said a woman's voice.

He didn't recognize the voice so he remained still. But curiosity finally got the better of him, and he cracked his eyes open. Immediately, he squinted against the murky sunshine coming through a large picture window in front of him. He heard sounds of the street coming through an open side window, and smelled freshly-baked bread. It took his eyes a few moments to adjust. Once they came into focus, he gaped at what he saw.

He was back on Earth. It wasn't the Earth he remembered, but the scene looked very familiar. Outside the big picture window, a horse pulled a cart slowly down a cobblestone street from right to left. In the small cart were loaves of bread. No, that wasn't right. They were baguettes. The driver was shouting something. Martin recognized the language. It was French. He loved the sound of that language and had tried to learn it many times but it had always been hopeless.

Martin couldn't take his eyes off of the view. He was in Paris, overlooking the capital. In the distance, smoke came from a thousand chimneys, and he saw the Eiffel Tower through a gray haze. He knew that this was Montmartre, probably one of the most famous locales in all of Paris, high on a four hundred foot hill with a breathtaking view of the sprawling city below.

He looked away from the window. He was reclining on a chaise lounge in a small artist studio. "I know this place," he said.

His grandmother had often regaled him with stories of the great French painters. All the greats had worked in Montmartre – Matisse, Degas, Toulouse-Lautrec, Picasso, Monet, and so many more. And now here he was. But that wasn't possible of course.

"You should know this place," said the woman in a firm, clear voice. She was sitting in a decorative, upholstered chair at the end of his recliner. "Much of your planet's greatest art was created right here during this time period. It's the year 1913 by Earth's calendar."

"But that can't be," said Martin with a frown. He had learned not to trust anything his mind threw at him these days.

"Don't be afraid, Captain Martin. I'm a fellow artist. I would never think of hurting you."

Martin allowed himself a chance to look her over. She was beautiful, dressed in an old-fashioned, royal blue dress, complete with frills and lace. The dress covered her body all the way from her neck to the floor. Pinned to her shoulders was a white painter's smock with multi-colored splatters that covered her knees while she sat. Her brown hair was coiffed in a bun that sat on top of her head. It wasn't a tight bun like a librarian's but fastened more loosely so it bounced charmingly as she spoke.

She got to her feet and smiled at him with impossibly white teeth. "How do you like my painting?"

Martin swung his feet down to the worn, hardwood floor and sat up. He looked around the room. If this was really an artist's studio, something was missing.

"There aren't any paintings here," he said.

The woman chuckled and the sound was pleasing, like tiny bells tinkling in a slight breeze.

"They're coming. In the meantime, there's one right there," she said, pointing to the picture window and the scene outside.

Martin glanced behind her and saw the same cart he had seen moments ago, coming from the right once again. The driver shouted just like before. Then the cart moved back out of the picture to the left.

"It's repeating itself," said Martin. Even though he had never believed he was actually in 1913 Paris, he felt an ache of disappointment knowing it was just an illusion.

"It's very real," the woman said. "But you must forgive me. I've only started the painting. Hopefully, I can complete it soon. But your work is much more important. That's why I brought you here."

Martin continued to gaze out the window at the famous painting that had come alive. "You did this? It's amazing!"

She sighed. "*Merci*. But I'm afraid it's only a poor copy of another artist. I copy from all the greats, but alas, they are only that. Copies. You are the artist here. If only I could create work such as yours."

Someone else came into the room with her head down. In her two hands, she carried a portable easel with a black canvas on it, layered in paint. She looked up and Martin gasped. It was his grandmother. He jumped to his feet. He had seen incarnations of his grandmother before since all this craziness with the *Campbell* began, so he was very leery about this one. She stared at him with no emotion as she moved closer. He looked down at her feet. They weren't human, but instead, she had small tentacles peeking out from the hem of her black dress, swirling and shuffling in an odd way, causing her to glide smoothly along the floor. Martin tried to back away, but the chaise lounge blocked him. When she reached him, she simply set the easel down and stood there.

The younger woman came over and lifted the easel. It was small and portable, the kind of device an artist could easily travel with. With a few quick turns of her head, she glided to the center of the room. Martin could see small tentacles propelling this woman as well. They were hidden by her long dress, but they occasionally peeked out as she moved.

"I don't understand any of this," said Martin. "Who are you?"

"That's a question you shouldn't ask," said the younger woman over her shoulder, as she finished setting up the easel. "The question you should ask is, 'Why this place? And why this time?'"

The grandmother smiled at him, and it seemed to make the room brighter. He wanted to say something to her, to maybe hug her. But again, he didn't trust anything that he saw here. She waved at the easel as if to say, "There ya go. Now get to work!" Then she glided out of the room on her strange, tentacled feet. Just like that.

"I brought you here to paint another masterpiece like this one," said the younger woman.

Martin felt a stab of fear when he gazed at the easel and the ominous, black canvas it contained. "But I didn't paint this," he said. "My grandmother did. It's the one I saw in the dream. And it wasn't a good dream." His fingers stung as he remembered. "Okay," he said, "I'm going to count backward from three and wake myself up. I remember being on the *Simpson*. I was dragged away by one of those tentacle things. And my teeth were missing."

Martin ran his tongue across the front of his mouth. His missing teeth had been restored. "And I was missing an eye." He brought his fingers up and waved them in front of his face, first on one side and then the other. Apparently, he now had two eyes again.

"I healed your mouth and replaced your eye," said the woman with a smile. "While you slept. It's no different than the mechanical healer on your ship. Ours is more advanced, but it still works on the same principle."

Martin used his healed eyes to examine the black shrouded canvas more closely. It was still covered in glass and he could see smudges of blood. His blood. It was beautiful and terrifying at the same time. "But I didn't paint this," he protested.

His grandmother returned. This time she carried an old basket filled with a variety of brushes and a multitude of oil paints. She set them on the chaise lounge and smiled once more. Even while standing still, the tentacles below the hem of her black dress rotated against the wood like an alien floor cleaner.

Martin grimaced. This was truly bizarre. Then the creature that was his grandmother turned and glided across the floor and back out of the room.

"I simply don't get this dream," said Martin.

"It's not a dream," said the alien. "You've been brought to a place I thought you could understand. A place that is sacred to many on your home planet. To you."

"I guess that's right," muttered Martin.

"You are in this time period so you can help prevent a war. You need to understand something important. That war is ready to begin outside of this studio. It's on your people's doorstep right now."

She paused and looked at him with shining eyes. "I brought you here to stop it before it destroys your entire race."

47

SS JOHN W CAMPBELL JR

Molly Mackintosh was a fighter. She'd been fighting since this whole thing began, first with the guards on Ganymede, then with Oscar, then with Tormod, and then with a tentacle monster. So she wasn't about to run screaming into a dark corner and collapse into a fetal position while sucking her thumb. Oh sure, a lumpy, mucous-like alien creature stood there staring at her with hideous eyes. And an unexpected voice had just spoken her name from behind the engineering console on the *Campbell*. But what else was new?

She glanced round the engine room and was impressed. She didn't only have the skill and experience to manage something as simple as a shuttle. The workings of this huge, complicated freighter were as familiar to her as the back of her hand. She'd studied diagrams of it for hours on end before heading out to this part of the solar system. She felt like her life had been preparing her for this moment. She'd traveled so many miles and fought so many battles to get here.

"We've been expecting you for a very long time," continued the voice.

Someone stepped out of the shadows.

It wasn't an alien creature like the ones she'd seen so many of lately. It was a fully-functioning human being. A man.

Molly looked closely. He hadn't been desecrated like Tormod. As far as Molly could tell, he didn't have a spider-cat implanted on his head. He had dark hair speckled with gray, and he wore a tattered green uniform. The word *Campbell* was stitched in red across the upper left side of his shirt, along with a logo in the shape of the space freighter, with the letters JWC sewn in. So he must be a member of the *Campbell's* crew. But hadn't they all been killed?

"You're Clement Mackintosh's daughter," said the man after he let Molly patiently look him over. "I'm Job Bradshaw. I've been the engineer on the *Campbell* since your father took it over. Is he still alive, Molly?"

Molly didn't answer. Instead, she said, "I thought this was a dead ship, and that the aliens killed everyone on board. So why are you still walking around?"

Bradshaw looked towards the mucous-bodied alien. Something passed between them but Molly had no idea what. Then Bradshaw met Molly's eyes. "I'm the last crew member of the *Campbell*. At least the last one that's...intact. This is one of the Explorers. At least that's the closest I can get to what they call themselves. In their language, the name sounds something like Tvex. Anyhow, I work for them now. I keep the engines running on this ship, just like always."

The alien didn't move or blink its eyes. Maybe it had no eyelids to blink.

"I think I might be able to take that thing," whispered Oscar, standing stiffly next to Molly. "It looks kinda mushy and..."

His words stopped when someone else stepped out of the shadows. This one had the same kind of green uniform as Bradshaw but that's where the similarity ended. Sitting on top of his head was another one of those spider-cat things, the same kind of abomination that had controlled Tormod. The body moved mechanically, like a puppet on a string. Molly could see the spider-cat that had impaled itself on the back of the corpse's skull. There were similarities between the spider-cat and the mucous-bodied alien. These creatures were probably like dogs. While two breeds might differ in size and shape, they were all still canines. But Molly had been trained as an engineer. It would take a biologist to figure this one out. Well, maybe they could find one after the aliens had been defeated. The thing to do now was to stay strong and not show any fear. And to rein in her emotions.

Evidently, Oscar had the same idea. "You say you're working for them," he said. "That's gotta be a crock. You're just their lap dog. How does it feel to be a slave?"

Bradshaw grimaced and his eyes flashed. "What was I suppose to do? They took over the entire ship. I couldn't hide forever. When they found me, they told me I could either work for them or end up like this guy here." He nodded towards the corpse with the spider-cat on its head. "You have no idea what they can do. They're centuries ahead of us. You have to believe me. I had no other choice. And neither do you."

A few more dead crew members came out of the shadows like a small army of marching zombies. Some of them had been very damaged. One was missing an arm. Another's head was barely attached to his shoulders. The spider-cat controlling that one must have been performing a delicate balancing act to keep it in place.

"I need your help, Molly," said Bradshaw. "If you contact your father, he can help us bring the *Campbell* home. To Earth."

Molly laughed out loud. "And if I don't, I suppose I end up like them." She waved her arm to encompass the animated corpses still coming out of the shadows.

"I'm afraid so. The Explorers would love to have your help. But if you decide not to cooperate, they'll find another way. As I said, they're centuries ahead. There's nothing we can do to stop them. Nothing."

Oscar spoke up. "You're wasting your time. She'll never cooperate. And neither will I."

Bradshaw frowned and looked over at the mucous-bodied alien. After a moment he turned back. "The Sub-Commander insists you help. One way or another. These corpses are not mindless. They retain the consciousness of their former selves."

Molly felt like she had been punched in the gut. She hadn't seen that one coming. What would it be like to be controlled by one of those spider-cat things poked into your brain, to do whatever it made you do, while still knowing what was going on? What you used to be. It would be a living hell.

She sighed and felt the defenses she'd built up all this time began to crumble. She'd come so far and had gotten so close. She'd wanted so badly to make her father proud. The information she needed was all there within the control panel, not more than ten feet away. But it might as well be across the solar system.

"The Sub-Commander insists you answer him now," said Bradshaw firmly, just as two spider-cat things appeared from the shadows, crawling along the deck. "He will only be happy when you convince your father to let us pass safely by the fleets protecting the inner-planets."

Molly knew who those two spider-cats were meant for. She glanced at Oscar, and for the first time, she saw real fear and confusion in his eyes.

"Okay, okay," she said. "I'll do what you want. I mean, what choice do I have? After all, who wants to end up like those poor suckers?" She pointed at the zombie-like crew members. "But it's not that easy to get in touch with my father. There are a lot of safeguards and I have to remember all the passwords. Let me use the Interspace com and I'll get started. I'll work as fast as I can."

Bradshaw looked back to the Sub-Commander. After a few seconds of silence, he looked back at Molly and smiled. "My master is very pleased, but he says you must begin right now. And you must hurry."

"Oh I will," said Molly, glancing down at the spider-cat creatures, looking like ghastly creations in an alien pet shop.

48

PARIS

Captain Martin stood in the center of the room and gaped at all the paintings that had suddenly appeared on the walls of the rustic Paris apartment. These were works he had admired all his life – paintings his grandmother had done with such care and skill. But this place wasn't in Spokane, Washington, where she had lived, and where he had visited so many times. It wasn't even in Paris, 1913, not really. Oh, it looked just like Paris, but that was an illusion of course. The animated scene outside the picture window was evidently one of the female alien's…paintings.

Martin knew Paris, The Eternal City. He'd been there often. A few superficial changes had taken place over the years because time marched on. But even though he hadn't been back to Earth for a while, he knew that the city would still be the same. The ancient town was deep in the marrow of his bones, no matter what century it happened to be.

So where was he really? Where had the aliens taken him? He didn't think he was still on the *Simpson*. He wasn't in Spokane and he wasn't in Paris. The only things truly familiar were the paintings. They were still close friends. If they were copies, then someone or something had done a very good job.

The paintings brought him great comfort as he ran his eyes over them. All except one. That was the large, black painting perched in front of him on an easel, the one he himself had done. Or had he? He'd cut himself on shards of glass while he was working on it and large areas were still covered with his blood. The remaining black part looked like deepest space, maybe a black hole waiting to collapse everything into it. Just standing in front felt like it would suck all the air from his lungs.

"It's beautiful....is it not?" asked the female alien, standing next to him. She ran a human-like hand in front of it, nearly touching its surface. "This might be the most alluring work of art your species has ever created, Matthew. You're a great artist. This is proof of that. It's truly a masterpiece. This is what taught us how to confine your race to the inner boundaries of your solar system. We hope it will also teach us more about your kind. It gave us the idea for the Curtain. You are incredibly skilled."

"But I don't have any skill," protested Martin. "My grandmother was the artist in my family."

"That isn't true. You were the artist, or you will be the artist. The painting will be painted or it has been painted. The past or the future. It doesn't matter. Everything is eternal, just like this city." She waved a hand to encompass the Parisian street scene outside the window.

"I don't understand," said Martin, shaking his head. "Not any of this."

"I know this must be hard for you. This is the first layer of the Dark Curtain. You probably think it's intended to keep your people confined within your solar system. And yes, it does that. But it also protects your species from those who would look inside. You wouldn't live in a house without a curtain over its windows, would you? So it's good that you painted it so long ago. Or in the future."

Martin ground his teeth in frustration. "I have no idea what you're talking about. Did I paint it in the past or will I paint it in the future? And how can it keep my species safe? You're making my head spin."

"You comprehend so little about the universe. The past and future are the same. When you paint the Dark Curtain isn't important. The canvas is in front of you right now. The first layer of the Curtain is done. Aren't those your brush marks? Now you must paint the rest."

His grandmother reappeared from a side door, carrying an easel with a glowing, white canvas already on it. She set it down next to the other easel and then retrieved the old basket of paints from the chaise lounge where she had set it before. It was just like the basket his grandmother had used so long ago. She held it out to him and he felt a twinge of nostalgia and emotion. He took it from her and glanced down. Inside were tubes of paint in all their colors, along with brushes in a variety of shapes and sizes, and a clean palette. He looked at the new, glowing canvas. It was bright white, filling the room with light. Martin found himself drawn to it. Instinctively, he took out the pallet and placed it on the easel. He couldn't help himself. Then he perused the variety of colors waiting patiently inside the basket. A dark cadmium red caught his eye, but he wanted to take his time, the way his grandmother had always done.

"You need to hurry," said the alien.

"Hurry?" asked Martin. "I thought the past and future are all the same. Why does it matter how long it takes me to do this?"

"Yes, the past and future are all the same. But something is about to happen at this point on the timeline. Something momentous. A war. You need to begin painting right now."

"I simply don't get this dream," muttered Martin. But the glowing white canvas kept drawing him in. He set the basket down onto the floor and pulled out the tube of dark cadmium red. He squeezed some onto his pallet.

"Excellent," said the alien with a smile. "Paint, Matthew. Paint."

49

SENATOR ALAN K SIMPSON

Jelly Roll looked around, pleased. Yes, terrible things had just happened. Captain Martin had been dragged off by one of those horrible tentacle creatures. The same creature had tried to force its way into Jelly Roll's mind. Constance had tried to blow them all up until Jelly Roll talked her out of it. And the rest of the crew was dead.

But there were still three of them left.

He and Constance and Michaelson were all gathered in engineering, the only compartment on the ship not surrounded by Bryantonium. Those creatures couldn't get in here. At least that's what Michaelson had said. The place stank of shorted out wires and circuits, and an overpowering smell of body odor, but at least they were safe. For now.

Jelly Roll knew he was so out of his league. Since the beginning of this voyage, he had been a simple cook. And yes, a secret Political Officer on the side, so now he was technically in charge. But that didn't matter any more. Now, they were simply three people fighting for their lives.

What was that his high school history teacher used to say? "Great events turn ordinary people into heroes." He didn't know about that, but he would try his best. The *Simpson* had been pushed around for far too long. The aliens on the *Campbell* were worse than bullies on the playground because they killed. They read minds. They could do things no human had ever seen. But in spite of all that, he had made up his mind. They would fight. If this was to be their last stand, they'd go out with weapons blazing.

Constance was busy at Chief Onion's control panel. She didn't seem to be suffering any adverse effects from what had happened and was back to her usual, tough, efficient self. From the way she pressed lights and flipped switches, she was probably close to bypassing damaged circuits and bringing all the weapons back online. He didn't know if he completely trusted her, but when it came right down to it, what choice did he have?

Michaelson manned the com, hailing the Swedish ship over and over, one frequency at a time. The com had been damaged and there was no guarantee he would get through. "*Trollslända*," he repeated yet again. "Come in, *Trollslända*. Broberg, are you there? Jenny, please respond."

If they did get through to the Swedish ship, this would be a coordinated attack, coming from two directions at once. Both ships would simultaneously throw everything they had at the *Campbell*, kind of like a gunfight in the old west...

"Uh oh!" blurted Constance. "Missile away!"

"What?" blurted Jelly Roll. "Our missile?"

"I'm afraid so. I finally got things back online and accidently fired. We just sent a Phillips' missile towards the *Campbell*."

"But you were supposed to wait until we could fire everything at once!" complained Jelly Roll.

"I know that!" shouted Constance.

They all waited. The view screen had fried, so all they could do was bide their time as Constance followed the missile's progress on the control board.

"Our missile just hit the *Campbell*," declared Constance flatly. "Dead on." Normally, at a time like that, she would have sounded elated. But this hadn't been part of the plan.

There was silence for a few moments. "Damage?" asked Jelly Roll.

"None that I can see."

"Are they firing back?"

"Not yet."

"Well," said Jelly Roll, trying to sound upbeat, "maybe we just pricked the giant's toe and he won't wake up from his nap."

"We should be so lucky," answered Constance.

But no missile came back their way from the *Campbell*. Maybe the *Simpson* had caught them napping.

Michaelson went back to hailing the Swedish ship. "*Trollslända*, are you there? Come in, *Trollslända*."

And then the Swedish ship finally replied.

"This is *Trollslända*."

The voice on the com was female and spoke with a slight Swedish accent, barely above a whisper. It sounded like she was in a small, enclosed space, which made sense because Michaelson had told them how Jenny Broberg had escaped the tentacle monsters by hiding out in a wooden sauna on the bridge.

"Are you okay, Jenny?"

"So far so good," she answered. "Those creatures couldn't get in here. I guess they don't know anything about wood. Is this Michaelson? George?"

"That's affirmative," he answered.

"How are things with you?"

"Not so good. There are only three of us left. It's probably a pipe dream but we've decided to fight. We're gonna hit that ship with everything we've got."

There was a pause. "What can I do to help?"

Michaelson kneaded his forehead with his fingers. Jelly Roll came over and stood behind him. Constance gazed on intently from her seat at the control panel.

"Can you safely get out of that sauna and over to your weapons console?" asked Michaelson.

There was another pause, this one a bit longer. "I think so. I haven't heard anything from outside of here for quite a while. Maybe they gave up on me."

"Good," declared Michaelson. "Then here's what we have in mind. If both ships can fire all their weapons at once, maybe it will overwhelm the *Campbell*. I know our firepower hasn't done much until now, but we've never tried a concentrated attack, especially from two directions. Do you have a good supply of weapons there?"

This time there was an even longer pause. "Affirmative. In fact..."

Michaelson waited. "In fact what?"

Broberg sighed. "Well, this is against every protocol in Swedish Space Fleet. But under the circumstances, I guess I don't have a choice. We've got a brand new weapon on board. Top secret. We tried firing it once at the *Campbell*. Or rather, the *Campbell* made us fire it. It gave us quite a show. At first it looked like it was going to do real damage. It's kind of like a green net that encircles the other ship, trying to crush it I think. But after a few minutes, the *Campbell* spit it out. Then it healed the damage the net had made. But that took a little while."

Jelly Roll felt a rush of elation. He glanced over at Constance and their eyes met. Hers were sparkling.

"That's fantastic," said Michaelson. "Do you think you can engage it again?"

"Affirmative."

"Then why don't you, carefully, get out of that sauna and..."

Boom!

Something hit the *Simpson* and the deck shook beneath Jelly Roll's feet.

"Uh oh," said Constance for the second time in the past ten minutes. "I think the giant just woke up."

Boom!

This time the concussion was stronger.

Boom!

The *Simpson* shook for a third time, like a dog coming out from under a sprinkler. The concussion knocked Jelly Roll's feet out from under him and he fell to the deck. He landed on his elbow and gave a cry when it hit the metal floor.

"They just hit us with their secondary armaments," said Constance, starting intently at the control panel. "Small concussion bombs. But they seem to have a bunch of them. Here comes about a dozen more."

This time, Jelly Roll actually bounced into the air from where he had fallen to the deck. After another series of concussions, he managed to get to his feet, massaging his injured elbow. "Status," he said, suddenly feeling like the acting captain he was supposed to be. After all, they had just started a war.

"We're still intact," said Constance through clenched teeth. Those bombs are for close-in fights. They haven't penetrated our hull. Maybe they're just feeling us out. Toying with us."

"Very good," answered Jelly Roll. In spite of the tension, he suddenly felt relaxed. Constance was back to her old self, reacting smoothly and professionally. Michaelson had resumed talking to the woman on the Swedish ship. His voice was calm. If this was going to be a last stand, at least Jelly Roll knew he had two of the very best at his side.

He flexed and un-flexed his arm. This ship was like his injured elbow. It might be bruised, but it still had some life left in it. "How close are we to having everything ready to fire at once?" he asked.

"Very close," answered Constance.

Jelly Roll strolled over to Michaelson and eavesdropped on his conversation with the Swedish ship. Broberg was speaking. "Okay, I'm out of the sauna now and talking to you from the bridge. I don't see any of those creatures, thank Odin."

"Good," answered Michaelson tersely. "How long before you're ready to fire that new weapon?"

"Five minutes max. I'm not actually a captain. I guess you could say

I'm a pirate. And second in command at that. But I watched Aaron do it before."

"Tell us the exact moment you're ready. The exact moment. We have to coordinate this perfectly if we're gonna have any chance at all." Michaelson's voice rose in pitch as his calm demeanor finally gave way to excitement.

"Affirmative," answered Broberg.

The seconds ticked away. Jelly Roll rubbed his hands together. "We're gonna throw the biggest, fattest punch since the Colonization Wars at the bastards. And those bullies are finally gonna get what they deserve."

50

SS JOHN W CAMPBELL JR

Gugu's pace had picked up after the sudden explosion outside the ship, the one that had thrown them both onto the deck.

"Someone's firing on the *Campbell*! "she exclaimed. "That means someone is still alive out there. And they're fighting back!"

The first thing Aaron thought of was *Trollslända*. Was that the ship that had fired? He could only hope because that would mean Jenny Broberg was still alive. Several minutes later they heard rumbling sounds from somewhere far ahead and below. "That's the weapons room," said Gugu quickly. "The aliens are firing back. We have to get down there and try to stop them. Create a little havoc behind the lines."

Aaron struggled to keep up as they raced around yet another corner in yet another corridor. Any sense of direction he had was long gone. After the fight outside Gugu's quarters, in which she had first cried like a baby and then snotklapped the alien tentacle-creature, he'd been following her blindly. Well, not blindly. Gugu was still naked.

It's remarkable that humans can get used to anything in a very short time. At first, when Gugu had stood naked and dripping in front of him after her shower, Aaron had been completely flummoxed. She was an attractive woman after all. Actually, once out of her grimy, masculine ship's fatigues, she was quite a babe. But now, after ten minutes or so of wandering down corridors, he had actually become accustomed to her gleaming, naked body, bluish in the flickering safety lights of the *Campbell*. It almost seemed normal to be strolling along beside a naked woman on a spaceship somewhere in a black void near Europa. Okay, he still occasionally found himself staring at her backside, or catching up so he could glance sideways at her firm breasts.

She held out her arm and stopped him. He felt his face flush as he realized that he'd been gaping at her like a horny teenager.

"Sorry," he mumbled.

"Never mind that," she muttered. "We're here. The weapons room."

A series of loud clicks emanated from just around the next corner, followed by rumblings that they could feel beneath their feet, much stronger now.

"Concussion bombs," said Gugu. "The *Campbell* is firing back. Probably trying to feel out whoever attacked this ship. They won't do much damage with those though. But I'm sure they have something much nastier planned for all of us."

"All of us?" asked Aaron. "You mean me and you and Erik?"

She shook her head and waved her arms as if to encompass the entire solar system. "All of us, as in people. If this ship gets loose in our solar system, humanity will be up a dragon blood tree."

Aaron felt a fluttering in his stomach and this time it wasn't from looking at her naked body. He'd come on board this ship to rescue his friend Erik Juergenson. But now he was part of something much bigger than he had ever imagined.

"Wait here," said Gugu. "They're probably firing remotely from the bridge. But the weapons room might be guarded. I'll let you know if it's clear. Be ready to fight. And don't forget to use your emotions if you have to."

She raced ahead and around the corner, leaving Aaron standing alone once more, the way he had been alone outside her quarters. By now the fluttering in his stomach had turned into a churning wave. Emotions? Yes, Gugu crying like a little girl had caused the tentacle monster to pause in confusion. But how was he supposed to pull off something like that? He hadn't cried since he was a little boy sitting on his mormor's lap. Not once. Yes, he did have emotions. They were there all right. But they were buried deep, like water beneath the ice on Europa. And he didn't know if he could ever produce the drill that would set them free.

It turned out that, at least for now, he wouldn't have to. Gugu came back around the corner and motioned to him. "All clear," she said.

Aaron breathed a sigh of relief and followed. She led him into a large room, brightly lit by harsh, white lights in the overhead. Aaron squinted against the glare. Now he could see every blemish on Gugu's naked body, not that there were many.

She seemed oblivious to the clicks of concussion bombs firing from ports all around them. Instead, she began to point out the various weapons systems in different sections of the huge room, using terms that he mostly didn't understand. She was the proprietor of a candy store, proudly showing off her wares. "Of course, the *Campbell* was originally just a freighter, with basic weapons for self-defense. But Mackintosh had them put in lots of other goodies for when we headed out through the Curtain. He put in the latest generation of Phillips' missiles. He changed the ion accelerators so they would..."

She stopped midsentence. Aaron hadn't been paying the slightest attention to what she was saying. The bright lights had him staring once again at her naked body.

"Men," muttered Gugu. She walked over and grabbed a green fatigue jacket that was hanging on a peg and tossed it on. It was too big for her and hung down to the tops of her thighs. But it covered what Aaron had been staring at. She clucked and shook her head, glaring at him with flashing eyes. "Is that mo' better? Are you going to be able to concentrate now so you can actually help me?"

He nodded meekly, feeling like a schoolboy who has just been scolded for something he has no control over.

"Like I was saying," she continued as she walked towards the far wall, "Mackintosh boosted the ion accelerators on the Phillips' missiles, which are behind this wall." She pushed a button and a large bank of Bryantonium panels began to slide smoothly back with a soft hum. "That way, their acceleration would greatly increase, while their mass..."

"My God," exclaimed Gugu, as the panels fully slid back to reveal what was waiting there.

Aaron had seen Phillips' Missiles before, but none like these.

"Did Mackintosh do that?" sputtered Aaron.

"Not in a million years," answered Gugu. "He had some alterations made but nothing like this.

This is simply... *uitheemse*."

"What?"

"Alien. And I think they're alive."

The missiles were stacked like cordwood in their usual trays. They retained the same, basic cylindrical shape of missiles since the early days of ICBM's, minus the fins, which weren't necessary in space. But instead of the usual dark brown covering of most Phillips' Missiles, these had a dull purplish tint. That in itself wasn't remarkable or ominous. But the surfaces of these missiles were infused with slithering, purple tentacles, phasing in and out as they watched. They reminded Aaron of those deadly creatures in the corridors, one stacked on top of the other, waiting to break loose and wreak havoc on anything that got in their way.

"We have to do something," said Gugu. "We need to disarm these things." She reached out her hand.

"No!" shouted Aaron, his voice ringing in the now quiet room. The concussion bombs had ceased firing. "Don't touch those!"

Gugu flinched and pulled her hand away. "Of course. What was I thinking? But we have to do something before they decide to fire these."

"Isn't there a way to control them from down here?" asked Aaron.

"Well," muttered Gugu thoughtfully, "there's an old auxiliary control panel in that far corner. It hasn't been used in a long time. But maybe I can reconnect it."

Aaron gaped at the sinister-looking missiles. The entire bay resembled a nest of writhing snakes.

"That would be a very good idea," he said.

51

SS JOHN W CAMPBELL JR

Erik Juergenson wished he was dead. He didn't know if there was a Heaven or Hell or simply oblivion. But anything had to be better than this. This was slavery of the worst kind.

One of those tentacle things had forced its way into his mouth and nostrils again and dragged him away from his friend Aaron. It always felt like rough, quick sandpaper when they entered his sinuses and brain. And now, here he was again, deposited back in a far corner of the bridge like a rag doll, exhausted and sick and gagging.

He desperately tried to shut off his thoughts to them, to block himself away where they couldn't go. Maybe that place was death. But no, he'd seen what happened to the crew members who were supposed to be dead. They weren't. Yes, he himself was at the mercy of those infernal, slithering tentacles, but at least he still had some semblance of free will. He didn't have a hideous, spider-cat thing impaled on the top of his head, controlling his every move.

No, he wouldn't kill himself, only to be brought back to life as a zombie. Instead, he would continue to resist. One way or another.

He gazed around the bridge. Those two mucous creatures were staring up at the view screen on the wall. Once again, it showed the American ship. There were no stars behind it. Evidently, the *Campbell* still had them trapped in the black bubble, with *Trollslända* undoubtedly somewhere just off the screen.

Ten minutes before, he'd seen a bright flash from the American ship. Seconds later an explosion had followed. The deck of the *Campbell*'s bridge lurched and he had felt a rush of elation. Someone was still alive on one of the other ships.

The aliens had waved their stick arms like branches in a strong wind, pressing lights on the consoles in front of them. A few minutes later, Erik had heard a series of clicking and humming sounds from somewhere far below deck. On the view screen, a series of bright yellow streaks moved towards the American ship. Flashes burst from its hull. It seemed to shudder for a moment, but then stabilized.

Erik had gaped at the screen, expecting the American ship to fire back. But it hadn't.

Now he could only breathe hard and wait, his poor, damaged throat feeling like a hunk of raw meat. He watched the American ship for any sign of action, like an observer looking over the hill with binoculars after the first exchange of a huge battle.

And then the American ship finally fired back. With a vengeance. This wasn't simply a few missiles or bombs heading towards the *Campbell*. Instead, the American vessel seemed to explode into a cascade of flame. Projectiles hurtled out from every possible weapons port, growing larger by the second. All of them hit the *Campbell* at once, causing the view screen to flash bright orange. The deck beneath Erik bucked like a bronco in an American western on SpaceNet. A cascade of explosions sounded in an ear-piercing roar. Erik nearly laughed out loud. The Americans were hitting the *Campbell* with everything they had!

He wanted to rise up and cheer, the way he would have at a fotboll game back home. But that would have been like trying to stand up in a hurricane as the *Campbell* continued to take damage. Lots of it. Objects flew around the bridge as the alien creatures desperately hung onto their consoles. The view on the screen changed from bright orange to black.

And then, there it was.

Trollslända. Hanging in space like a diamond-studded dragonfly.

This time Erik did let out a ragged cheer and pump his fist. That was the glittering pride of Swedish Space Fleet right there. And since the view screen had shifted, it probably meant that *Trollslända* was getting ready to fire. And then it did.

Something blinked away from the hull of the Swedish warship. Erik Juergenson had seen that weapon before, the one that would morph into a ship-sized, green spider web. It's hadn't destroyed the *Campbell* before, but this time, maybe it would. After all the damage it had just taken from the American ship, its defenses had to be almost gone.

When the green web engulfed the view screen, the *Campbell* began to rock and shake. The artificial gravity switched off and Erik flew into the air, banging off the overhead and walls. It felt like he was in a giant blender with a cockeyed gear. The walls emitted a series of clicks as the hull groaned inward on itself. Erik shouted defiance with the ragged remains of his voice. Whatever the strange new weapon was that had come from *Trollslända*, it was about to crush the *Campbell* like a tin can. But that was perfectly fine with him. If he was going to be ground into space dust, then he would take those alien bastards with him.

52

SS JOHN W CAMPBELL JR

Aaron Ljungman felt like he was on an ocean liner in a hurricane. A deafening series of explosions rocked the *Campbell* from all sides. The artificial gravity in the weapons room phased out as the bright lights in the overhead flashed like strobes. He and Gugu were tossed around like popcorn, bouncing off walls and deck and overhead. Aaron managed to grab onto the overhead grate with one hand, narrowly avoiding being thrown into the bank of Phillips' missiles. Gugu flew by him and he just managed to grab her hand and hang on. They stayed like that, hanging precariously, with the overhead above them one moment, below them the next. It was impossible to tell which way was up. It had been a long time since Aaron had experienced zero-grav and his stomach began to churn. Beneath him, or maybe above him, Gugu shouted, "Feels like they're throwing everything they got at the *Campbell*! I think this whole ship is gonna get snotklapped!"

All around them, the outside hull creaked and groaned as if the ship was being squashed by a giant hand. The air pressure increased.

"I think we're gonna die," shouted Aaron through clenched teeth.

"I hope so! Cause then those *bliksems* die too!"

Aaron tried to digest this information. Did he really want to die? He'd survived a bunch of scary things since coming on board this cursed ship. Would it just end here in the next few moments?

Evidently not.

The pressure on the hull ceased suddenly. The sound of explosions wound down. He heard a deep hum as the artificial gravity kicked back in. He found himself hanging from the overhead with one hand, while still holding onto Gugu with the other. His upper hand chafed on the metal above because he was holding the weight of both he and Gugu. He looked down. Her feet were just a few inches off the deck.

She looked up at him. "You can let me go now."

He did as he was told, and Gugu dropped lightly onto the deck, leaving him to dangle six feet up.

Gugu reached up her hands. "Let go. I'll catch you."

Aaron swallowed hard. In spite of all his years in space, he'd never much cared for heights.

"Come on! I'll catch you!" she repeated.

He gritted his teeth and let go. Sure enough, she caught him smoothly under his armpits and eased him down. It was the first time he had actually been in close contact with her body, even though it was through the rough surface of her fatigue jacket.

She pushed him away. "We have work to do."

Abashed, Aaron kept his distance. They both stood there panting for a minute or so, trying to get their bearings. Things were scattered all around the deck. It looked like the room had just been through an ice tornado on Europa.

"We're still alive," muttered Gugu. "I always knew the *Campbell* was tough as an old rhino, but I'm amazed it made it through that."

"Me too," replied Aaron, not sure if he was happy or not. "What now?"

"I imagine the *Campbell* is going to fire back. Which means..."

They both looked over at the Phillips' missiles, slithering ominously in the harsh glare of the overhead lights.

53

SS JOHN W CAMPBELL JR

Molly had been punching in numbers on the Interspace com when the first, small explosion hit, setting things buzzing in the engineering room. Sub-Commander Bradshaw had glanced back and forth to the mucous-bodied alien, his eyes flashing, while the alien waved its stick arms in the air. Clearly, they were having some sort of frenzied conversation through telepathy. But then Bradshaw had folded his hands in front of him and said to Molly, "That was nothing. Just a pin prick from one of the Earth ships. The pilots on the bridge are preparing a response. Please continue."

But after the *Campbell* fired back, the real cataclysm had begun. Deafening explosions rocked the engineering room. The hull had made groaning sounds and the artificial gravity went out. Molly found herself flying around the room with her arms pin-wheeling. Sub-Commander Bradshaw and Oscar were tossed about as well, along with a host of zombie-like crew members. It was like a ghastly amusement park ride, or maybe a drug-induced hallucination. Strangely, the mucous-bodied alien didn't seem to be affected by the loss of gravity, and simply stood firmly on the deck in the center of the maelstrom.

When things finally settled down and the gravity kicked back in, Molly fell to the deck and breathed a sigh of relief. She had thought she was going to be smashed against a wall, but her body was still intact.

Something was beneath her.

It was fairly small, about the size of a cocker spaniel. And it was moving. With horror, she realized she had landed on top of one of the spider-cat things. She shrieked and leaped to her feet. The creature reared up and moved towards her. She kicked at it in revulsion. Immediately, Oscar was beside her. He pushed her away and reached down. He grabbed the spider-cat thing with his left hand and held it into the air. He began to pummel it with his right, using quick jabs, savagely beating it while grunting loudly. The spider-cat dripped venom onto his left hand from its gaping mouth and hissed like an alley cat. But the creature was no match for Oscar Gunn. Soon it began to go limp. Finally, Oscar threw it into the corner of the room, where it smacked against the wall and slid down onto the deck, oozing black blood.

And then it was finally quiet in the engineering room, which now looked like a war zone, with objects scattered all across the deck. Bradshaw got to his feet and stood beside the alien Sub-Commander. Most of the zombie-like crew members, all with spider-cats implanted in their heads, were standing around and shuffling their feet, at least the ones that had feet. The zombie whose head had been hanging by a thread had actually lost it, and its separated body had collapsed to the floor. The spider cat that had been controlling it crawled away from the disembodied head and moved randomly around the deck as if looking for a new host."

The attack failed," said Bradshaw with a smile. "Now it's our turns. The Earth ships will have no defense against what's coming their way. You will soon be completely alone. So you have no choice but to contact your father." He pointed at the remaining spider cat, which was still wandering around the deck like a windup toy. "Then again, maybe we should just implant that one onto you and save ourselves some trouble. Or, if your friend kills it, we have more. Lots more."

Several more spider-cats entered the room from the corridor. They made three-quarters of a ring around Molly and Oscar, waving their spider legs and hissing. The implication was loud and clear. The only way for them to go was back over to the Interspace com.

Molly felt her heart sink, for now, she really did have no other choice. She had stalled for as long as she could. She glanced over at Oscar. God, he was a beautiful man. But how beautiful would he be with a spider-cat sticking out of his head?

"Whatever happens, you need to kill me before you let one of them latch onto me," she whispered.

"I'll find a way to kill us both," he answered.

She let herself be herded to the com box. She glanced longingly at the engineering control panel, lights blinking like a Christmas tree, ten feet away. If she could somehow access that, there was one last, desperate thing she could do. But with the way they were surrounded, the beckoning panel might as well have been on Ganymede.

54

SS JOHN W CAMPBELL JR

Much to Erik's dismay, *Trollslända* hadn't fired again. And there was no sign of additional fire from the American ship. Instead, the aliens on the bridge gathered themselves, their mucous-like bodies shuddering once or twice before settling back in. One of them pushed a light on the console with its pink, lily-pad finger. Erik watched in horror as he realized what was happening. The Campbell was going to fire back.

As he watched on the view screen, a red streak raced towards *Trollslända*. It looked like a Phillips' missile, but then it spread out, just like the Swedish weapon had done. But this one blossomed into tentacles. They grew and grew until they dwarfed *Trollslända*, making it look like a child's toy. The tentacles writhed and swirled, finally latching onto the hull of the beautiful Swedish warship. Even on the view screen, Erik could see them seek out entry ports, the way tentacles had sought out Erik's mouth and nostrils. He could only imagine the nightmare that must be going on aboard *Trollslända* as the massive, slithering abominations found their way inside, crawling down every corridor, filling every space.

Soon *Trollslända* was completely covered by a jumbled, writhing mass. It pulsed and squirmed, looking like an octopus pulverizing its prey, while the hapless creature still alive in its gullet struggled to get out.

The pulsing slowed.

And then it stopped.

The tentacles went slack and fell away, fading into bits of purple that scattered into space like dust after an explosion, leaving nothing in their wake. Nothing at all.

Trollslända had simply ceased to exist.

Erik hung his head and tears came to his eyes. He felt a deep, deep despair, the worst of his life.

But that only lasted for a moment.

His sadness and shock were replaced by something else, something primal that began to build behind his eyes like a smoldering piece of charcoal. He had had enough of these aliens, enough of feeling helpless, enough of being dragged up and down corridors, body and mind violated.

He struggled to his feet and held his weary head high. Slowly and deliberately, he limped towards the creatures that perched in front of their consoles like steaming piles of mucous.

Erik Juergenson reached out one trembling hand and then the other.

In a voice like gravel, he said what he used to say while piloting his ship alongside another to dock, like talking to a lover he was getting ready to seduce.

"Come to me, my little Flickväns."

55

SS JOHN W CAMPBELL JR

Aaron and Gugu had both whirled around when they heard the loud, metallic click from somewhere in the overhead. They'd been trying to reconnect the old auxiliary control panel. Instead, they'd ended up watching in dismay as a panel below the slithering missiles hummed open. The bottom missile had dropped down with the panel closing behind it, with the rest of missiles clicking down a notch.

They had heard the missile fire.

"Kak!" Gugu had exclaimed. "We're too late!" She'd raced over to the far wall and pushed a button. A small section of wall rotated 180 degrees to reveal a small view screen. It had given them front row seats to something truly terrible.

"It's *Trollslända*!" Erik had exclaimed when the glittering, elegant ship came into view. "It's still out there!"

But his elation had been short-lived. When the red streak on the view screen spread out into monstrous tentacles and engulfed the Swedish ship, he had screamed. But for all the effect it had, it was like screaming into empty space.

And now, *Trollslända* was gone.

"*Min* Gud," said Aaron, reverting to his native Swedish. "Broberg. Jenny. *Min* Gud." The emotions he had so successfully managed to bury all these years began to bubble up and tears came to his eyes.

"No time for that now," grunted Gugu. "Look at the view screen."

The scene had rotated. There in the blackness was another space ship. "I think it's American," said Gugu. "And I think they're next."

Both of them glanced over at the modified Phillips' missiles, stacked like cordwood in their bay. Aaron felt his own grief pushed into the background. Someone was aboard that American ship. Someone human. And they were about to be swallowed up by the most frightening weapon any human had ever seen.

"Quick!" shouted Gugu. "Pick up anything you can find and toss it into those missiles. Maybe we can jam them until I get the auxiliary panel working."

Aaron began to do just that, starting with an overturned chair. It was amazing how many things had broken loose during the zero-grav chaos. And he threw or jammed most of them into the missile bay. The tentacles infused in the surfaces of the missiles phased in and out as the objects piled up. Some of the objects intermingled, while others stuck out at odd angles.

At that moment, they heard another loud, metallic click from the overhead. "Uh oh," said Aaron.

They heard the panel slide open again. Both he and Gugu watched as the bottom missile shifted. But it didn't drop down. Instead, it made a soft, repetitive, grinding noise, like from a gear knocked out of alignment.

"That worked," muttered Gugu. "But who knows for how long? I'm sure they'll send an attack dog down here to clear things out so they can fire another missile."

An ear-piercing shriek came from the level above, along with a faint scraping noise. "That was fast," said Gugu. "I need some time to get this panel working. You're going to have to go out there and stop it by yourself. Use your emotions. Grief would be good."

Aaron swallowed hard. Of course, he would have to do this. There was no one else. So he headed into the corridor alone.

56

PARIS

Martin had seen the Eiffel Tower through the large studio window as he flew into the air. Then the entire Paris street scene flickered out. He hated to see it go. Yes, he knew he was not really in Paris, but the illusion had brought joy to his heart. He'd even been able to smell the baguettes from a nearby bakery and cigarette smoke coming through the window. But now it was all gone. Things had flown everywhere, bouncing off walls and floors. That told him he was somewhere on a spaceship with the artificial gravity out.

When the gravity switched back on, he fell to the floor and pulled himself to his feet. The Paris studio apartment was gone. His grandmother's paintings on the wall were gone. He was in a room on a space ship. It wasn't his ship, but, given everything that had happened, he knew what ship it must be.

The *John W Campbell Jr.*

Somehow, they'd gotten him here from the Simpson and he was their prisoner. And they'd made him think he was in Paris. But his own ship was undoubtedly still out there. Who else would have fired on this ship and caused the artificial gravity to go out? He was proud of his crew, and the fact that they were still fighting back, even without him there.

But he was still the captain.

In the middle of the room sat two canvases, the black one he had painted in the AutoMed, and the white, glowing canvas he had been working on when all the concussions and explosions had come. The female alien stood by them, looking in his direction. He'd already painted a cadmium red circle in the middle of the white canvas. It reminded Martin of Jupiter's Eye, its Great Red Spot, which was actually a hurricane-like storm that had lasted over four hundred years, a storm three times the size of Earth. At least that's what the scientists said. And Martin had seen it up close. So why had he painted it? For that matter, why had he painted the original canvas with black paint and his own red blood? None of it had ever made sense to him.

"The attack is over," said the alien female. "You were not in time to prevent it from happening, but if you finish your new painting now, it will not take place at all. So please continue. You still have a chance to follow in your grandmother's footsteps."

Martin saw his grandmother standing off to the side, a calm, serene look on her weathered face. But, like before, this grandmother had tentacles whirling below the hem of her dress.

"You've been playing me all this time," he said. "That is not my grandmother. She died thirty years ago in Spokane, Washington of Fanatia's Disease."

Martin felt emotion well up, even after all this time. His grandmother's death had hurt him deeply, for he had loved her more than any other woman, more than even his own mother. And now this...this...abomination was standing here on tentacled legs, pretending to be her.

He walked up to the white, glowing canvas and grabbed the palette knife perched on the easel.

"I'm glad you're ready to begin again," said the female alien.

"No," answered Martin. "I'm going to end this."

He plunged the palette knife into his grandmother's chest. She made a high-pitched, shrieking sound, like a mountain lion crying in the woods. He plunged the knife in again and again, causing bright, red blood to gush out of her chest and mouth, turning her shrieks into gurgles. The tentacles below her dress slowed, and then finally stopped whirling altogether. She toppled onto the floor and was still.

"I just killed my grandmother," muttered Martin.

He turned back to the female alien, the one who had been goading him all this time, controlling him, playing him like a puppet. "Now it's your turn," he said, holding up the dripping knife.

"But wait!" she sputtered. "You need to finish your painting! It's the only way to stop what's..."

He plunged the knife into her left eye. Clear liquid gushed out, along with bright, red blood. "An eye for an eye," he said in triumph. "That's what my grandmother taught me. My real grandmother."

Martin thought how strange it was that the aliens would have the same color blood as his own. It was an odd thing to notice at a time like this.

There was something else he should have noticed. The alien reached into the pocket of her dress and produced a pistol. She pressed it firmly against his chest and fired.

Martin gasped in surprise as the bullet tore through him. He let go of the knife and watched it hang from the alien's eye socket, quivering like an arrow in a target. She fired two more times and Martin felt his eyes go dark.

This time, they would stay dark forever.

The alien gasped and pulled the knife from her eye. She threw it across the room. Her biology was not the same as humans, so losing one eye meant that she was now completely blind. At least until someone could fix her up. But at least she'd had the foresight to hide the pistol in her dress. Human fashions were useful for that sort of thing. And if you were going to simulate a human environment, it was good to have a human weapon.

What now? The faithless human had barely begun the second painting. The first one had helped them immensely by creating the Dark Curtain. Who knows what the second one would have done? It might have destroyed the humans completely. But now she'd have to do things the hard way. And the battle was already underway.

She shed her human form like a snake shedding its skin. It didn't take long. But she was still blind. She'd have to feel her way out of this room, because in her species, the telepathy part of the brain is located behind the left eye, and the human had thrust the knife in deep. But once she found her way to engineering, Bradshaw or the Sub-Commander could be her eyes.

Even though humans had built this ship, she was now the captain.

And she would get her revenge.

57

SS JOHN W CAMPBELL JR

Erik Juergenson said the words again. "Come to me, my little Flickväns."

But the two mucous-bodied aliens seemed oblivious. They were still staring up at the view screen with their huge, unblinking eyes, rolling in beds of mucous. The fat, misshapen bodies were wobbling like gelatin. That was the first time Erik had ever seen that. Were they laughing at what they'd just done to *Trollslända*? Probably. If these ghastly alien creatures had any type of feelings at all. But the thought of them laughing made Erik all the angrier, and every bit of his rage, frustration, and shame finally bubbled over like an exploding volcano.

He leaped into the air with both trembling hands out in front of him. He landed on one of the aliens from behind, wrapping his hands around its neck as the creature's chair spun around and dumped him sideways onto the deck. Erik turned it onto its back and climbed on. It was like climbing onto a pile of firm mucous, or maybe wet, clammy clay. The creature opened up the gaping mouth that was set just beneath its eyes. The voice that came out was low and metallic, just like it had been the first time Erik heard it. But this time Erik detected something else. Was it fear?

"What are you doing?" it said. "We control you. We can make you suffer even more." The voice came from both the creature's mouth and from inside Erik's own head. It sounded like the voice of God in there, and Erik flinched momentarily. But then his anger returned.

"Shut up!" he sputtered. "I'm sick and tired of this! Now it's time for you to suffer. But not for long."

He squeezed the creature's neck. It felt like he was rolling Play Dough as a kid, except that this glob of material had a pulse beneath its surface, growing more rapid as he squeezed. The creature's wide eyes grew wider, rolling frantically back and forth within their mucous beds. He felt stick arms on his shoulders and then clasping, lily-pad fingers as the creature tried to push him off. But the alien wasn't nearly strong enough. Of course not. With their mind control abilities and tentacle creatures to protect them, why would they need physical strength? But there were no tentacle monsters here now. Not yet. But then he heard them coming from far down the corridor. It sounded like a lot of them.

Erik squeezed harder. They'd kill him for sure this time. But he'd take at least one of these bastards with him. He felt the pulse in the creature's neck slow. It's gaping mouth opened and closed, thick, mushy lips flapping like a bass on the beach. But Erik continued to squeeze. Finally, his fingers burst through the putty-like skin. Red liquid gushed out onto Erik's face and into his eyes, momentarily blinding him. But he held on. "Die, you bastard!" he shouted.

The clenching fingers of his hands met amidst a squishing sound like a rotten pumpkin hitting the sidewalk. Through a film of the creatures blood, he saw that he had decapitated it. With his bare hands.

He got to his feet and wiped his eyes with the sleeve of his filthy pilot's shirt, his hands dripping blood. The other mucous-bodied alien was frantically punching lights on the control panel with its lily-pad finger. On the view screen above, the American ship was still hanging in the black void. But Erik knew that it probably wouldn't be there for long. Unless he could do something.

Behind him, he heard the shriek of tentacle monsters, very close now. The lights on the control panel cycled in a circle. In the center of that circle was a single, purple light. It began to blink slowly as the other lights went out. The creature raised its hand.

"No!" shouted Erik.

He grabbed the fallen chair and smashed it into the creature's midsection, knocking it off its seat with a dull, liquid thud before it could push any more buttons. Behind him, a cluster of tentacle monsters shrieked like the trumpets of Armageddon. He only had a second or two at best.

Erik raised the chair over his head and brought it down onto the control panel as hard as he could. The plastisteel surface cracked, and a few sparks flew. The purple light went dark. Erik smelled hot wires. He hoped it would be enough.

The tentacle creatures closed in a like a pack of wolves. This time they didn't crawl up Erik's nose or mouth. They simply wrapped around his body and dragged him down onto his back. He looked up as they raised their triangle heads. Just before they struck, he had time to say one last thing.

"Come to me, my little Flickväns."

58

SS JOHN W CAMPBELL JR

Something was happening in engineering and Molly thought it just might give her the distraction she needed. There had been noises from above, a loud shrieking from several tentacle monsters. It sounded like it came from the bridge. And then the mucous-bodied alien had simply waddled out of engineering and into the corridor.

"Where are you going Sub-Commander?" Bradshaw had called after.

But the creature merely waved its stick hand as if in dismissal. And then it headed down the corridor, followed by a slithering tentacle monster.

"Whatza matter?" mocked Oscar. "Massa leave poor ol' Jeb alone?"

Bradshaw grimaced. "Mind your own business. And just make sure your girlfriend keeps on working. Or else we'll hook you up to one of these nasty, little guys."

He waved his hand at the spider-cats along the deck. But they were no longer in their herding posture. Some of them had wandered off, and the others we moving jerkily, as if whatever had been controlling them had momentarily taken its hand off the switch.

Molly knew that this was her chance. "Cover me," she said to Oscar.

She inched away from the Interspace com box and moved one step towards the control panel. None of the spider-cats followed.

"Get back to work!" thundered Bradshaw.

"Here's the thing," said Molly, continuing to inch her way back. "My father sent me here to represent him in all matters about this ship. He trusts me and has given me full authority. And...I don't think he would appreciate it if I called to interrupt him every time there's a minor problem. Mister Bradshaw, you have never been the child of one of the most powerful men in the solar system. You were only an engineer on my father's ship. And I don't take orders from engineers."

Bradshaw paused, as if listening to something in his head. "The Sub-Commander demands that you return to the terminal and contact your father immediately! Or else he'll make you a slave like the rest of the humans on this ship!"

Oscar held up his fists in a boxer's stance. "Your little pets seem to be confused. So now you're gonna have to get past me yourself."

Molly reached the control panel and sat down. She could only hope that Oscar would give her enough time. But then again, he was Oscar. Of course, he would.

She calmly began, pressing lights and buttons while staring at the computer screen. She hoped that all of her training would come back to her now, because, after all, she'd never actually been at this control panel, just on simulations.

Duncan Mackintosh was a savvy businessman. He had taught Molly that when a business is no longer profitable, it's better to burn it down than hand it over to your competitors. Of course, you have to sacrifice the inventory that way, but with a good fire insurance policy and a poor arson investigator, the company's balance sheets will always end up in the black. And he had taken out a very good insurance policy. He'd programmed a self-destruct sequence into the *Campbell* with his own hands.

Behind her, Bradshaw was talking to Oscar. "I don't know what you two think you are doing. You might as well give up. The Tvex are simply too powerful. They're centuries ahead of us. Can't you see that? The only chance we have to survive is to do what they say."

Molly smiled knowingly as she worked. Her father had purposely placed a weak-willed crew on this ship. Every year he spent a fortune on personality profile tests. He always knew who to hire. The perfect employee was one that was smart enough to do their duties, but not ambitious enough to think for themselves. It was always a fine line, but he had hired the perfect guy in Job Bradshaw.

She got to her feet and turned around. She put her hands together and cracked her knuckles. "Okay," she said.

Bradshaw looked relieved. "So, you'll contact your father now?"

She ignored him and walked up to Oscar. "We're done here," she said.

"What?"

"Let's go!"

She stepped into the corridor, with zombie crew members and spider-cats wandering aimlessly around behind, and Bradshaw calling after them with no effect.

59

SS JOHN W CAMPBELL JR

Aaron Ljungman stood outside the weapons room and faced down a monster. The tentacle creature paused right in front of him, about ten feet away. It wasn't the biggest one they'd seen, maybe about two thirds the size of the one that Gugu had battled outside her quarters, and much smaller than the one that had dragged Erik away. But it was an alien tentacle monster just the same. And it was Aaron's job to stop it. If he failed, then he would either be killed or dragged away and then it would come for Gugu. He'd grown quite fond of the South African woman since he'd come on board the *Campbell*.

This tentacle had acted strangely. When Aaron first stepped into the corridor, it had raced around the corner and he thought he was done for. But then it stopped abruptly as if whatever was controlling it had gotten distracted or something. It was giving him a chance to gather his thoughts, to think about how he would battle the thing.

He knew what Gugu had told him to do. And now he had to find a way to follow her advice. "Use your emotions," she had said. "Grief would be good." Not anger or fear. He already had plenty of that. But it was grief that had worked for Gugu.

The creature stirred, as if it had just reconnected with its master. It slithered forward a few feet and raised its triangular-shaped head, yellow eyes blinking. Then it crept a little further, moving smoothly. If he was going to do anything, now would be the time.

It took all his courage, but he closed his eyes. He felt that at any second the creature would tear its razor teeth into his body or wrap itself around him, but he kept them closed, squinting tightly. He made himself think of *Trollslända*, the beautiful, shining warship that he had pirated from Europa Station, and how it had been swallowed up by that terrible alien missile. Remembering how that looked on the view screen made him furious all over again. But furious wasn't what he needed right now. He had to think of something else.

No. Someone.

Jenny Broberg.

He'd worked together with her on Europa for four years. They'd slept together. And now...

He imagined the helpless look that must have crossed her face as those gigantic tentacles broke through every available port on the *Trollslända*, filling up every corridor. Where had she been when they came? On the bridge? Probably. She would have been torn apart or crushed. He could almost hear her screams in his head. And now she was gone. He'd never see her again. Ever.

Aaron felt a tremble in his throat. A sob escaped his lips. And then full-on tears began to flow from his tightly-shut eyes. "*Min Gud*," he wailed. "Jenny is gone. And I will never see her again."

When he opened his eyes, the tentacle creature was gone.

60

SS JOHN W CAMPBELL JR

Molly pulled on Oscar's arm. "Run now! Back to the shuttle!"

Oscar followed her down the corridor, his mind racing along with his feet. They'd wandered together all over this ship since coming on board. He'd lost direction countless times. But he knew that the shuttle dock was on the opposite end of the ship, far from the engineering room they'd just left. And this was a huge ship.

"What's going to happen?" he asked as he caught up with her.

"The whole things is going to self-destruct. What do you think I was doing on that control panel anyway, playing video games?"

"Self-destruct? How long do we have?"

"Thirteen minutes."

Oscar felt his guts clench. "We'll never make it."

"I think we will," said Molly. "I know this ship like the back of my hand. And if I'd programmed it for any longer, they'd figure out how to disable my commands."

So he ran. It wasn't hard to keep up, considering all the adrenaline that was coursing through his body.

A blast from an energy weapon just missed his head. The discharge struck the wall to his left and he felt the heat on his cheek. He kept running and looked back. The Sub-Commander was coming after them, surprisingly swift with its strange, wobbly gait. It held a bulbous-shaped pistol in its lily pad hand. It fired a second blast just as they turned the corner. Pieces of wall kicked up behind them.

"I think we'd better run a little faster," said Oscar.

"No shit," answered Molly. "I was wondering where that mucousy bastard went."

Oscar could only hope and pray that she wouldn't run them into a dead end. "I'm trusting you, Babe," he said.

"Don't worry. I've got this. As long as we don't run into any more surprises, we should be there in plenty of time."

Just as they approached another intersecting corridor, a tentacle dropped down from the overhead, coming through a Bryantonium grate and landing right on Molly. It was fast. Before Oscar could do anything, it had wrapped itself around her neck. He grabbed it with both hands and pulled. But the monster was strong and didn't want to let go. Molly made choking sounds and Oscar felt real panic rise up in his gut. He was not going to lose her after all they'd been through together.

He found hidden strength in his hands and arms. He grabbed the tentacle's head and twisted with both hands. Slowly, agonizingly, the monster's flesh moved and the pressure on Molly's neck eased slightly. She took a quick gasping breath. But she wasn't yet free, and the monster clamped down once more, fighting and wiggling like a fish on a line.

Oscar saw the alien Sub-Commander round the corner behind them, still holding up the strange-shaped pistol. Oscar knew what was coming and pulled Molly towards him with all his might, so the tentacle ended up between Molly and the Sub-Commander. When the shot came, it caught the tentacle creature full on its body, the part that was strangling Molly. Bits of purple flesh flew through the air and there was a hot smell of burned, alien flesh. The tentacle relaxed its grip, and Oscar twisted the damaged ends until the whole thing came apart. As it dropped away, Molly coughed and gasped. Blessedly, she was still alive.

"Come on!" shouted Oscar. "I don't know how many rounds he can fire with that thing."

Molly stumbled, but he grabbed her arm and pulled her around the next corner.

"Which way?" asked Oscar.

Still coughing, she looked around. "To the left," she croaked. "We're almost there."

And sure enough, they were.

They rounded one final corner and Oscar found himself looking at the shuttle's docking bay with the hatch still open. The two of them jumped through and Oscar struck the door's closing mechanism as he went by. Both of them hit the deck wheezing. The hatch hissed closed and sealed behind them. Oscar began to laugh with joy and relief. They'd made it.

They were alive. Pistol blasts bounced off the outside of the hatch, but the shuttle was designed for space, and even a meteor couldn't pierce it. They were safe.

Molly turned over and hugged him, her body trembling. He could see ugly, red marks on her neck, but he knew she would be alright. How many minutes since she had set the self-destruct sequence?

"I suppose we should get as far away from here as we can," said Oscar.

Molly was ahead of him, already getting to her feet. She took up her place at the controls and started the shuttle's engines. The small craft came to life. She punched in a few more keystrokes, and Oscar felt the docking clamps let go and they were free.

Molly goosed the shuttle's thrusters and Oscar felt the G-forces as they raced away from the big freighter.

An alarm sounded. He looked over Molly's shoulder and saw a blinking red light. "What's that?" he asked.

Molly hit a few buttons and the alarm stopped. But the light kept on blinking.

"Incoming," she said.

Oscar let out a breath and said, "Out of the frying pan and into the fire."

61

SS JOHN W CAMPBELL JR

Aaron staggered into the weapons room with legs trembling and tears still trickling down his cheeks. Gugu looked up from the auxiliary control panel she'd been working on. "Eich!" she exclaimed. "Did you snotklap that thing?"

"Never had to," answered Aaron bemusedly. "It just crawled away."

Gugu smiled as she turned back to the control panel, which had now come to life. "I told you. They don't know nothing about emotions. It freaks them out."

Aaron came forward to stand beside her. "Looks like you got it working."

"Yep, I did. And now let's see if I can disable those missiles and...uh oh."

"What?"

She stared at the control panel. Then she pressed some buttons. "There's a program running in the background."

"What kind of program?"

"A self-destruct sequence."

Aaron sputtered. "Self-destruct? But why would the aliens do that?"

"I don't think it was the aliens. Maybe Erik managed to do it. Or some other humans on board that I don't know about."

"How much time before it goes off?" asked Aaron.

"Nine minutes."

"Nine minutes?" sputtered Aaron. "Can you shut it off?"

"Now why would I want to do that? This will kill every last one of those bastards. And probably save the solar system."

Aaron looked into her eyes. "I suppose that means we're going to die for sure now."

"I suppose you're wrong," she said. "There are a bunch of escape pods on this ship. One of them is only two corridors over. Do you want to stand here and discuss this like a *babbelbekkie*, or do you want to get off of this ship?"

She didn't need to say more. They both raced out of the weapons room, with Aaron following her down the corridor. But as they rounded the first bend, she pulled up. A mucous-bodied alien was limping down the corridor towards them, holding onto the wall with one hand. Instead of the usual two, bulbous eyes rolling around in mucous, this one only had one, and where the left eye should have been was a gaping, black hole. It didn't seem to notice them but continued to make its way cautiously forward.

"For God's sake, what's that?" whispered Aaron.

"One of the head honchos," Gugu whispered in reply. "I think it's heading for the bridge. And I think it's blind."

They pressed themselves against the side wall. Aaron held his breath as the alien approached, feeling the seconds tick off in his head, wondering how many minutes were left until the self-destruct blew them all to kingdom come. It was agonizing, but they managed to keep completely still as the alien made its clumsy way by. After it had rounded a corner, Gugu whispered, "Go!"

They ran down one more corridor before pulling up in front of an escape pod hatch. Gugu punched a button on the wall and the door swung open. Beyond was a tiny bubble craft with plastisteel windows all around and a metal floor below. As they ran inside, the starless, black void beyond the windows made it seem as if the pod was hanging on the edge of an abyss.

Gugu sat down at the controls and strapped herself in. She punched a button and the control panel blinked to life. She gazed at it for a few seconds to get her bearings and then pressed one of the lights. The hatch closed behind them, sealing them off from the sounds of the *Campbell*. "So far, so good," muttered Gugu. Her voice sounded flat in the enclosed space of the pod.

There were seats for four people and Aaron jumped into the one directly behind Gugu. He strapped himself in, feeling his heart beating fast, and the seconds counting down even faster.

"As far as I know, these old pods have never been used," said Gugu.

"I hope this one works." She slid a lever forward and nothing happened. Frowning, she pushed a few lights on the panel. Then she slid the lever forward once again and this time the engine hummed to life. "This thing's not gonna be fast," she said. "But it'll get us away from the *Campbell*. I just hope it gets us away far enough."

The tiny craft separated from the huge freighter. All around them, the black void grew and grew outside the windows. There was no artificial gravity here, so Aaron felt himself float up against the straps that held him in. Gugu rotated the pod so they could watch the huge bulk of the *Campbell* dwindle as they floated away. It felt to Aaron like he was on a very small lifeboat, retreating from a huge ocean liner on a pitch black ocean. But this ocean liner was getting ready to explode. And it just might take them under with it.

62

SENATOR ALAN K SIMPSON

Jelly Roll's spirits had sunk down to the soles of his shoes. The massive, two-pronged attack had failed. They'd fired everything they had at the Simpson. It had been exhilarating to be acting captain during the attack, especially after Constance got the view screen to flicker on at the last minute. They'd watched the whole thing unfold as their weapons lit up the *Campbell* like a Christmas tree.

Then had come the *Trollslända*'s secret weapon, which had covered the Campbell with a giant, green spider web. But after a few minutes, the web fell away and the *Campbell* was still intact.

And then came the worst part of all. Jelly Roll, Constance, and Michaelson had looked on in horror as the *Trollslända* was swallowed up by ship-sized tentacles, leaving nothing in their wake. Nothing at all.

And now, there wasn't anything they could do but wait. What would the *Campbell* do next? Probably send another of those tentacle weapons their way.

But Jelly Roll was still the captain. "Lieutenant Constance, did I tell you about..."

"Please don't," she said.

"Please don't what?" asked Jelly Roll. "I was only going to say..."

"You were going to tell me a story that involved your cooking. So when you were done, I could mend the error of my ways."

The hefty cook found a chair and sat down uncomfortably. "You don't like my stories."

"I didn't say that. I just don't feel that all of life's lessons can be learned from baking, grilling, and frying. And besides, what good will it do now? We shot our wad. Unless there are some humans alive over there on the *Campbell* who can do something, we're out of options. So far the aliens haven't fired one of those tentacle missiles at us, but I'm sure they will any minute."

Jelly Roll sighed. Old age didn't mean you had patience. You had to learn a skill like that. Barbecuing was good for learning patience. Not the backyard kind, but the real thing, like in Kansas City or Memphis. He wanted to tell her about a Pit Master in Georgia who would pay attention to the pig all night to make the sure the heat was the right temperature and...

"You're still thinking of telling a story," said Constance. "I don't want to hear it. I just want to find a way to defend ourselves." She fidgeted in her chair, reminding Jelly Roll of a small child ready to throw a tantrum.

Jelly Roll held up his hands in surrender.

"What?" she asked.

"Nothing," he said. "You want me to keep quiet, so I'll shut up." He stretched his legs out in front of him, trying to get more comfortable in Chief Onion's chair. The engineer had been much skinnier than Jelly Roll. But then again, so were most people.

"I didn't say you couldn't speak," said Constance. "I just said please not another story about cooking. I can't take another one of those."

Jelly Roll paused, feeling a bit stung. "Well then, what should we talk about? Politics? About how you became a revolutionary? And how you made it this far out into space without ending up in prison?"

"I don't want to talk about that either."

"Well, frankly it doesn't bother me, except when you were going to blow up the ship. I don't care if you're one of the generals. I still like you all the same."

She looked away from the control panel. "They made me a lieutenant."

Jelly Roll laughed. "Just like on this ship. Well, if I were going to join an outlawed political army, I'd make sure they gave me a higher rank than I already had. Like general, maybe."

"They don't have generals. It's a fleet. They have admirals."

Jelly Roll finally pried himself out of the seat and stood. "That's why I'm a better cook than ship's captain. I'd rather hang out in the galley than try to figure out military ranks and politics."

Constance laughed. "You know, by all rights, I should be Captain now and you should be under my command."

"But then I'd be sitting where you are. And I couldn't hit the broadside of a barn. How about I keep pretending to give you orders and you keep pretending to follow them?"

She laughed again. "Deal. And when the revolution is over, I'll make sure you're the last one they lock up."

"Because revolutionaries still need to eat."

"Yes. You can't overthrow a corrupt government on an empty stomach. We get cranky when... "

The control panel beeped. Constance whirled around and looked up at the viewscreen. "Look at that!"

"What?" asked Jelly Roll.

"A shuttlecraft just launched from the *Campbell*! And another craft as well from the far side. Looks like an escape pod!"

Michaelson came over. "Who do you think it is?"

"I don't know," answered Constance. "But whoever is on that shuttle is about to get jostled. The Campbell is firing at them. Concussion bombs."

"Can we do anything?" asked Jelly Roll.

"All we have left are a few concussion bombs of our own."

Jelly Roll thought about gunfights in the old west on Spacenet movies. "Fire 'em off. I'm sure whoever is in those crafts could use some cover."

63

SS JOHN W CAMPBELL JR

Job Bradshaw stood in the middle of engineering feeling helpless. The Tvex Sub-Commander had left the room. Molly Mackintosh and her boyfriend had left the room. And now he was alone among shuffling spider-cats and zombie crew members amidst the sounds of concussion bombs exploding outside the hull. Evidently, the American ship had not been finished off yet. Why hadn't the Tvex fired a tentacle missile at them? Well, he supposed that was the reason the Sub-Commander had headed for the bridge, to get things straightened out. It wouldn't be long before the battle was over.

On the original *Campbell* crew, before they had set off through the Dark Curtain, he'd been a miner, an expert on Bryantonium. Well, he wasn't an expert on that metal anymore, not after he'd seen what the aliens were able to do with the stuff. And what they'd been able to do to the brains of the humans. So he'd chosen a side. No one could have survived intact and untouched on this cursed ship without joining the aliens. They could read minds, after all. They could alter matter. And they could certainly stop anyone who resisted.

So what was he supposed to do now? He'd thought of going after Molly, but she'd surprised him when she ran and would have gotten a clear head start. Besides, he needed to stay here for when the Sub-Commander returned. In the meantime, he should probably try to figure out what Molly had done at the control panel.

He walked over, just managing to keep his feet clear of spider-cats, who seemed to be wandering aimlessly about. Those things still gave him the creeps, especially since they had impaled themselves on so many of his former crewmates and friends. The only thing keeping him from getting one himself was his cooperation.

He sat down at the control panel. Most of the lights were blinking rhythmically in sequence, the way they had always done here in engineering. Green lights, yellow lights, purple lights. Not that he'd paid much attention. That was up to the Sub-Commander. But everything looked normal, he thought. Except for a tiny red light in the upper left corner. It was blinking rhythmically as well, slower than the other lights, but steadily picking up speed.

There was a thunk from the doorway behind him. He whirled around. The alien captain had just fallen into the room.

"Captain!" cried Bradshaw, jumping to his feet. But there was no answer. Normally, the captain would already be inside his head, giving him orders. But that didn't happen. He ran over and helped her to her feet. He gasped as he saw the black, gaping hole where her left eye should have been.

She opened her jack-o-lantern mouth and spoke. "Sub-Commander?"

"No, Captain. It's Job Bradshaw."

The captain's remaining eye rotated in its mucous bed as if trying to see him, but it was clear that she was blind. "Where is the Sub-Commander?"

"He's gone up to the bridge, I think. There was an attack."

"Of course, there was an attack," said the captain in her low, metallic voice. "The human weaklings think they actually have a chance against us. Take me to the control panel."

He led her by the arm, cringing at how her alien skin felt clammy, like inanimate clay, but with faint pulses of life.

When they reached the control panel, she said, "Tell me what happened here."

He told her briefly that Molly Mackintosh, the daughter of Duncan Mackintosh, had been here in engineering. And about how she had done something on the control panel before escaping.

The alien moved her stick arms up and down. Her remaining eye whirled like a spinning top. "Look at the control panel," she said quickly. "And describe to me what you see."

He told her about the normal blinking lights. And then about the tiny red light in the upper left corner. "It's blinking very fast now," he said.

The alien captain shouted something in her native language. It was incomprehensible to Bradshaw, but from the tone she used, it might have been, "Oh shit!"

64

ESCAPE POD

Aaron and Gugu saw the flash before they felt the effects. One moment the *Campbell* was there, and the next moment the entire, huge freighter was a mass of white-hot flame. It was like a supernova, lighting up everything in the escape pod and washing out all detail and shadow. They shielded their eyes with upraised arms. And then the concussion hit, a blast that flung the pod through space like a pebble on a beach, tumbling over and over and over. Somewhere they heard a supply locker click open and things began to clatter around the small cabin, filling up their vision with packets of freeze dried food, canisters of air, and who knew what else. Gugu was wrenched violently against the straps of her captain's seat. She hung on, feeling the G-forces tug at her from every direction. It was like being in a barrel going over Victoria Falls, only this waterfall kept tumbling and tumbling.

It was fortunate that these pods were so small, because objects flying around didn't have far to go before they hit something, so they never picked up much speed. The *Campbell* had been designed with a dozen of these pods, the thinking being that in an emergency, it was better to put your eggs in different baskets instead of putting all the escapees in one, large pod. But they hadn't been designed to go through turbulence like this. Gugu could only hope that this particular basket wouldn't break up in the swirling chaos.

Finally, the Armageddon-like explosion began to sputter and die. It grew dark in the escape pod. Through the windows, the *Campbell* faded into a billion bits of flying debris, rocketing in all directions. But the pod was still spinning out of control, silently now, and Gugu knew she had to find a way to stabilize its path.

All the lights on the control panel were simply streaks of color as Gugu struggled to get her bearings. She reached out against the G-forces and pressed a random, green light. She heard a thruster kick in and the motion of the craft changed. She pressed more lights and the spinning began to slow. After a lot of experimentation, she got the craft under control. Soon they were floating gently in space like a cork on a calm ocean.

"Wow!" she exclaimed breathlessly. "That was a real stormloop! Are you okay back there, Aaron?"

There was no answer.

"Aaron?" She turned in her seat and looked back. It was hard to see in the dim, colored light from the control panel, but she could make out Aaron's shape. He was still strapped in, but his head was lolling. His body floated limply against the straps.

"My God," muttered Gugu. She undid her own straps and floated up and away from her chair. She pushed down from the overhead and parked herself in front of Aaron, hanging onto the arm of his chair to stabilize herself. She reached up to touch his face and felt blood trickling down his forehead.

"Aaron," she said softly, shaking him gingerly. "Aaron. Are you still with me?"

She moved her face close to his. Was he breathing? It was hard to tell. She grabbed his wrist, feeling for a pulse. If there was any pulse at all, it was very weak, and she didn't know if that was just wishful thinking.

"Aaron," she said, "I know you're not a *babbelbekkie*, but please wake up and say something."

For another minute, it remained deathly quiet in the small, enclosed space of the pod. Gugu wanted to shake him harder, but she was afraid that if he was alive, he might have internal damage and...

He emitted a weak, shaky breath, followed by a groan.

"Thank God," whispered Gugu. She hadn't known this man for very long, but they'd been through a lot together. A lot. She thought that maybe...

Aaron lifted his head slowly and groaned again. "Gugu?" he said. His eyes fluttered open in the dimness. She saw specks of light there. That should have told her something, but she was too preoccupied to notice.

"I'm here," she answered.

"What happened?" he asked.

"The *Campbell* blew up. It's gone. Completely snotklapped."

"That's good," muttered Aaron. "But what happened to me?"

"You got conked on the head while we were spinning. How do you feel?"

"I got a headache. And I'm seeing stars."

"That's normal. I think one of those canisters hit you."

"No. You don't understand. I'm seeing stars."

And then Gugu understood what he was trying to tell her. She looked through the plastisteel windows that completely surrounded them. Everywhere, like a carpet of jewels, she saw stars upon stars upon stars. In the distance, Europa hung among them like a majestic snowball, and behind it, Jupiter.

"We're free," she said. "The black void is gone."

65

SENATOR ALAN K SIMPSON

"Is everybody okay?" asked Jelly Roll.

"Affirmative," said Michaelson.

"Yep," said Constance.

"Me too...I think," muttered Jelly Roll as he got to his feet with a groan. "That was one hell of a concussion bomb you hit the *Campbell* with, Lieutenant."

They'd all been tossed around like rag dolls when the *Campbell* had exploded. The *Simpson* had been pelted with debris like a metal garbage can getting hammered with rocks. But the good old *Homer* had survived.

"Status, Lieutenant Constance?" asked Jelly Roll.

"We're intact. And that was not a concussion bomb."

"No, of course not. What do you think it was?"

"Hell if I know. Maybe a self-destruct. Looked like a nuke."

"But who would have set it off?"

"No idea."

"And the *Campbell*?"

"Completely gone, Sir. Destroyed without a trace."

"Well, hallelujah for that!" exclaimed Jelly Roll with glee. "That son of a bitch was worse than a cake that won't rise, no matter how much yeast I use. Oh...I forgot. You're tired of cooking analogies."

"Never mind that, Jelly Roll...uh...Sir. The news gets even better. You need to see this."

He limped over to the control panel and gazed over her shoulder. "Well, what do ya' know about that?"

The Campbell was gone. But as nice as it was not to see it perched on their screen like a nasty relative who won't go home after Christmas, what he did see was even better. Stars upon stars. Jelly Roll had been in space for most of his adult life and he'd seen billions of them – blue tinted, red tinted, supernovas, meteors, you name it. But no field of stars had ever looked sweeter than this.

"We're free!" he exclaimed.

"Yes, we are," answered Constance. "And I suppose we can go anywhere we want now. No more plasma bubble to hold us."

"Mr. Michaelson, send out an S.O.S.," said Jelly Roll. "I imagine there are a lot of people that would love to hear from us right now."

"Will do, Sir," he answered. "But we've still got a problem."

"What's that?" asked Jelly Roll.

Instead of answering, Michaelson motioned with his head towards the corridor. At first, Jelly Roll wondered what he was looking at. But then it sunk in. Of course. The *Campbell* might have been destroyed, but at least one of the tentacle monsters it had spawned was still out there. And though the ship was free, they were still trapped in engineering.

As if in answer to that thought, a bang reverberated through the engine room as something big pounded on the hatch from the outside. Jelly Roll nearly jumped out of his skin. The bang came again. The iron hatch rattled, suddenly looking flimsier than it had a moment ago.

"It sounds pissed," muttered Constance. "It's probably cranky because its masters just got blown into space dust."

"Probably," agreed Jelly Roll.

"So what do we do?" asked Michaelson.

"Those things killed most of the crew," said Jelly Roll. "My crew. My friends. And I've had enough."

Jelly Roll felt part of himself step away from his own head and look on. What the hell was he thinking? But his elation had been so high when he saw the *Campbell* gone that he just couldn't be afraid anymore. He'd been afraid since all of this had first started. But not anymore. He was going to put an end to it right now. He reached down and grabbed a large kitchen knife hidden in a sheath on his pant leg.

"What are you going to do?" asked Constance.

"What does it look like?" answered Jelly Roll. "Or maybe you want to trade places. I'll fly the ship and you go fight the monster."

"No, Captain, us revolutionary Lieutenants are better at flying ships than fighting the evil proletariat rulers who enslave us like that monster out there."

"Uh huh," answered Jelly Roll.

"You're both crazy," said Michaelson.

"Of course," answered Jelly Roll. "We've been through a lot. Who wouldn't go crazy?"

Jelly Roll held up the knife and looked back at Constance. "This is going to cost you. You're gonna have to listen to one of my cooking stories when I come back."

Constance groaned and said, "Fine. I'll listen to two cooking stories if we survive. But not three. That would be too many."

Jelly Roll spun his knife in his hand. It had been a long time since he had been in a knife fight. But he was as ready as he was ever going to be. "See, Lieutenant? Who says our two sides can't sit down and come to an agreement? You just found common ground with an evil Party member like me. Neither of us would ever want to hear three cooking stories in a row. That would be cruel."

Then he opened the hatch and stepped into the corridor.

66

SENATOR ALAN K SIMPSON

The first time Jelly Roll got into a knife fight was as a teenager in New Orleans. He'd been a sous chef at a restaurant in the French Quarter, catering to the city's many tourists. He was in the alley by the back door, smoking a cigarette after a very long night. He was exhausted, and his feet hurt so bad that he had brought a stool to sit on. Many of the kitchen staff had already gone home, and he needed to go back inside to finish up before calling it a day.

He heard voices from some diehard tourists still wandering Bourbon Street, along with cops telling a few of the louder ones to go home and sleep it off. Two tourists rounded the corner and staggered into the alley. He knew he should throw away his cigarette and go back inside. But he didn't.

The fact was, Jelly Roll didn't feel like getting up. He wanted to finish smoking and sit a little longer. He liked it down here in the south, especially the nights, when the cooling, damp, Louisiana air embraced his skin.

The two men approached, singing a drunken song. He reluctantly got up from his stool and tossed the smoldering cigarette to the other side of the alley. "Good evening," he said, planning to go back inside.

But the tourists had other ideas. The bigger of the two stepped behind him, blocking his way back into the restaurant. The shorter man, wearing a purple LSU t-shirt, answered, "Good evening to you too! Don't y'all think it's a nice night to fuck you up?" He laughed and methodically unfolded a large jack-knife.

Jelly Roll had an advantage. He hadn't been drinking all night. He pulled out a knife of his own, hidden in a sheaf on his leg, something he'd started to do while working late in New Orleans, just in case. With a quick stroke, he leaped forward and slashed right to left across the shorter man's chest. Open-mouthed, the man looked down at the blood flowing down his shirt and screamed. He took a step back as Jelly Roll advanced, but his feet got tangled up and he fell, just as Jelly Roll felt a nick in his back from a knife in the hand of the big man behind him. But only a nick, because Jelly Roll had been moving away.

Jelly Roll spun around to face the big man, who came at him again. The cook dodged the attack and slashed the man's hand. His knife clattered to the ground and he yelled, covering his wounded right hand with his left, trying to stem the flow of blood. Jelly Roll whirled around and saw the smaller man still on the ground, clutching his chest.

Now he was the only armed man remaining. These men had attacked him. He knew he could kill them both.

But he didn't.

"Get out of here," he said, waving his bloody knife in the air.

They both scrambled to their feet and limped out of the alley, trailing blood. The last he saw of them, they were rounding the corner into the French Quarter.

And now, fifty years later and 400 million miles away, he readied his knife again.

"It's time for you to go," he said to the tentacle monster. Its triangle head reared up and waved back and forth. Its yellow eyes were not blinking like before. Why was that? Maybe because there was no longer a connection to the aliens on the *Campbell*. But that made it possibly more dangerous, a lone, mad dog with no restraints. Kind of like an angry, drunk tourist at 2 AM in a bar in the French Quarter after all his friends were gone.

"You don't have to go home, but you can't stay here," said Jelly Roll.

The tentacle attacked, striking like a cobra. But the old, overweight cook was still quick, parrying the attack with his blade. For a second, he felt like he was in an old-fashioned sword fight, with two blades clashing together, his knife and the creature's long, sleek neck. But since his blade was steel and the monster's neck was some sort of metal-flesh hybrid, his blade penetrated, not deeply, but enough to send a chunk of alien flesh onto the deck. The monster quickly pulled its head back out of harm's way, giving off sparks and dripping black liquid from its neck.

Jelly Roll stood his ground and looked the monster in the eyes as it slithered closer. In his peripheral vision, he saw its tail snap around, intending to strike him from the side. He jumped back and slashed down with his knife, cutting off a twelve-inch piece of tail. The monster shrieked and the sound went through Jelly Roll's backbone. But again, he held his ground. Once more the triangle head raised up, waving back and forth.

It was time to end this.

Just as he had done in that long ago alley in New Orleans, Jelly Roll leaped forward and slashed right to left, as hard as he could. He caught the creature's neck full on, and the knife sliced all the way through, severing the head. It fell to the floor with a dull thud, like a fish falling on a rock. The yellow eyes dimmed and went out.

The damned tentacle monster was dead. Just like that.

"Huh," muttered Jelly Roll. He wiped the black liquid off his blade and put it back into its sheath. Then he headed back into engineering to tell Constance and Michaelson that the coast was clear. They could head up to the bridge now and get ready to welcome the armada of ships that was undoubtedly on its way from Europa. Oh sure, there might be a few more tentacle monsters hiding out on the ship but he knew what to do about that.

Because he was no longer afraid.

67

EUROPA STATION

Aaron Ljungman sighed. He wasn't wired to be the center of attention, to be surrounded by so many people of all nationalities. All the noise and shouted questions at he and Gugu were worse than running away from tentacle monsters on the *Campbell*. Well, then again, maybe not.

"Mr. Ljungman, can you describe the tentacle creatures one more time for our viewers back in New Toledo?" shouted yet another reporter. Aaron's answer would be beamed on SpaceNet to all the outlets across the solar system, from Europa, to Mars, to Luna, and to Earth, as well as to ships in space.

He did his best to answer the question one more time, glancing over at Gugu who was answering yet another question of her own. This was the biggest story that had ever hit SpaceNet, the biggest story in the history of the human race. There had been extra-terrestrial contact for the first time, and the contact had not been good. To encounter aliens that could travel through the vacuum of space, read minds, and alter the molecular makeup of Bryantonium was simply terrifying. To find out that there was another galaxy beyond the Black Curtain where, in the words of Erik Juergenson, hostile alien ships roamed around like cockroaches, had brought humanity together like nothing else. Space Fleets from all the nations, and even most of the rebel factions, were on their way now towards Europa to gather together, in case any more of those aliens decided to come through. There was even talk of sending an expedition through the other way like the *Campbell* had done, but no one knew exactly how they had done it in the first place. A shuttle had gotten away during the chaos after the *Campbell* exploded. There was a search underway for whoever was on that shuttle, in hopes that they could shed more light on what had happened.

Aaron was gratified that his late friend Erik was being universally hailed as a hero, and not just in Sweden. He was the first human outside of the *Campbell*'s crew who had encountered the aliens when he docked *Skalbagge* with the doomed freighter. He'd suffered more than anyone during the crisis and had finally given his life. He's the one who let Aaron know so many important things about the aliens' minds before being dragged off. Aaron was sure that he'd done even more heroic things, and that he probably had something to do with the *Campbell* blowing up. All of that would come out sooner or later.

He glanced across the hall at the three remaining members of Simpson's crew as they also fielded an army of reporters. They were the ones who had picked up Aaron and Gugu's escape pod before the armada of space ships from Europa had shown up. Aaron hadn't had much time to get to know them, but he really liked the old, fat cook named Jelly Roll, who'd made some amazing croissants for them when they first came aboard.

But now, he desperately needed a break.

He reached out and touched Gugu's arm, motioning with his head towards the hallway. She smiled gratefully and leaned over to say something to Alrik Nyland, who had been their handler on behalf of Swedish Space Fleet ever since they'd landed back on Europa. He nodded to Gugu and she stood up. Aaron followed her into the hallway.

Instead of heading for the restrooms, they snuck away to a spot in the next module, away from all the chaos. There was no one else here, and Aaron breathed a sigh of relief. Outside the plastisteel dome, the ice fields of Europa gleamed white in the starlight, with Jupiter hanging large in the distance. It was a view he would never tire of.

"Helvete," exclaimed Aaron, huffing through his cheeks. "It sure is good to get away from all those reporters."

"Amen to that," said Gugu.

They both gazed out at the ice for a few moments. Then Gugu spoke up. "What will you do now?"

"I suppose I'll go to jail. I did steal a warship after all. And got it destroyed. The jewel of the fleet, complete with its new secret weapon. And I got my friend Jenny killed. And two more of my countrymen." His voice broke a little as he said this.

"That wasn't your fault," said Gugu. "It was the aliens. And lots of people died during all of this."

"But if I hadn't taken *Trollslända*, Jenny would still be alive."

"Maybe. But then the aliens would probably be loose in the solar system."

He looked off into the distance. "I suppose. But I'm sure I'll go to jail. They don't make it easy on pirates these days. But at least Swedish jails are not so bad."

Gugu chuckled. "Always the *stoïsch*. Strong and silent."

She reached up and gently turned his head towards her. She looked into his eyes. "Strong and silent men make good fathers. Just the kind of man I'd like around to help raise my baby."

Aaron felt a fluttering in his stomach. He struggled to reply. Finally, he managed to blurt out, "But I'll be in jail! Who knows for how long?"

"They're not going to lock up a national hero. Besides, you already told me about the dirt you have on Nyland. You could use that info if you have to."

"But...but..." he sputtered.

"Maybe you don't want me. Don't you want to be my bru? If you don't, I'll understand...."

"No, no!" exclaimed Aaron. "I would like that. I'd like it very much."

"Good," she said. "Maybe, later tonight, if you're up for it, we could even have a jol."

Aaron stared at her. "Um...yeah. That would be nice. But aren't you pregnant?"

She clucked and shook her head. "Men. You really don't know much about women, do you?"

"I guess not," answered Aaron. "And, come to think of it, there's another thing I don't know. You only told me your real name once. In all the excitement, I forgot it. If I'm going to help you raise your little barn-barn, I should probably know what it is."

Gugu smiled, and it looked to Aaron like the distant sun. "Hansie," she said, offering her hand. "Hansie Addington."

Instead of taking her hand, Aaron kissed her for the first time. It turned out to be even better than seeing her naked.

68

EUROPA STATION

"So, what's next for you?" asked Constance. She and Jelly Roll were having dinner in the cafeteria on Europa after a long, long day of questions. They'd found a spot away from everyone else after Michaelson had wandered off with a female reporter from Ganymede.

"I'm not sure," answered Jelly Roll. "I suppose I could find another ship. Or maybe stay with the *Simpson* after they find another captain. Or maybe I could work here on Europa. I've never been much for Swedish food, and this is particularly awful." He looked at the lump of herring on his fork and let it drop back onto the plate.

She chuckled. "I suppose. But you make ethnic food all the time. Didn't we have gumbo last month?"

"Yes, we did. But if you compare Cajun cuisine to Swedish, it would be no contest. And I can also do Italian pretty good. And French. And Tex-Mex. And Asian. And..."

"Okay, okay!" said Constance, holding up her hands. "I get the point. You're a master chef, and everyone in the solar system needs to eat. You'll find another job.

"They continued to poke at the food on their plates, trying to find something that would go down better than the herring. Finally, Jelly Roll spoke up. "What about you? Where will you go now?"

She looked down at her plate and then back up. "That all depends on how much you tell Space Fleet about what happened. You're the P.O. after all. I'm sure they're going to want a full debriefing."

Jelly Roll looked away for a long moment. Then he returned her gaze.

"As far as I'm concerned, every member of the crew was good and loyal and brave during the recent crisis. Especially Lieutenant Helen Constance." He raised his glass of aquavit in a toast.

She didn't immediately reply. Finally, she picked up her own glass. "Thank you...Uncle."

After swallowing some of the brutally strong liquor, Constance coughed twice and said, "I imagine that the Revolution will take a break for quite a while anyhow. Nothing like hostile aliens to bring together the whole human race."

"Amen to that," answered Jelly Roll. He raised his glass one more time and downed the whole thing.

"And now," he said, "I think I'll just waddle into the kitchen to see if I can knock some sense into those so-called chefs."

69

BRAHE STATION

Oscar Gunn watched Ganymede on the view screen, the intricately carved grooves on its surface growing larger as they approached. He and Molly had managed to slip by the entire armada of ships from Europa after the *Campbell* had self-destructed. Molly said she didn't think it was a good idea to face anyone until she had a chance to talk with her father. They knew there would be questions galore, and a firestorm of speculation from here to Earth. There had been hostile alien contact after all.

"Are you sure you want to land here?" she asked him. "They'll probably kill us both after what happened when we escaped. And we got Tormod killed as well."

"Sometimes you have to face the music," said Oscar. "That's one of the things my grandfather always said."

It looked like the O'Neils had just finished repairing the landing docks, and the autopilot took them smoothly in. The shuttle gently touched down and was pulled back into a special airlock. Molly received notice that it was safe to depressurize, and the hatch hissed open behind them. Oscar unbuckled his seat belt and stood to face whatever was coming. He fully expected to find a bunch of O'Neils waiting to arrest them or worse. But that didn't happen. There was no one to greet them at all. They headed out into the newly-repaired hallway, looking down at bits of construction materials littering the floor.

"So you're back," said a woman's voice. She'd just stepped out of the docking control booth. They pulled up short and the woman stared at them. "I don't suppose that my son Tormod came back on that shuttle with you," she said, her inquiring eyes showing grief and pain." We've been watching all the coverage on SpaceNet. We heard about the *Campbell*. I figured you must have gone there when you escaped. I knew Tormod escaped with you. Did he survive?"

Molly and Oscar glanced at each other. Then Molly shrugged. Finally, Oscar looked back at the woman. "Tormod died when the *Campbell* exploded," he said softly. "But you need to know something. He died a hero."

As Oscar said this, a gruesome picture forced its way into his mind, a picture of Tormod standing in the door of the shuttle with one of those spider-cat things sticking out of his head. And then his whole body split apart at the seams as baby tentacles burst out...

Oscar shook off the vision with a shudder. He'd never tell this woman that part of the story.

The woman hung her head and burst into tears. "I still had hope," she sobbed. "I hoped he might come home to us."

They stood there uncomfortably and let her weep for a while. Finally, she gathered herself. "We need to go and tell the others. The O'Neils are a very tight clan. They'll want to have a memorial service right away."

Oscar knew he should just grab Molly and drag her back into the shuttle instead of seeing all the O'Neils. But then he remembered his grandfather.

Face the music.

Later, after everyone on Brahe Station had torn themselves away from continuous coverage on SpaceNet about the *Campbell*, they were all gathered in the gymnasium. Tormod's mother stood in the fight ring at the center of the room, encircled by six other women. It was the same ring where Oscar had fought Big O'Neil. But now, the huge man sat in the bleachers on the far side. Occasionally, he shot hostile glances at Oscar, but he couldn't do anything while the memorial service was going. But the service would soon be over.

The women in the ring continued to lead everyone in the long remembrance. It was a lot like an old ceremony Oscar had been to back on Earth. This one was particularly poignant, though, way out here at a lonely outpost on a faraway moon.

"Those we love don't ever go away," continued Tormod's mother in a chanting voice, loud and clear and confident. The sound echoed around the cavernous gymnasium. "They walk beside us every day. They walk unseen. They walk unheard. But they are always here."

One of the other women produced a penny whistle. Another pressed a violin to her shoulder and raised the bow. The two of them began to play an ancient song. Although the mood was mournful, the Celtic lilt made Oscar think of faraway mists somewhere on Earth, maybe Ireland or Scotland. All the O'Neils began to sing, filling the gymnasium with music.

"Amazing grace how sweet the sound.
That saved a wretch like me..."

Oscar knew that song well from growing up in South Carolina. He wasn't a part of this clan, and indeed, he had caused a lot of their pain, but still, he found himself singing along.

"I once was lost but now I'm found
Was blind but now I see."

By the time the song was over, there were tears everywhere in the crowd.

And then the ceremony was over.

People began filing out, quietly and respectfully. But several of the men lingered in the bleachers, looking towards Oscar.

Tormod's mother was the last to leave the ring. Oscar approached her and touched her arm. "Ms. O'Neil," he said, "there's something I need to say to you."

She turned and looked into his eyes. "Go on."

"I know you can never forgive me for what happened to your son. And what happened to this station. But I want you to know that I am sorry. That might sound hollow coming from a bare bones fighter like me. But you should know that my guilt will stay with me as long as I live."

Once again, tears brimmed at the edges of the woman's eyes. Unexpectedly, she began to sing the song again, a capella and sweet. But this was a verse Oscar had never heard.

"The earth shall soon dissolve like snow
The sun forbear to shine
But God who called me here below
Will be forever mine."

When she finished, she took a deep, cleansing breath and said, "Life is short, especially in a place like this. And now we have aliens to worry about. I don't know what God has in mind for all of us. But I do know there's no time for bitterness. So I forgive you."

Oscar tried to think of something to say, but he could only nod his head in thanks.

The woman spoke again. "But now, Mr. Gunn, I think you should go. Those men over in the bleachers certainly don't feel the same way I do."

Molly grabbed his arm and soon they were hurrying down the hallway towards the shuttle. He tried to pull up, but she kept tugging on his arm.

"But I came here to face the music," he complained.

"You already did. You made peace with Tormod's mother. What else do you want? Now you have to go!"

Oscar screwed up his courage and asked, "You're not going with me, are you?"

Molly looked down at the ground. "I can't," she said. "I have to make things right here. It was to rescue me that you came to Ganymede in the first place. And then me and my father opened the door to those aliens with our ship. I'll tell everything I know about what happened so we can fight back better next time. And I'll have the full backing of the Salome Corporation. But right now, these people on Ganymede need me. Believe it or not, I grew quite fond of them while I was hostage here. I think they'll accept me. But not you. Never you. You wounded their pride, and that's something the men will never forgive."

She reached up and touched his cheek. Then she kissed him. "I've grown quite fond of you as well. But I'm sorry, I just can't go with you."

With that, she turned and headed down the hallway. He could only stand there and watch her walk out of his life.

Someone rounded the corner from the opposite direction. Oscar heard the footsteps and whirled around.

Big O'Neil.

Oscar thought the man looked like a cartoon character as he advanced – oversized feet, sleeves rolled up, mouth moving as if chewing on something. Oscar could practically see smoke pouring from his ears. He couldn't help but laugh. He had faced alien monsters that were a lot tougher than this guy.

"You think I'm funny?" asked Big O'Neil in his oddly high voice. "You're not going to laugh when I beat you to death. Only I'm allowed to laugh today."

Oscar raised his arms into the air. He didn't know if he was raising them to God, but he knew that he wouldn't fight this man. He wouldn't even defend himself.

Face the music.

Big O'Neil punched him in the gut. Oscar doubled over in pain. The pain felt good. Big O'Neil used an uppercut that landed below Oscar's chin, sending him flying up and dropping him to the floor on his back. He looked up at Big O'Neil and smiled. He wondered why he was smiling.

Maybe he deserved this? Maybe he should have died on the *Campbell* with everyone else? Whatever the reason, he could accept dying here now. In fact, he would welcome it today.

Big O'Neil stomped around to the side and kicked him several times. "Quit smiling, you punk," he said. "I'm going to keep kicking until I wipe that smile off of your face."

Oscar felt several of his ribs snap from the man's oversized boot. He tasted blood trickling from his lips. It was strange that he didn't feel the pain anymore. Maybe he was just embracing it. He continued to smile up at the big man as the kicks rained down. The man was taking great pleasure in this like Oscar had done so many times in his fighting career. But no more.

Behind Big O'Neil's head, Oscar saw a flash of silver. The big man's eyes suddenly rolled back in his head and he toppled over on top of Oscar. Now Oscar felt the pain as his broken ribs screamed at him. He was able to push the big man off and he looked up, gaping. Tormod's mother was standing above him with a large wrench in her hand. Behind her stood Molly. They helped Oscar to his feet, and he came up coughing and spitting blood.

"Are you okay?" asked Molly.

Oscar shook his head to try and clear it. It felt like he had just gone ten rounds with the entire O'Neil clan. "I've been better," he said. "I thought you had walked out of my life forever."

"I had," she answered. "But now you're going to fly out of mine."

The two women half-dragged Oscar to the shuttle bay, his rubbery legs wobbling and his feet kicking up construction debris and dust. They took him into the shuttle and strapped him in the pilot's seat. Molly produced a first aid kit from a cabinet overhead. As he watched her patch him up, he could only think, 'I love this woman.' When he tried to actually say it, she put a finger to his lips. "I know," she said. "Me too."

She punched some commands into the control panel. "I'm putting it on autopilot," she said. "I'm sending you to the Swedes on Europa. They'll help you."

He wanted to cry, but his ribs hurt too much to even breathe. And then Molly was gone, with the hatch closed behind her. He heard the shuttle's autopilot start the countdown. When it reached ten seconds, the engines kicked in. By the time it reached zero, the craft had lifted off. And he was back in space.

Oscar woke several hours later. He saw Jupiter on the view screen, with Europa hanging next to it like a veined, white ball. It would take at least two days to get there. He began to cough, and the pain in his ribs flared like needles. But at least he was alive.

What would he do with his life now, a life without Molly? He would no longer make his living in the fight game, he knew that much. But life threw battles at you that weren't always in the ring. And the human race certainly had a battle on its hands now. Maybe he could help fight that one. After all, he knew a lot about the aliens, more than just about anyone else.

Or maybe he could go back to Earth. To South Carolina. Spend some time fishing in the coastal lowlands.

No, that was another life.

Oh well, those thoughts could wait. Because right now, he had to pee.

He unstrapped himself and struggled up from the captain's chair. He limped painfully over to the head. There was blood in his urine. Big O'Neil had done a number on him alright.

He made his way back to the control panel and stared at it for a few long moments. He wouldn't go to Europa. Not now. Eventually, he would, because he'd need supplies. And then he would find a ship that was going further out.

To the Dark Curtain. That's where he decided to go. Because the aliens would be back. He would become a space fighter. Because fighting was all he had ever known. It was all he was good at.

He pushed a few buttons and the shuttle gently changed course. He'd wander around out here for as long as air and supplies held out. Then he'd go to Europa and look for a spaceship. After what had happened, there were bound to be flotillas of them heading for the Dark Curtain.

Oscar limped over to his bunk and settled in, pulling a blanket up to his chin. He needed to sleep some more and heal. But before he drifted off, he began to sing. In spite of the pain in his ribs, he sang it strong, the way his grandfather used to do.

"I once was lost but now I'm found
Was blind but now I see."

He'd been blind for so long, in so many ways. But now he could see clear enough. Clear enough to know it was time to help out his fellow humans.

And he would do the best he could.

STORY CREATORS

Wayne Faust

Wayne Faust has been a full-time music and comedy performer for over 40 years, playing in 40 states and overseas in England, Scotland, and Holland. His funny songs have been heard on the radio all over the world and on the Internet. While on the road, he writes science-fiction and has over 40 stories published in various places, including Norway, Australia, and South Africa. He's published two full-length books, "Thirty Years Without A Real Job," a fast-moving and entertaining memoir of his life in show business, and "12 Parables," a collection of short stories.

You can find more than you'll ever need to know about Wayne on his website at:

www.waynefaust.com.

Charles Eugene Anderson

Charles Eugene 'Chuck' Anderson is a poet, painter, baker, runner, hospital volunteer, and writer who lives in Colorado. He spends most of his days with his pup, Champ. Chuck is a husband and father, and he has a weakness for muscle cars. Chuck's stories are found at:

www.charleseugeneanderson.com

Click Here To Join Charles Eugene Anderson's Email List
https://goo.gl/ai9YQj

Valdas Miskinis

Cover art by Valdas Miskinis, miskinis.valdas@gmail.com

CHARLES ANDERSON BOOKS

Mad Cow Press is an Imprint of Charles Anderson Books

Charles Anderson Books
15986 E 17th Pl.
Aurora, CO 80011 USA
candersonbooks@gmail.com